SEVEN
Stones

An Eric Logan Novel

Novels by Gary Kassay

Eric Logan Series

Under My Thumb

Best Served Cold

Seven Stones

Warren Temple Series

He Who Laughs Last

Out of the Abyss

Circle of Death

Inspector Duke Becker Series

Murder in Silence

Murder by Prophecy

Classic Murder

Murder by the Invisibles

Murder by Blood

SEVEN
Stones

An Eric Logan Novel

by

Gary Kassay

WWW.OAKLEAPRESS.COM

Dedication

This is dedicated to those who read and review novels. I recently had a review for **Stone Murder,** and the reviewer was disappointed in the grammar and some of the story plots. I reread it and he was right. I'm not sure what happened but I rewrote it, and it appears here as **Seven Stones.** You have to take the good with the bad and I hope my readers enjoy this new novel.

Author's Notes

There are many myths and legends told by the Shoshone Native Americans, as well as other Native American tribes. The story in this novel is not a true story told by the Shoshone. It is fiction, a story from my imagination only.

The names of the Shoshone are again made up by me alone. There is no disrespect intended and if the names are not actual names, if I have written them wrong or not in the proper way, I hope the readers and especially the Shoshone will forgive me.

Some of the Shoshone language which appears in the book is correct, or as correct as I could find. Again, any mistakes are unintentional and there is no disrespect intended by the author.

Foreword

Four hundred years ago, before white men began their conquest of what is the United States of America today, the land was inhabited by many tribes of who we call today Native Americans. In the land now known as Wyoming and the area both north, and south, were the Plains Indians. The tribes were numerous, some of them being the Shoshone, Arapaho, Arikara, Bannock, Blackfeet, Cheyenne, Crow Sioux, Ute, and others.

The Indian back then and today had a deep respect for the Earth, and all the things upon it which lived. From the bear to the lion, to the bird and butterfly, to the trees and waters that flowed. They believed they were not above other living things, but part of all which lived. They were in tune with their surroundings, and never destroyed or wasted resources. They hunted to feed themselves, never for sport as the white man did. If they needed five buffalo to feed their tribe, they hunted and killed five buffalo. Conservation was an unknown term to them, but they practiced it always.

There are many legends and myths which have been told by the Native Americans of North America through the centuries. Some have been told and retold without many changes in the story, while others have taken on different beginnings and endings, as many stories tend to do. Many of these stories are attributed to the Earth and all the living things upon it.

Unlike many societies, the Native American lives by "Indian time," today as it has for thousands of years. They are connected to nature, the Earth, and their beliefs which we call mythology. Power exists in all of nature, in its lakes, rivers, land and forests, and in stones, some which have fallen from the sky.

There are many legends and myths concerning mountains of the western plains. Some are considered sacred, and others have stories told about their creation or their power in the world of the Native American.

Some of the different tribes warred with each other at times, but not as often as believed. They mostly got along with each other, trading and living on the land in relative peace. There was even a council of Elders made up of several tribes. One man would be the overall leader of this council. It was decided by many factors including the wisdom, bravery, strength, and age of the one elected.

There was a leader of the council at the time of the event, a Shoshone Chief named *Kettaa Piatukkuppiccyh*, which roughly translated into English, meant Strong Mountain Lion. Chief Mountain Lion had been respected by many Indians in many of the tribes. When he had been only twelve winters, he came upon a mountain lion attacking two small children of his tribe. He only had a knife made of stone, but he didn't hesitate. He came up behind the lion, jumped on its back and stabbed it to death. The story of his bravery became well known and his name had been changed forever. He was a fair man, slow to anger, decisive and at the time of the event was seventy three winters old.

In the land of the Shoshone, is where our story begins. It is a creation from the author's mind only. For now, put aside your reality, your analytical mind, your disbeliefs and read about the events which are to follow. And most of all, enjoy!

Prologue

Four centuries ago, on a pleasant spring evening, when the snows had begun to withdraw from the land, several young Shoshone Indians were at the base of a scared mountain known to them as *Tahna Pia Na-Nankha*. Loud Place is the closest translation, but to the Shoshone it meant much more. At times the mountain rumbled, and massive rocks would tumble down its sides. Clouds would sometimes cover the peaks, and snow covered the top of it all year long.

On this particular night, Chief Strong Mountain Lion's grandson whose name was *Kettaa Ciwox Huu-Pin*, meaning Strong Tall Tree, was sitting near a fire. He had been named for his long legs and arms, and his strength even as a baby. Strong Tall Tree had lost his father in a hunting accident, and now looked to his grandfather to teach him what was necessary to become a warrior.

He was sitting with five other boys, all roughly the same age, having lived through fifteen winters. The boys would soon no longer be looked upon as boys but recognized as men. In the coming week there were going to be tests for bravery, endurance, strength, wisdom, and other attributes for a young Indian to be recognized as a man and a warrior.

The boys huddled around the fire and spoke in whispers. They were excited and nervous about the tests in the following week. Over the many years, there had been boys who failed to pass the tests, and it would mean waiting all four seasons before they could test again. None of these six boys believed they would fail, but they could not help but think and talk about the possibility. They spoke of the coming trials, of what they would entail, how they would pass them and then about becoming warriors.

Once they had passed all the tests, they might be given new names, in accordance with their skills and completion of the trials. They would now be included in the hunts, in defending their people and would be able to choose a wife, for they would be men and warriors. Many did not choose a wife immediately, but Strong Tall Tree had his eye on a beautiful young girl named *Juun-Katy Donziape*, or Still Flower. She was almost the same age as Strong Tall Tree, and she was beautiful, with long silky black hair and dark eyes, which when she looked into the eyes of Strong Tall Tree, made him shudder and feel as if she were looking into his very soul. It scared him a little, but her eyes intrigued him more than the fear. He had made up his mind, as soon as he was recognized as a warrior and a man by his grandfather and the other warriors, he would marry Still Flower. Of course he would need her father's approval, but what mattered most to Strong Tall Tree was if Still Flower wanted to marry him. He believed she did.

The boys talked in whispers because they did not want to waken the sacred mountain. As the boys joked quietly and made fun of each other, wrestling at times, or sitting in quiet thought, something appeared in the night sky. A bright object with a glowing stream of light behind it was falling from the stars.

Now this event was not unheard of by the Shoshone or other tribes. It was looked upon as a gift from the Gods in the sky. Perhaps a God sending down one of his children to walk among the tribes, or to give the tribe a gift. Usually it was looked upon as a good omen. It might mean a calm winter or a bountiful spring. Although their understanding of what a meteorite was did not matter. Sometimes these stones from above were broken up and used to make tools, but they were always considered spiritual in nature and sacred. There were some tribes who formed their villages near a crater where a meteorite had struck, mining the nickel and iron. In any case, all the boys stood and watched as it streaked across the skies.

As they watched it fall, it struck on the side of the mountain, close to the top of the Loud Place with a bang as loud as any thunder they had ever heard. The boys watched as snow and large boulders tumbled down the mountain sides. The boys quickly took shelter waiting for the boulders to stop rolling. When they did, the boys stood with their mouths open, in awe and scared of what they had seen. Looking at each other and not giving it another thought, all six boys began to climb the sacred mountain. It was not forbidden for a warrior, a Chief, or a Medicine Man to climb the mountain, but not the boys. Still, in their excitement and wonder, the rules were not observed, and the boys climbed as fast as they could.

Soon the climb became too steep for all but two of the boys. In the lead was Strong Tall Tree and right behind him was *Kwipuntahkanten Nymypoai*, Crooked Path. Because Strong Tall Tree was almost taller than most of his tribe, with strong long legs and arms, he moved quickly up the mountain. Crooked Path continued up, trying to keep Strong Tall Tree in sight.

It was colder the higher they climbed but it did not slow them down. Soon the tree line fell behind them and the ground was covered with snow and all sizes of rocks and boulders. Shivering, they continued to climb. Then suddenly in front of Strong Tall Tree was a large crater, a hole in the side of the mountain. The ground surrounding it was steaming and free of snow. As Strong Tall Tree kneeled by the edge, Crooked Path finally caught up and kneeled beside him.

In the center of the great hole, the boys saw an almost round object, only slightly larger than a grown man's fist. Strong Tall Tree took a tentative step into the hole. He quickly jumped back because the ground was still hot.

"Help me throw snow into the hole," he said to Crooked Path.

Together they began to throw snow into the hole. As the snow landed it would melt from the heat. The boys kept throwing the snow until it started to remain as snow, not melting any further. The stone had been covered with snow over and over again, but it remained uncovered.

Crooked Path slowly entered the hole, with Strong Tall Tree directly by his side. They slowly moved closer to the stone and could still feel heat coming from it. In the dark of the night, it seemed to glow with a soft light. Both boys had never seen anything like it.

Crooked Path said, "If we gather a few sticks and lash them together, we might be able to lift the stone out."

"A good idea," Strong Tall Tree replied. "Let us gather some branches from the pine trees lower down. The pine needles will hold the stone better."

The boys climbed out and made their way back down to the tree line. They collected branches and sticks and returned to the hole made by the stone from the sky.

"Maybe we should go back down and tell your Grandfather what we have found," Crooked Path said.

"It is a gift from the gods Crooked Path," Strong Tall Tree said. "Maybe it was meant for we two to find it, since we saw it and made the climb."

"Maybe, maybe not. It is sacred and taking it might cause us great pain and disaster."

"Or it might make us mighty among our brothers."

The boys thought about what they should do for a few minutes, and then decided.

"We will carry it down to the Chief," Strong Tall Tree stated. "Together we will present it to him and the tribe. We will have songs sung about our bravery."

"Do you really think there will be songs sung about us?" Crooked Path asked.

"Of course. The women will make the songs, and the warriors will sing them."

"It still looks hot. Maybe more snow will cool it down enough to carry it."

"Yes, more snow. I don't think we should touch it."

It took many handfuls of snow to cool down the stone, but once it had, the boys were able to place it onto the branches, rolling it with sticks they had lashed together. Both boys were unable to believe how light the stone was. It felt as if they were carrying a small rock or pebble. Slowly and carefully they made their way down the sacred mountain and into the village. When they arrived, the entire tribe was waiting for them, having been awakened by the explosion and avalanche of boulders and snow. They were also alerted by the boys who did not make the climb.

Strong Tall Tree and Crooked Path made their way to where *Taikwahni Kettaa Piatukkuppiccyh*, Chief Strong Mountain Lion stood. There was no expression on his grandfather's face, so Strong Tall Tree did not know if he was going to be praised or punished. Either way it was too late now. He and Crooked Path stood with their heads held high, their chests puffed out and then knelt before the chief.

"Strong Tall Tree and Crooked Path have brought you and our brothers and sisters a gift from the gods," Strong Tall Tree said, with only a slight quiver in his voice. Chief Strong Mountain Lion said nothing. Next to him his medicine man, *Pia Taikwawoppih*, Great Talker, whispered in the Chief's ear.

Chief Strong Mountain Lion nodded and said, "Bring this gift from the gods into the council teepee. We will discuss your punishment later. Great Talker will be the only other to enter, for now. It is still too early to start our day. Back to sleep all of you."

The Chief and Medicine Man walked into the council teepee together, as the tribe listened to their Chief, and went back into their teepees. The council teepee was large enough to seat close to twenty in a circle. On the outside it was adorned with drawings of animals, lakes, rivers, and mountains. It had taken many buffalo hides to make it and it represented the strength of not only the chief, but the council as well.

The two boys entered slowly and placed the branches holding the gift on the ground in front of the Chief. Before the Chief had a chance to say anything, Crooked Path reached out and touched the surface of the gift.

Crooked Path's eyes rolled back into his head, and he fell backward, unconscious.

Great Talker jumped up and began to touch Crooked Path. He saw he was still breathing and touched his chest to feel his heart beating. Finally he began to shake him., softly and then more violently.

Strong Mountain Lion stood silently, looking from the boy to his grandson and back again.

"Is he *tei Kenu,* is he dead Grandfather?" Strong Tall Tree asked.

"No, look upon him," Chief Strong Mountain Lion said.

Crooked Path was coming awake and shaking his head, sat up.

"What did you feel Crooked Path?" Great Talker asked.

"I...I don't know?" Crooked Path said.

"I will take him to his mother and father," Great Talker said. "We must go slowly with this gift. We must not rush our thoughts about it."

"I agree," said Strong Mountain Lion. "At first light we will gather the council, and we will decide what is to be done. Strong Tall Tree, help Great Talker and say nothing of what happened."

"But Grandfather..." Strong Tall Tree began to say.

"Silence! Do not speak of this and we will discuss your punishment for climbing Loud Place at another time. Now go."

The next day as the council met, Crooked Path was visited by Strong Tall Tree.

"Are you well?" Strong Tall Tree asked.

"I am fine but my mother refuses for me to get up. As if I were a weak girl."

"Maybe she is right. You don't look well. And you have a streak of white in your hair."

"I know. My mother and Father think I have been touched by evil. But it isn't evil. It is power, and strength, and...and much more."

"The council is meeting now, and they will decide what is to become of the gift."

"I must have it!"

"You cannot have it Crooked Path. If it stays here, it will belong to all."

"What do you mean *if* it stays here. They cannot take it away from me! I will not allow it!"

"Rest Crooked Path. Rest and then we will hear of what is to become of the gift."

Strong Tall Tree was scared of the way Crooked Path was talking. He knew he should not enter the Council meeting, but he had to say something to his Grandfather. He waited outside the teepee for hours and when his Grandfather and the council exited, Strong Tall Tree spoke to him.

"The gift must not stay here Grandfather!" he blurted out.

"And why do you say this?" Strong Mountain Lion asked.

"I am not sure, but the gift scares me. Crooked Path is talking about taking it for himself. He said it has great power."

"Yes, Crooked Path is right. It does have great power. Great Talker touched it and had a vision. Nothing else will ever be said of the gift again. You must never talk of it. Do you understand?"

"I do not but as your grandson and soon to be a man and warrior, I will obey you."

"That is good. I must now speak with Crooked Path."

Unknown to the Chief, Crooked Path had snuck out of his teepee and made his way to the back of the council teepee. Taking his knife, he cut a slit and stepped into the teepee. He thought he could hear the gift calling to him. He knelt next to it and using a stick, rolled it into a pouch. Then he placed the strap holding the pouch over his shoulder. He then left the same way.

Strong Tall Tree did not know why, but he made his way to the back of the council teepee just in time to see Crooked Path walking off, something in his hands.

Strong Tall Tree cried out, "Crooked Path stop! I know what you have in your pouch. You must not take it."

"Stay away Strong Tall Tree!" Crooked Path called out. "It is mine and mine alone. I was chosen by it."

Crooked Path began to run as fast as he could. Strong Tall Tree followed and other warriors who had heard Crooked Path yell out, began to follow as well. Crooked Path could not let them have it. It was his and his alone. He ran wildly, soon coming to the cliffs that bordered the tribes land.

He stood looking down and decided the only way to escape would be to climb down. He began to descend slowly. Looking up, he saw Strong Tall Tree and other warriors looking down. He took another step, but the rock was loose. Suddenly he felt himself falling, and as he did, the strap on the pouch caught on a jutting stone. Crooked Path held onto the strap but felt himself falling.

"Now no one will have the gift," Crooked Path said, and he reached out to open the pouch..

"I am coming Crooked Path," Strong Tall Tree yelled out, and began to climb down.

Before Crooked Path could remove the gift from the pouch, his grip loosened.

Strong Tall Tree saw his friend fall, crashing into the stones below, his blood staining the rocks on his way down. Crooked Path hit the water of the river below and disappeared below its surface.

"I will get the pouch and the gift inside," he said with a quiver in his voice. "I brought this gift, or maybe this evil to our people, and I will return it to the Chief."

Strong Tall Tree wiped away his tears as he climbed down to the pouch. He lifted it off the rock slowly and climbed back up. Upon returning to the village, he met with his Grandfather in the council teepee. The council was gathered, and Great Talker was there as well. He then told what had happened to Crooked Path.

"I will go now to Crooked Path's mother and father. If they wish, I will take them to the place where Crooked Path fell."

Strong Tall Tree then left. The council was hesitant, but they still believed in Great Talker's vision.

Thus the story of the gift from the gods was lost to most but not all. The tale was told throughout the generations, to a select few, and to no one else.

CHAPTER 1

Sunday Sunrise, present day

As the sun slowly rose over Eagle Mountain, it painted the sky with deep reds, yellows, and orange hues. The land in front of me was covered with undulating tall grass, soon to be cut down, made into bales of hay for the upcoming winter. Here and there were slight elevations of hills and rocks and looking west I could almost see for miles. The sky above was turning a deep blue, the kind of blue only seen in Wyoming. This was the same land my ancestors, pioneers and Indians crossed and lived on. I tried to imagine the way it was, the hardships, the joys, the fighting, and the living and dying. Sitting atop Justice, a two year old palomino, it wasn't very hard to do.

Since we bought the horses and started spending every Sunday out here near the res, I constantly was amazed at the beauty of the land and the sky. We were on the Double T's land, but we weren't trespassing. The Double T was where we stabled our horses, and we were given permission to ride anywhere we wanted. The ranch was owned by the Tremont family. Their family had been on this land for almost two hundred years. They had fought through summers with hardly any water, winters cold enough to freeze your soul and Indians on the warpath. They were a proud family, and Gus Tremont ran the ranch today, with his wife Fran, and three sons. Since the ranch was just south of the Wind River Reservation, in Freemont County, we usually rode to the east or west. The Double T was several thousand acres, so we never had to worry about going off the ranch.

I looked out about two hundred yards to the west and saw my sons, Ben and Bear riding towards us. To my right was my beautiful wife Bell, sitting on her chestnut brown mare. Being a Detective Sergeant in the Eagle Police Department meant I spent most of my days with criminals of all kinds. I loved my job but there were times when the stress was pushing down on me and these Sunday rides gave me some peace and relaxation. Since getting the horses and spending time out riding with my family, my nightmares didn't bother me each night.

"Here they come," I said.

"Looks like they are racing again," Bell said. "I wonder if Ben is going to let Bear win this time."

"I think he will. After the last three Sunday's with Ben whooping Bear, I had a little talk with him."

We watched as the boys galloped toward us, throwing up dust and rocks as they rode. Ben was on Blackie; an all-black stallion he had gotten last year on his 13th birthday, while on vacation at Bell's parents ranch in Whispering Rock, Montana. Bear was on an American Quarter horse, with a mishmash of colors. He had named it Naruto, after an anime cartoon hero.

It looked like Ben was going to win again, but at about fifty yards from us, I saw Ben pull up slightly, letting Bear roar to a win!

"Whoo-hoo!" Bear cried out. "I finally beat you Ben."

"You sure did Bear," Ben said as he reined his horse in. "You're really learning how to ride little brother," he said and gave me a wink.

"Okay boys," Bell said, "time to head back. Remember we have to unsaddle our horses, walk them around, brush and feed them before we can head to church."

"Aww mom!" both boys called out.

"Knock it off boys," I said. "Let's not spoil the great morning we just had. We can come back next Sunday for another ride. And don't forget, at the end of July, Paul, Caroline, Tara, and Abigail will be coming to stay with us for a few weeks."

"Ben's girlfriend is coming!" Bear said.

"You better knock it off Bear before I knock you off your horse!" Ben said.

"Oh yeah, I'd like to see you do it!"

"That's enough," I said. "You two start in right now."

Both boys turned their horses toward the stable and slowly trotted off.

"Seeing the boys tease each other brings back memories of my brother and me growing up," Bell said. "Did you and Ashley fight as much as those two?"

"Honestly I suppose we did but I don't really remember. But boys will be boys and it's only natural for them to fight and tease each other. But they're both pretty good kids, and I wouldn't worry about it."

We started following the boys back to the stables, slowly, trying to take in the beautiful sunrise.

Reading my mind, Bell said, "It is beautiful out here and I know the boys love our rides. Since Paul and Caroline will be coming down in July, any ideas on what we are going to do?"

"I figured for the first few days we can show them around Eagle. The boys will love showing Tara and Abigail the hangouts, arcade, and all around the town. You can find things for you and Caroline. I will bring Paul down to the department, let him see our Dispatch, our holding cells, introduce him to some of the guys."

"Sounds to me like you're going to be giving him a full tour. I think you have something up your sleeve mister. Give."

"I guess being married to a detective is rubbing off on you lover. Well, one of my detectives is retiring around the end of June and I spoke to Will and the Chief about possibly recruiting Paul for the job."

"Really? Has he said anything about moving his family to Eagle?"

"We've discussed it a little bit, and that is one of the reasons he is coming down with his family. He wants them to check out Eagle and see if they want to move. He was really disappointed when his department hired a new Chief. He went back to being a detective, which he loves, but he thought he was going to get the job after being interim chief for nearly nine months."

"I would love it if they moved here, and I'm sure the boys, especially Ben would be thrilled, if you know what I mean."

"Yeah, I know, and it scares me a bit, but our boys are growing up. Ben will be 14 soon and I think he has discovered girls."

"He certainly seems to like Tara. And Bear is taking after Ben, liking Abigail. Who knows? Maybe one day our boys and the girls will get married."

"Take it slow," I said and laughed. "We still have plenty of time before our boys will be considering marriage. Let's catch up to the boys."

"I'll race you. On the count of three. One, Two..."

Bell took off like a shot and all I could do was laugh. We caught up to the boys and together we rode in and brought the horses into the stables. An old ranch hand named Tom Brown Shirt was standing and watching us. Tom was an Arapaho Indian and he worked and lived on the Double T ranch.

"Morning Tom," Bell and I called out, and the boys said hi.

"Morning to you Eric, and your lovely bride," he said. "How was the ride boys?"

"I finally beat Ben!" Bear called out.

"Did you now?" he said with a wink to Ben.

"We probably won't be out to ride too many more times Tom," I said. "We have some company coming in by the end of July. Let me know how much I need to pay you to watch over the horses."

"Awww, don't worry about it Eric. You pay enough for the food and use of the stables, and I don't mind taking care of these beauties. Arapaho and horses are brothers."

"You're brothers are horses?" Bear asked.

"The Arapaho and Shoshone are brothers to all animals Bear. One day I will tell you some of the old stories, if your parents say it is okay."

"Absolutely Tom, I think a little knowledge about your people would be a good thing," I said. "Thanks for taking care of the horses, but if you change your mind, just let me know."

Tom waved his hand at me and slowly walked off.

"Okay boys let's get to work," Bell said. "I'll come up with something to give Tom for his help."

"I didn't have a doubt in my mind Bell. By the way, do we really have to go to church today?"

Bell tried to playfully slap me, but I ducked and moved my horse, Justice, into his stall. I was a lucky man, and I knew it.

CHAPTER 2

I finished my breakfast and gave Bell a kiss as I headed out the door for work. The boys only had a few days left of school, and they were excited about the upcoming summer. Bell had said she was coming into town to meet with some people, but she refused to tell me who or why. I figured when she was ready she would let me know what was up.

Last night I had one of my nightmares. Even though they were becoming far and few between, I still suffered from them now and again. As I drove down from our home on Eagle Mountain, remembering the nightmare, I thought back to a summer when I had just turned 16 years old. I remembered how excited I had been for my first real summer on my own. My parents had told me I was soon going to be a senior and it was time for me to be more responsible. They said I could get a job, or just hang out, it was up to me.

On the first day of summer vacation, I had been sitting in a secret spot near Tranquility Lake, making plans. A boy, a few years older than me had disturbed my thoughts and he almost destroyed my life. He was crazy and dangerous, calling himself DeSade. He had called me Runner, a nickname given to me by some of my friends after seeing a movie, *Logan's Run*. I was terrified of him and with good reason. He had photos of my family; intimate photos and he blackmailed me and nine other boys. He formed us into a gang, committing burglaries around town.

We burgled several homes and stores exactly as DeSade had laid out, until one night when we met at a secret disheveled cabin out in the woods, it all ended. We ten were standing outside, waiting for DeSade to call us in, when the cabin went up in flames. We all had moved closer, trying to see a way in, and help DeSade. Seeing a chain around the door, locking DeSade in, and the flames engulfing the cabin, there was nothing we could do. We heard his cries, and in my mind, I could still hear them today. Soon after, we went our separate ways, never talking about DeSade, the burglaries or his habit of tossing a human thumb into the air.

Twenty years later, I had been a detective in charge of Person Crimes which included assaults, rapes, sexual assaults against children and of course, homicides. One of our local drunks, Big Joe, had been found in an alley. He had his throat slit and one other thing. His left thumb had been cut off. At first I didn't connect it to DeSade, but after another person was killed, and both he and the first victim had been part of the gang, I began to think about DeSade. I also thought about the burglaries I had committed, and the fire.

It turned out DeSade had not been killing anyone, but he had escaped from the cabin. There had been a trap door and a long tunnel beneath the old cabin. Making his way to a hospital because of the burns he had gotten. He had been treated by a compassionate nurse and eventually he married her. They had adopted a girl, and DeSade had told her all about the gang and the fire which destroyed his life. When both DeSade and the woman he married died, she decided she would have revenge upon us and find out who had set the fire.

After attending law school in California she adopted an alias, Michelle Carlyle, and got a job as an Assistant District Attorney in Eagle. She hunted down the old gang and was finally stopped, before she ever found out the truth about who had set the fire. She was now in prison, serving a life sentence.

As for the person who had lit the cabin on fire, it turned out it wasn't anyone from the gang. My best friend and now the District Attorney, Benedictus Angelo Carmelo Impeletti, called Imp for as long as I could remember, had done the deed. He had been away in Italy for the first part of the summer. But when he returned, he knew something was wrong with me. He decided to follow me, and he had found out about the gang and DeSade. He had snuck up on the cabin and learned about the blackmail and the burglaries. He decided to do something about it, and it was Imp who had set the fire. He had thought he would scare DeSade off, not kill him. For many years he had carried the thought he had killed DeSade.

After Carlyle was caught, Imp and I saw no reason to bring up the past, especially because I was being black-mailed and DeSade hadn't died in the fire. The statute on our crimes had also expired. I still felt guilty, and I know Imp did as well. But we both agreed to do penance for our crimes, and we would help the citizens of Eagle to the best of our abilities.

Soon after the case had been solved, my Sergeant and friend Will Toliver was made Detective Lieutenant. The acting Lieutenant, John (Hoorah) Mitchell had been feeding information to a news reporter, against police policy. He had been fired and no one was sad to see him go. I was promoted to Detective Sergeant and my partner on the case, Chuck Blackwell, was put in charge of Person Crimes. Things were always changing and sometimes they were for the betterment of all, and sometimes not. But nothing ever stayed the same.

I put those thoughts away as I pulled into my spot at the back of the Eagle Police Department. Every space was filled, and I was glad I didn't have to search for one. Being the Detective Sergeant, I had my own space. A small perk but one I loved having. The city of Eagle was growing, which also meant an increase in crime. The department was now at 120 sworn officers and the Police Department building was overcrowded. It would soon be necessary to get a larger space. The decision would be up to the city council, and so far there has been some disagreement as to whether to build a new building or renovate an old one.

Walking toward Will's office, I said good morning to several other detectives and officers. I was looking for Chuck or Jimmy but didn't see them. Chuck had been mentoring Jimmy Bridges, a great cop who had been made detective a year or so ago. He was a bright guy who also had a talent as a locksmith. More than once, Jimmy had opened up a lock for me, saving a door from being broken down. Since I didn't see him or Chuck, using my deductive reasoning, I figured they were out on a call. Take that, Sherlock Holmes.

"Good morning Lieutenant," I said and sat down in one of two chairs in front of Will's desk.

"Sergeant," he replied.

Although Will and I were best friends for over twenty years, while in the office we had both agreed to be professional. Only if we were alone with the door closed would we revert back to Will and Eric.

"Close the door please Sergeant," he now said.

I closed his door, sat back down, and said, "What's up Will?"

"Chuck and Jimmy are over at CAP."

CAP stood for the Child Advocacy Program, and it was staffed by mostly women who had been trained in methods to talk to children of all ages. They were the ones who conducted interviews once a patrol officer or detective had discovered a sexual assault. The interviews were recorded and the detective on the case would be able to see and hear the interview from another room.

"How old?" I asked.

"Seven year old girl. I think it might be a good idea for you to head over there. You have more experience than Chuck and it couldn't hurt."

"Okay Will, but Chuck still needs to be lead on this."

"No argument from me. But see if he needs any... guidance, okay?"

"Okay. I'll let you know what's up when I get back."

"Thank you Eric."

I walked back out to my car and headed for the CAP building. It was only a few blocks from Police Headquarters, but I had to prepare myself for the case where a seven year old girl had probably been sexually assaulted. Driving up to it always turned my stomach. I had overseen numerous cases, and they always were the worst kind to me. Children should never have to live with an assault, but if they were assaulted, it was up to me and our other officers to put away their monster. The people who assaulted children were always thought of by cops as some of the worst criminals out there. Even other criminals in prison, would place pedophiles on the bottom rung of the criminal ladder.

Stepping out of my car I took a deep breath and prepared myself for the horror I was about to hear. Catching the person who assaulted this seven year old would not be an easy task. Some cops thought catching someone who sexually assaulted a child would be easy. I even had a boss who called them "Cookie cutter crimes", meaning they were all the same. He thought they were the same because the perp was usually known and was able to be identified by the victim.

Usually it was someone in the family, or a boyfriend of a single mom. But the reality was the victim wouldn't come forward for weeks, months or sometimes years. Any evidence such as clothing, blood, hairs, and DNA would be hard to find. The only time any evidence could be found would be if the victim spoke up immediately. Then the possibility of DNA or semen might be found. Since most assaults occurred in private with no witnesses, the proof needed to put the perp behind bars usually came down to a confession.

I took another breath and rang the bell at the front door. I looked up into the camera, and I was buzzed in. Security at CAP was of the utmost concern. I walked to the back room where detectives would watch and hear the interview. Sitting there was Chuck and Jimmy.

"Okay guys, what do we have?" I said.

CHAPTER 3

"I would say good morning Eric, but it's not," Chuck said.

"Morning Sarge," Jimmy said, and I noticed he was looking a bit shaken and pale.

"You okay Jimmy," I said. "Need a little air?"

"I'm okay Sarge, and I don't want to miss a word. Whether for good or bad, this is my first case as a detective of a child sexual assault."

"Okay, even though it sucks, you need the experience. Run it down for me Chuck."

Chuck took a deep breath and began. "Victims name is Charlotte Campbell, age seven. Seems she told a friend at school how she and her grandfather..."

"Grandfather?"

"Yeah. She told her friend how they would play something called the *monkey game*, and she and her grandfather would always be naked. Her friend told their teacher, the teacher asked a few questions of Charlotte, and then we were called. I asked Charlotte about the game, and after she told me a little bit about it, about her and her grandfather being naked, I didn't ask her anything else and we brought her here."

"Good job guys. Have her parents been notified?"

"Both parents are deceased. Charlotte lives with her grandparents, Tammy, and Gordon Summers. Gordon's daughter and her husband went off the road a few years ago, and they went over a cliff, and both died."

"Have we found any other relatives?"

"There is an aunt who lives in Cody, ummm, Candace Hart. We have contacted her, and she and her husband are driving over. Should be at the department by the time we finish here."

"What is the monkey game?"

"Don't know but Charlotte is just about to tell us."

We stopped talking and I sat down to watch and listen. I saw a pretty little girl, in a pink tee shirt and blue denim pants. Her hair was blonde and was in a pony tail. She looked as innocent as any other little girl. But I knew she would never be innocent again. Sooner or later the assault her grandfather committed, would affect her. I always got angry whenever these cases showed up, and today was no different. But I had to put my anger aside if I was going to be of any help.

There was also a very slight chance this was a false accusation. It happened rarely with children so young. Sometimes an older girl, say around fifteen or so, would accuse a father or mother's boyfriend of a sexual assault. Sometimes it was a lie, a way to be noticed or get back at their mother. I didn't think this was going to be one of those times.

I looked at the monitor and saw Leslie Turner was conducting the interview. I had seen her do too many interviews to count and I was happy she was conducting it. Leslie had a real gift in getting children to talk. She was a good looking woman, around 35 years of age. She had shoulder length dark chestnut hair and striking blue eyes. I saw she and Charlotte were coloring with some crayons.

I heard Leslie ask, "Okay Charlotte, I'd like to hear about the monkey game now."

Charlotte just shook her head, and continued coloring.

"I have an idea Charlotte. I have a few dolls and stuffed animals here. Would you like to see them?"

Charlotte nodded yes and she and Leslie moved over to a box. Leslie reached in and pulled out a male doll, which was a bit bigger than the others. Then she pulled out a pretty girl doll, smaller and more like a child. She handed the girl doll to Charlotte and then returned to the table.

"Let's make believe your doll is you, and this doll is your grandfather. Okay?"

"Okay," Charlotte said.

"Great. Now how about you show me and if you could, tell me about the monkey game. Remember, you are completely safe here and you won't get into any trouble at all."

Charlotte took her doll and began to undress it.

"Should I undress my doll too?"

"Yes," Charlotte said quietly.

All the dolls used at CAP were anatomically correct, to help victims show what the assault had been if they couldn't or wouldn't say it out loud.

"When Grandpa and I play the monkey game, we take off all our clothes. Grandpa stands and is the tree and I'm the monkey. I climb up Grandpa, putting my hands around his neck, and then he carries me and lays me down on the bed."

"And what happens next Charlotte?"

"Then I die and a little while later, Grandpa makes me come alive again."

"Can you tell me what happens when you die?"

"NO, I cant! Grandpa told me when I'm dead I won't be able to remember anything."

"I see. Okay Charlotte. How about how he brings you back to life?"

"He says some magic words."

"Why don't you draw some more, and I will be right back."

"Okay," she said and began to draw again.

Leslie came into the room, shaking her head.

"This bastard has really done a number on her," Leslie said. "He basically has brainwashed her. He has made her not remember anything he does to her, or at least tried to. She really may not remember anything about the assault. I don't think she is going to go into any details, possibly never."

"We still have enough to bring him in," Chuck said. "Him getting naked with her is enough for me."

"Are you going to keep trying?" I asked.

"I'll try for a little while, but I don't want to push it," Leslie said. "I can try to interview her again in a few days. If I have to, I will drive up to Cody if her aunt gets custody. In the meantime, why don't you guys do your magic and get the grandfather to confess. Maybe if he gives some details, we can use them to get her to talk. Maybe Charlotte will be able to remember some details and talk about them."

"I know you will give it your best shot. As for a confession, you know it is easier said than done, but we will do our best."

"I'll come by later to get a copy of the interview," Chuck said. "If she gives you any more, you can call me to let me know. And thanks Leslie. Great job."

"Good luck guys," she said and went to return to Charlotte.

Chuck, Jimmy, and I walked out to the cars. We stood there for a minute, trying to get our thoughts and emotions under control. If this stuff didn't make you angry, you shouldn't be investigating this type of crime. A little anger can go a long way sometimes.

"Jimmy and I are going to go pick up the grandfather," Chuck said. "The grandmother too if she is there. What about you, Eric?"

"I'll run their names back at the P.D." I said. "Maybe he will have a record, maybe the grandmother too. You both know these guys don't just start out of the blue. He may have done this before. I'm thinking he might have done this to Charlotte's mom as a child."

"Right. A good possibility. I think I'm not going to tell him what this is all about till we get him in an interview room. Make him wonder and sweat a bit."

"Sounds like a plan to me. Just remember, don't get too physical with him unless you absolutely have to. We don't want anything to ruin the case and get it thrown out by doing something wrong."

"Got it boss. See you soon."

I watched Jimmy and Chuck take off and got back into my car. I knew the upcoming interview was probably going to be the hardest thing to do. Some of these Chimos as most cops called them, child molesters, needed to be coddled and others needed to be yelled at to make them confess. Knowing which way to go was something you had an instinct for or didn't.

I remembered a perp who had been sexually assaulting a five year old girl. He had been the boyfriend of a single mom, and when she went to work, he was left alone with her. It also turned out he had been in prison the last fifteen years, for the same crime. While in prison, he had therapy twice a week. So much for therapy working. In my experience, child molesters were never cured.

I decided on being his friend during the interview. I built some rapport, and then I told him how I completely understood how a five year old girl could be a turn on. Those short skirts, their smooth legs. He agreed and then told me how he had sexually assaulted her. I had gotten him to confess and after he was taken away, I felt like I needed three hot showers.

I had been in on several interviews conducted by both Chuck and Jimmy, and I wasn't too concerned. They both had a knack for knowing which way to go.

I pulled out my phone and called Dispatch. I asked them to get in touch with Detective Henry Walters, our department polygrapher. Sometimes if these guys weren't too bright, they would consent to a lie detector examination. Most criminals thought they could beat a poly, but in my experience, they never did. In any case, it was a good option to have handy.

I drove over to the department and filled Will in on what was happening. Then I went into my office to look up any record this guy might have. I knew it was going to be a long morning ahead of us. But if we could get a confession from this so-called grandfather, and get him out of Charlotte's life, anything we could do would be worth it.

CHAPTER 4

While Chuck and Jimmy were hunting down Gordon Summers, and I was searching for any past crimes by him, Charlie Two Horse was working on his daughter's home on the Wind River Reservation.

The Wind River Reservation was the seventh largest reservation in the United States, located in the central-western area of Wyoming. It was located in the Wind River Basin and was home to approximately 3,900 Eastern Shoshone and 8,600 Arapaho Native Americans. Near Lander and Eagle, it comprised approximately 2,268,000 acres of land. Like most of Wyoming, there were wide open fields, lakes and mountains on the res.

The living conditions for the tribes was extremely poor for many. Most of the Native Americans lived in squalid houses or trailers. A few without clean running water, or proper heat. The thought of having air conditioning never entered the minds of most of the reservation inhabitants. Healthy food was not plentiful, and crime was a large problem. It was committed by both the natives living on the res, and others taking advantage of the poor. One of the worst crimes was the disappearance of many American Native women, never to be seen again.

Most of the people on the res got by with small jobs, like working on nearby ranches, or working in nearby Lander or Eagle. Some made money by making trinkets to sell to tourists. Some would leave the res or travel to Riverton, where there was a casino. It was a sad situation, and most people never gave it another thought.

Charlie Two Horse was closing in on turning 75, but he still was strong, and his mind was clear. He usually wore old boots, denim pants and one of four shirts he owned. His face was lined with deep wrinkles and his black hair had only a few strands of gray. He usually kept his long hair in two braids, decorated with feathers. His daughter had two children and no husband to help them. They lived in a broken down home made up of different materials, scrounged from abandoned homes or junk piles. Her home was close to where Charlie and his wife of forty years now lived. Their home was larger and made of better materials. Charlie was very handy, and so the home he and his wife, Delores shared was considerably better than most on the res.

There was a great deal of work which needed to be done on his daughter's house, and today Charlie was trying to repair one of the windows on the house. It was well off square, and the wind would come in through the gaps and the broken glass in the top corner pane. He would need to remove the frame, build a new one, put in glass and then paint it. In the summer the broken glass and gaps wasn't an issue, except for the dirt pouring into the room from the strong winds. But soon it would be winter, and the family would freeze.

Charlie had driven his old truck over to his daughter's home just after sunrise, bringing his ladder, some tools, wood, paint, and several new panes of glass. Soon after arriving, Delores walked the three quarter mile and borrowed the truck to drive into Lander. His daughter and her two children had gone with Delores.

Charlie had been working for several hours now. The heat was rising, so he stopped for a minute to rest and get a drink. As he drank from an old canteen, he looked over his work. The window was looking good, with the frame now replaced by the wood he had brought. It was almost time to put in the glass panes, and then he would paint the frame. He couldn't find the same shade of brown the house had been painted, but it was close. It was something he had no choice in, and his daughter would never complain. It was not the Shoshone way to complain.

Glancing at all his supplies, he realized he had forgotten to bring any paint brushes. Maybe he had left them in the truck, or he had just forgotten them. Shaking his head, he thought to himself, he might just be losing his mind. He didn't want to walk back to his house once the sun was high in the sky. The heat would be much greater.

He took another sip of water and started slowly walking back to his house. He knew he had some brushes in a small shed in the rear of the home. He arrived back at his house and went directly to the shed. There was no lock on the door, because there really wasn't anything worth stealing inside.

As he was looking for the brushes, he heard a bang from outside. He stood still for a minute, listening and thought he heard another bang. Had Delores returned? No, he hadn't seen the truck and there was no one else who would enter his home.

Charlie Two Horse may have been an old man, but his courage was strong, and he had no fear. He didn't think to take any sort of weapon with him. Afterall, he was a Shoshone, who in his 15th year had passed all the ancient tests, becoming a man and a warrior.

Charlie slowly made his way to the back door and stood still, listening. Someone was definitely in his house, and from the sound of things, was tearing it apart. Charlie slowly turned the knob on the back door and quietly eased it open. He stood in the kitchen, looking at the open cabinets and things tossed all around.

Charlie saw a ceramic vase he had made and painted with his own hands years ago. It had been a present to Delores, and she always kept fresh flowers in it. Now it lay broken on the floor, shattered with the flowers trampled upon. Charlie's anger grew and without a second thought, headed into the main part of the home.

Charlie couldn't believe his eyes. There standing on a stool, was a young Indian he thought he recognized. The room was a mess, with every piece of furniture tossed over, the bottoms ripped out. The few books he had in a bookshelf were tossed about the room, as were some knick knacks Delores collected. His anger built and he strode into the room, grabbing the man by his shirt.

The man was younger, stronger and had no difficulty throwing Charlie off of him and to the ground. The man straddled Charlie and held a wicked knife against Charlie's throat. Charlie tried to speak but the man ordered him to be quiet, pressing the knife onto his throat, drawing blood.

"Listen to me Charlie Two Horse," the man said. "I will give you one chance, and only one chance to tell me the truth. If you do not, I will tie you up and when your wife comes home, I will kill her in front of your eyes. Then I will kill your daughter, and her children. Only then, will I kill you. Do not make the mistake in thinking I am lying to you. Nod if you understand."

Charlie could think of nothing to do, so he nodded, and he felt the knife at his throat move slightly away.

"Good. Remember I will only ask once. Now, where is the *tempin?*"

Charlie immediately knew what he wanted, but how could he give it to him? The *tempin* had been handed down to members of his family for four hundred years. But he couldn't let this maniac kill his wife and daughter. Couldn't let him kill his grandchildren.

Whispering, he said, "Give me your oath you will not hurt them if I give it to you."

The man smiled and said, "I give you my oath as a man, and a warrior."

"Under the bed, there is a loose floorboard," Charlie said. "The *tempin* is there. But it will be of no use to you. How do you even know of it?"

"It is no concern of yours."

The man tied Charlie's hands with some cord he ripped from a lamp. Then his feet and gagged him.

"If you have lied to me Charlie Two Horse, you will suffer, as will your family."

The man left Charlie lying on the floor and went into the bedroom. Charlie tried to get free, to stop this traitor to his tribe, but the cord was too tight. What could he do, he thought desperately?

The man returned and Charlie saw he had a small pouch in his hands. Charlie knew he had disappointed his ancestors.

"Do not beg for your life or cry tears, I feel nothing old man," the man said. "Now it is time for you to join your ancestors."

Charlie had tears in his eyes as the man came toward him. He knew what was to come and he silently asked forgiveness of his wife, his daughter, his grandchildren, and his ancestors. Although he knew he had no choice, he was ashamed of his actions.

The man stood over him, a smile on his evil face, holding the knife in his hands. He bent down and drew the knife forcefully across Charlie's neck. The blood spurted and in a few seconds, Charlie Two Horse no longer felt ashamed. He felt nothing at all.

CHAPTER 5

It had taken Chuck and Jimmy a short time to bring Gordon and Tammy Summers to the police department. They had found Tammy at home, but Gordon had gone shopping to Home Depot for some tools. Chuck and Jimmy had sat down with Tammy, not telling her anything at all. They stated they would wait till Gordon got home.

Tammy looked to be approximately sixty years old. Her hair was short, gray and she was what would be considered pleasantly plump. Her eyes were clear, and she wore no glasses. She had made some coffee and brought out some cookies as they waited. She didn't appear nervous and had only asked once what they were there for. As they had their coffee, Chuck and Jimmy looked over the living room. It was decorated nicely, with a large sofa, two recliners and a large flat screen tv mounted on the wall. There were two bookcases filled with books. In the corner was a small toy box, overflowing with stuffed animals and toys.

Seeing Chuck looking at the toy box, Tammy said, "Those belong to my granddaughter Charlotte. She is at school right now. Gordon and I are her legal guardians."

"What happened to her parents, if you don't mind me asking?" Jimmy asked, even though he knew the answer. He wanted to get her talking.

"About four years ago, my daughter and her husband had been killed out on the interstate. Some drunk had been driving on the wrong side of the road. Forced them off and down a cliff and killed them instantly. At least the highway patrolman said they didn't suffer, but who really knows. Of course the drunk driver walked away with only probation."

"I'm very sorry, Mrs. Summers for your loss," Chuck said. "Where was your granddaughter at the time?"

"She was with me and Gordon, thank god. His parents had passed on, so Gordon and I adopted her. Charlotte, that's my granddaughter, doesn't really remember them. We try to show her pictures and tell her things, but I think she will never really know who her parents were."

Gordon Summers then came home, and Chuck and Jimmy explained there was an investigation, and both of them needed to go with them to the station. Gordon at first wanted to know what it was all about, but finally agreed to come down. But he insisted on driving his wife and himself in their car. Chuck and Jimmy agreed, and the Summers' followed Chuck and Jimmy to the police building.

Upon arriving, Chuck had the Summers' wait in a conference room, brought them some coffee, and told them it would only be a few minutes. Chuck had closed the door but did not lock it. A lawyer might make something of a locked door before either of them had been officially arrested.

Chuck and Jimmy went straight to Eric's office.

"Are they here?" I asked.

"Yup, got them sipping coffee in the conference room," Chuck said.

"Any trouble? Do they know why they are here?"

"Nope. Obviously they are concerned but neither of them put up any argument. What did you find out?"

"I checked them both out and neither has any record at all. I was surprised but maybe he never got caught for doing anything like this before."

"He still might have assaulted his daughter."

"Right. So who is taking the lead?"

"I think Jimmy should conduct the interviews. I'd like to start with the wife."

"You ready for this Jimmy?"

"I am Sarge," Jimmy said.

I was glad he was confident, but hopefully not too confident. Chuck would be sitting in with him. I would be watching from my office on my computer. As always, everything would be digitally recorded. I would be able to see and hear every word while making a second copy on my computer.

"I'm okay with the plan," I said. "Remember to Mirandize them both before they say anything. Tell them it's policy. Also, if we need him, Henry Walters is here. Okay, go get em."

I turned on my computer, linking to the video camera and sound mike in the interview room. I watched as Jimmy escorted Mrs. Summers into the room, sitting her, so she faced the camera. Jimmy left the door open and explained to her she was not under arrest and could leave anytime she wanted to. Then Jimmy read her, her rights, and had her initial on a form.

"I still don't understand why my husband and I are here?" Tammy stated. "I hope this won't take too long. We have to pick up Charlotte at school at three."

Jimmy said, "Don't worry about Charlotte, Mrs. Summers. This will be over shortly. I'd like to ask you just a few questions. Okay?"

Watching Jimmy, I thought about the best way to conduct an interview. You asked questions, usually open ended, and let the person speak. The more they spoke the better. The initial goal was to build some rapport, and to let them talk as much as they wanted. When the time came to change the interview into an interrogation, the only thing you allowed the person to say would basically be yes or no. Cutting them off if they tried to say too much more.

"So Mrs. Summers, tell me a little bit about your life. How long have you been married?"

"Gordon and I will celebrate twenty-eight years next October," she said. "We've lived our whole lives here in Casper. I was a teacher for almost twenty-five years, and Gordon worked at the power plant. We both retired right after the accident, to take care of Charlotte."

It didn't seem getting Mrs. Summers to talk would be a problem, I thought as I watched.

"So the two of you are both retired," Jimmy stated. "How do you occupy your time, especially when Charlotte is at school?"

"Well, I like doing jigsaw puzzles, and gardening in the good weather. I read a lot and sometimes sew needle-point. And of course I play with Charlotte when she is home."

"And what about Gordon?"

"Gordon is always out in his small shop, working on this and that. He doesn't play with Charlotte too much though."

"Why is that?"

"Well, Gordon thinks it's not his place to play with her. Like with dolls or her make believe kitchen. Gordon thinks it best if I do those things."

Jimmy and Chuck both found that unusual and Jimmy gave Chuck a small nudge on Chuck's knee.

"Okay Mrs. Summers, just a few more questions," Jimmy said. "So, is there any time when your husband and

Charlotte are alone? Maybe he reads to her, or tucks her in, things like that?"

"No, never," she said, a bit forcefully. "Gordon doesn't like to be alone with her, so he never is. Now I think I want to know what this is all about."

"Charlotte has been placed into protective custody. She has made some statements which we believe are very serious. Based on what she has told us, we believe Gordon has been sexually assaulting her."

"That's impossible! Not only would Gordon never do that to her, but he is also never alone with her! Never! Now I want to leave and see my granddaughter!"

"Just one more question please. Did Gordon ever assault your daughter when she was a child?"

"NO! I am not going to listen to one more word of this...this blasphemy! I'm leaving right now."

"For the moment you will have to wait in another room," Chuck said. "At least until we have interviewed your husband. Come with me."

Mrs. Summers stood and angrily followed Chuck out of the room. She was placed in a room away from her husband, so they could not talk to each other. She was advised she could leave at any time if she so desired, but it would be better if she stayed. She had replied she would wait for her husband. As soon as Chuck had escorted her out, Jimmy ran to Eric's office.

"What do you think Boss?" Jimmy asked.

"You're doing a great job Jimmy," I said. "But getting through to our perp might be tougher. Remember to build some rapport first and get him talking if he wants to. Don't interrupt him if he is talking. Don't break the reason he is here too quickly. And if you need any help, Chuck will be right there."

"That's right Jimmy," Chuck said as he entered the room. "Mrs. Summers is pissed off, but I think she might know what has been going on. I think she protested too much. I told her she could leave if she wanted to, but she wants to wait for her husband. If we get a confession, it might be twenty years or so."

"Let's hope. You ready to interview Mr. Summers now?"

"I am," Jimmy said and stood up.

"Okay, go get him."

CHAPTER 6

I watched on my monitor as Chuck and Jimmy brought Gordon Summers into the interview room. He was a large man, maybe 6'3 or more, weighing about 240 lbs. He had thick black glasses, reminiscent of Buddy Holly. He was mostly bald with a fringe of white hair, and he sported a long beard, mixed with gray and white. A white tee shirt and denim coveralls completed the picture. Looking at him, I got angry thinking about this hulk of a man assaulting little Charlotte.

He sat down at the table, facing the camera the same way his wife had done. He didn't say a word, just stared at Chuck and Jimmy.

"Okay Mr. Summers," Jimmy began, "it is policy to read you your rights."

"Uh huh," was all he said.

Jimmy ran through them, advised him he was not under arrest and could leave anytime he wanted to. He then offered him a pen to sign the form.

"Not gonna sign anything till I know what this is all about."

Jimmy began to say something, but Chuck interrupted, saying, "No problem Mr. Summers. But I will need verbal confirmation you understand your rights as I have read them."

"Fine. I understand them."

"Let's start off with a few simple questions," Jimmy said. "Could you state your name, your birthdate and where you live please?"

"You damn well know where I live, you picked me up there, you know my name and my birthdate is February 12, the year don't matter. Where is my wife?"

"Your wife is waiting in one of our conference rooms sir. Now, do you work or are you retired?"

"Retired."

"And do you spend most of your days at home, with your wife and granddaughter?"

"Where else would I be?"

I heard Jimmy ask him a few more open questions, but Summers' didn't want to say more than a word or two. Building rapport was not going to work on him. It was time for Jimmy to get a bit tougher and get to the heart of the matter.

"Do you ever spend any time alone with Charlotte?" Jimmy asked. He also leaned forward a bit, a trick used to make a person feel blocked in.

"Why do you..."

"Just answer the question."

"Never."

"Never? Very interesting. You never read to her, or play with her, maybe with her dolls or toy kitchen."

"Never."

"Okay, you want to explain what the monkey game is?"

Summers glared at Jimmy and then said, "I don't think I want to talk to you anymore."

"That's your right Mr. Summers, but it doesn't mean I can't talk with you. You can just sit there and listen." Jimmy took a deep breath and began. "Charlotte has been placed in protective custody for now."

"You can't do that!" Summers said and started to stand up.

"Sit back down...now." Chuck said, half rising off his chair.

Under other circumstances, I thought it would be funny, watching Chuck, who was just under 5'10 trying to put Summers back in his seat. But thinking about what this man allegedly had done, took all the humor out of it. Plus, I thought Chuck would probably take him.

After Summers sat down again, Jimmy said, "We know all about the monkey game. Your wife told us."

"My wife has no idea what it is!" Summers yelled out.

"So there is a monkey game then."

"Yeah, yeah. But it's not what you think it is."

"Why don't you tell me then, if you want to continue to talk to us of course."

I was glad to see Jimmy was being smart. Once someone said they didn't want to talk anymore, you had to get them to agree to talk again. Otherwise anything else said might be thrown out of a court of law.

Summers said, "Yeah, okay, I'll talk. The monkey game was just hide and seek. I made believe I was a tree, with bananas, and I would hide them. That's all it was."

"And your wife played the game with you?"

"No."

"Well then, that would mean your game, would have been played while alone with Charlotte, right?"

"Umm, yeah, I suppose so."

"Charlotte told us, when you both play the monkey game, you are both naked."

"That's a lie! Charlotte has a very vivid imagination."

"So you never have been naked with your granddaughter?"

"Never. I would swear on a stack of bibles. She's lying for some reason."

"Relax Mr. Summers", Chuck said. "We told you; you aren't under arrest. We're just trying to find out the truth. Let's step out for a second Detective."

"Excuse us for a minute Mr. Summers," Jimmy said. "Can I get you a coffee or soda?"

"A coke would be fine," Gordon said, crossed his arms across his chest and glared into the camera.

Jimmy and Chuck left the interview room and left the door open. Outside the room, a uniformed officer stood in case Summers wanted to leave. He couldn't stop him legally, but his presence alone might keep him in the room.

"What do you think Sarge?" Jimmy asked me as he and Chuck came into my office.

"I think you are doing a good job Jimmy," I said. "But you will never build rapport with him. His body language indicates he isn't going to say anything. And I don't think you are going to get him to confess. Remember, we only have Charlotte's word on this. No physical evidence, or at least none until we get her examined by a doctor. The wife knows something has been going on, but she is ignoring the truth."

"What about using Henry?" Chuck asked.

"Might be the only hope we have."

"But how do we get him to take a poly?" Jimmy asked.

"Stay here and watch and learn Jimmy," Chuck said, and left the room.

Jimmy pulled a chair around my desk so he could watch the monitor. A few minutes later, we saw Chuck enter the room with a can of coke in his hand.

He sat down, handed over the soda and smiled.

"Gotta love these young kids, right?" Chuck asked.

Summers didn't say anything but took a few swallows of the soda.

"Don't get me wrong. Detective Bridges is a good kid but maybe a bit overzealous. He doesn't have the experience I do. I know most of the time, when kids say someone is assaulting them, it's some kind of, well, not a lie but a fib."

"Well, fib or lie, Charlotte isn't telling the truth about me," Summers said.

"I believe you Gordon, can I call you Gordon?"

"Yeah, sure."

"I'm Chuck. So here's the thing Gordon. It really doesn't matter if I believe you because Detective Bridges is lead on this case. He wants to take you to jail right now and go to see the District Attorney."

"He's nuts. I haven't done a damn thing. Maybe I should get a lawyer."

"That's one way to go, but I don't recommend it. I have a better idea."

"Oh yeah, what?"

"First, do you want a lawyer, because if you do, I have to stop talking with you. Detective Bridges will take you to jail."

"No lawyer yet. Now, what do you have in mind?"

"Ever heard of a polygraph? A lie detector?"

"Yeah."

"Well you know, a polygraph is not allowed in evidence. The courts look at it as if it were some kind of magic. The thing is most people believe a polygraph is meant to make you look guilty. But really, we use them to clear a person. You can pass a poly, can't you Gordon? I mean if you are not lying."

Gordon thought for a few minutes and then said, "Sure, I can pass one cause I'm not lying."

"Okay then. I can get it set up in about ten minutes."

As I watched the monitor, I got Henry on the phone and told him he was needed immediately. He would get all his equipment set up in another interview room. Then he would go over the questions with Jimmy and Chuck. The way the questions would be worded was extremely important.

"I'll go get our guy and then you can take it. Once you have passed, you can go home, and all of this will just disappear. Okay?"

"Yeah, Yeah. Let's get it going so my wife and I can go home."

"Okay then, just wait right here."

Chuck returned to my office and took a seat.

"You get Henry started?" Chuck asked.

"Should be ready in ten minutes," I said. "Great work in there Chuck. What did you think, Jimmy?"

"I thought you were fantastic," Jimmy said. "Can I sit in on the poly? I have never seen one, other than the one I took to get this job, of course."

"No can do, but I can tell you how it will go, and we can watch on the monitor. First Henry will put the equipment on him. Two springlike things on his chest, one under his backside, a blood pressure cuff on his arm and a clip monitor on his finger. Then he will tell Summers the exact questions he is going to ask. He will ask for his answers. Then he will use something to prove to Summers he cannot lie and get away with it."

"How does he do that?"

"Usually, he will ask Summers to think of a number between 1 and 6. Then he tells him to answer every question with a no when he asks about the number he chose. He will say is it number one, number two, and so on.. He will also hand him some paper and a black marker. Tell him to draw his number, large on the paper, fold it and put it in his pocket."

"What if Henry can't guess the right number?"

"It's not a guess Jimmy. I've never seen it fail. Henry will pick the number Summers wrote down. Then, Summers will realize he might not be able to lie. He will try, but he will fail."

"And then what?"

"Then he will ask Summers the questions he has already given him. He will ask in a monotone voice, slowly and carefully. The way the questions are worded are of the utmost importance. He will ask the questions twice, and then excuse himself to score Summers' answers."

We sat and waited and in about forty-five minutes, Henry came walking into my office. He looked from me to Jimmy and then to Chuck. Then he smiled.

"We got him!" Henry said.

CHAPTER 7

"He lied?" Jimmy asked.

"Of course he lied," Henry said. "He was overall deceptive on every question concerning the monkey game and Charlotte. I did ask one question about his daughter, and he was deceptive again. He did it, the sick son of a bitch."

"Then we got him!" Jimmy exclaimed.

"Slow down Jimmy," I said. "We can't use the poly except to make him confess. I think we should let Chuck take lead now. You go in with him but watch and learn."

"Can I watch with you, Eric? Henry asked.

"Of course. You ready Chuck?"

"Absolutely!" Chuck said with a smile. "Gotta get a few props first."

Henry and I watched as Jimmy entered the interview room, took a seat, and waited. A full five minutes later, Chuck walked in with a large folder in his hands, and a thick looseleaf book. Without any hesitation, Chuck slammed the whole thing down on the table, making Summers and Jimmy jump.

"You lied!" Chuck said. "I believed you, and you made an ass out of me! You fucking lied!"

"But I..." Summers began but Chuck cut him off.

"Bullshit! You failed the poly Gordon. You failed it bad, and I know..., I know you assaulted that little girl. Now the only thing I want to know is if you are going to be a man, and a grandfather who supposedly loves her..."

"I do love her!"

"Prove it! Tell me the truth."

I watched as Gordon hung his head and began to weep. It was as good as done. Chuck would get a full confession and have Gordon write it down. I shut off the monitor and waited for it to be over.

In the interview room, after confessing and writing it down, Summers asked Chuck for a favor.

"Can you bring my wife in here, so I can tell her myself please?" Summers asked.

"Sure, give me a second."

Chuck and Jimmy walked out, telling the uniformed officer Summers was now under arrest, and not to leave the room.

A minute later, Mrs. Summers was led into the room. She sat down across from her husband. Chuck and Jimmy came into my office, all smiles and clapping their hands.

"We got him Eric," Chuck said. "All tied up with a neat ribbon on top."

"Great work guys," I said. "Did he say anything about his daughter?"

"I didn't bring it up, figured once he is over at the jail I would pay him a visit and try to get the truth out of him."

"I just hope Charlotte isn't permanently destroyed from that bastard. Once her aunt gets down here, you guys will have to go in front of a judge with all the paperwork and the confession. I'm sure the judge will not let Mrs. Summers retain any legal right to her."

"Turn on the monitor Eric," Chuck said. "Let's see how Mrs. Summers is taking his confession."

"I bet she's pissed!" Jimmy said.

I turned on the monitor and couldn't believe my eyes. Gordon Summers was on the floor, his hands across his face. Mrs. Summers was straddling Gordon, her heavy pocketbook swinging through the air, striking Gordon on his head and face!

"Get in there!" I yelled.

Chuck and Jimmy raced into the interview room and pulled Mrs. Summer off of him. The uniformed cop took control of her and said he hadn't heard a thing.

Once everything was under control again, Summers was handcuffed. They could've arrested Mrs. Summers for assault, but they thought she had the right to hit her husband. Maybe she really didn't know what kind of monster her husband really was.

Jimmy and Chuck led him out of the room and would take him to the jail, where he would be booked. Then Jimmy and Chuck would be looking at four or five hours of paperwork. But they wouldn't mind, they had just slain a monster.

CHAPTER 8

Monday 3:45 pm

The truck made its way up the dirt road, leaving a dust trail behind it. The truck was white, underneath the dirt and grime covering it. An old F-150 with rust here and there. The sound of its engine was loud, straining as it pulled in front of Charlie Two Horse's home. The driver's door opened with a squeal, and the dust from the road had all but covered the shield, stating this truck belonged to the Wind River Reservation Tribal Police.

Lieutenant Robert (Bobby) Black Bear stepped out of the truck. Bobby was a tall man, standing 6'6, unusual for a Shoshone. His long black hair hung straight down, past his shoulders. He wore a button down white shirt, denim pants and black boots. His gun, a nine millimeter Glock was on his hip, and a pair of handcuffs hung off the back of his belt. Bobby Black Bear had been with the Wind River Tribal Police for almost eighteen years. He had a force of thirty men, both Shoshone and Arapaho Native Americans. He needed sixty or more, but getting anyone from either tribe was hard work. Plus the government wouldn't pay for many officers.

He reached into the truck and came out with a weathered, sweat stained white cowboy hat. Placing it on his head, he stood looking all around, taking everything in, burning it into his memory. He knew Charlie Two Horse well, his wife, their daughter and her two children. He saw the house, which was better than most, two children playing on the side of the house, and an old truck sitting to one side. Then he saw one of his men, Daniel Red Shirt, striding toward him. Daniel was twenty-four years old and had been on the force for almost two years. He was an Arapahoe and did not wear his hair long, in the traditional way. He was always bothering Bobby about modernizing the tribal police department. Bobby would if it were possible, but the money just wasn't available. As he looked at his officer, Bobby saw Daniel didn't look too well, in fact he looked as if he had tossed his cookies, maybe more than once.

"Lieutenant," Daniel said with a tremor in his voice. "Bad in there, really bad sir. I never..."

"Take a deep breath Dan," Bobby said. "Take another and remember, you are an Arapahoe, and a police officer. Get control."

Daniel took a few deep breaths, regaining his emotional control. "I'm better now Lt., thanks. Old Charlie Two Horse has been murdered. Throat slit almost taking his head off. Entire house has been tossed."

"Who found him?"

"His wife Delores and his daughter Lisa. Luckily, the kids were playing outside as soon as they returned from shopping. The kids didn't see anything."

"Where is Delores and Lisa now?"

"I have them in the kitchen, sitting at the table. I would have put them outside, but it's way too hot."

"Good job Dan. Might earn you some stripes one of these days. Get on the radio and have George Running Deer come on out. Then call for the Medical Examiner from Eagle. After that, stay out here and make sure no one tries to enter the house. You can sit in your car with the ac running."

"I'm on it Lieutenant."

Bobby took one more look around as he stepped up to the front door. He looked at the door frame but didn't see any unusual marks. House was probably unlocked, like most houses on the res. He stepped into a small foyer and then into the living room.

Bobby had been in this house before. It was a small but comfortable house. There had been family pictures on the walls, shelves with books and some reminders of the history of the Shoshone. He remembered a drawing of one of the ancient Chiefs, *Kettaa Ciwox Huu-Pin* Chief Strong Mountain Lion.

Daniel hadn't been kidding about the home being tossed. There wasn't one picture, one piece of furniture or one book not torn or ripped or broken. Fragments of pottery were scattered all over the floor. Even the drawing and frame of Chief Strong Mountain Lion had been torn to shreds. In the center of the room, lay Charlie Two Horse, with a pool of blood under his head and shoulders.

Stepping closer, he noted none of the debris from the home was on top of Charlie. He lightly turned Charlie on to his side, seeing debris under him. That meant whoever had killed him, did not continue to break anything, after Charlie had been killed. More than likely, Charlie had surprised the killer while he was destroying the living room. The search had ended when Charlie was killed. Maybe the killer had only been intent on destruction, or maybe he had been looking for something, some money, or valuables.

Bobby stood looking around, once again taking in everything. Who would want to kill old Charlie, he thought. There wasn't anything worth stealing here, at least he didn't think so. Maybe he would get some information from Delores or Lisa to shed some light on this.

Bobby made his way into the kitchen where he saw Delores and Lisa, sitting at the table. Delores was a few years younger than her husband and was still a beautiful woman. She had on a buckskin top, decorated with small trinkets. On her wrists were two turquoise bracelets and she wore only her wedding ring on her fingers. Her daughter Lisa was dressed in Levi's and a blue tee shirt. She took after her mother and was very pretty. No one understood why her husband abandoned her. Bobby removed his hat and knelt down by Delores.

"*Tamshe gomia tsa*, Delores, Lisa." Bobby said, meaning 'My heart is sad with you.'

"Why would anyone kill Charlie?" she sobbed. "Why?"

"If you want some time, we can speak later."

"No. I will speak now. Ask me your questions."

"Was there anything in the house worth stealing and killing for?"

"No, we were poor, the same as most. There was nothing."

"Did Charlie have any arguments or had trouble with anyone lately?"

"No. Charlie was a peaceful man. There wasn't anyone who hated my husband. Can you think of anything Lisa?"

Lisa just shook her head, tears running down her face.

"Can you give me an idea of what Charlie had been doing today?"

Lisa answered quietly, "My father came to my home early this morning. He was going to replace the frame of a broken window and put in new glass."

"I walked over at about 10:30", Delores said, "and took the truck so Lisa and my grandchildren could drive into Eagle for some shopping."

"My father was a good man," Lisa said. "You must find the man who did this."

"I'm going to do my very best Lisa," he said. "The medical examiner will be here soon. He will have to take Charlie in for an autopsy. I will make sure he moves quickly so you can make a funeral. Do you know if Charlie wanted to be buried or cremated?"

"My husband wanted to be buried," Delores said. "We know of a place up in the mountains. He will be buried with the things he loved."

"For now, why don't the two of you go back to your house Lisa. I don't want your children to see their grandfather taken away."

Delores and Lisa stood, slowly walking out the back door of the kitchen. Neither wanted to see Charlie lying in his own blood again.

After they left, Bobby figured he would look around until the Medical Examiner and his evidence tech showed up. The only good thought he had, was the Shoshone and Arapahoe who knew Charlie, would now look after Delores and Lisa. It was the Native American way.

The living room was such a shambles, he didn't think he would find anything right now. Maybe after the place had been photographed and Charlie had been removed. He gathered the pieces of the drawing of the Chief, thinking he might be able to tape it together.

He walked down a small hallway where there were three doors, all closed. Opening one he saw a bathroom. The fixtures were old, but everything was spotless. The killer hadn't been in here, he thought. Next he found a small bedroom. It probably had been Lisa's at one time. Now there were bunk beds, more than likely for the two children to sleep in when they stayed with their grandparents overnight. Again, nothing was disturbed. Either the killer never got this far or found what he was looking for.

Finally, Bobby opened the last door. The bedroom was larger than the other one, but not by much. It had a full bed, covered with a colorful blanket, probably made by Delores. Two end tables and some pictures on the walls. There was a large dresser against one wall, and a trunk at the foot of the bed. There was only one closet. Looking into the closet and trunk, Bobby thought they too hadn't been searched. Nothing was broken or moved as far as Bobby could see. Moving around to the far side of the bed, Bobby saw something out of place. Bending down, he saw it was a small plank of wood. It was approximately six inches long and three inches wide. It matched the color and type of wood from the bedroom floor.

"Now where did this come from," he said to himself. He looked in the closet and all around the small room, finally getting down on his belly, looking under the bed, with his flashlight.

There he saw an opening in the floor. Standing up, he pushed the bed against one wall. He knelt next to the hole. It was empty. He took the small plank and tried to fit it onto the opening. It fit perfectly.

Taking the wood back off, he stood thinking. Something had been in the hole in the floor. Something someone thought was worth killing for. But what would it be? The opening couldn't hold anything too large. Gold maybe? Some papers? Bobby had no clue. Still, he would have George his evidence tech dust the opening and gather any evidence from it.

Bobby returned to the living room and kneeling next to the body of Charlie Two Horse, said a silent prayer, and waited for the others to arrive.

CHAPTER 9

Monday 8:30 pm

Bell and I were sitting in the den, having some coffee and a slice of pie. The boys had finished their dinner and headed up to do their homework. In a week or so, school would be over, and the boys were excited. I thought Ben was more excited about Tara coming down for a few weeks in July, than school being over.

"This pie is delicious," I said. "If you keep baking like this I'm going to have to go on a diet."

"You look fine honey, and you definitely don't need a diet" Bell said. "But you are a bit flabby, so I think some exercise is called for."

"Flabby? Did you just call me flabby?

I stood up, pulling my shirt up and grabbing my stomach. Unfortunately, I had quite a handful. Maybe I was getting flabby.

"Besides for your job," Bell said with a smile, "how would it look for a councilwoman's husband to be lugging around a big fat belly."

"I do not have...wait a minute. Did you say councilwoman?"

"I was meeting with a group of our most prominent businessmen today in town. They seem to think I would make a great city councilwoman. They want me to run. The election is in November, still a ways off."

"Well what did you tell them?"

"I said I would have to pass it by you. Afterall, it would affect both our lives if I won. Less time at home, less time with the boys."

"First of all, the boys and I will be just fine. You have no reason to worry about it. But more importantly, do you want to run?"

"Well, it's been nearly 14 years since I was working. I loved being a teacher but we both agreed it would be better if I stayed home when Ben was born. Now that the boys are older, I think I would like to do something meaningful again. What do you think?"

I acted like I was thinking it over, getting up and pacing.

"Are you going to walk a path in the floor or tell me what you think Eric?"

"I think I am looking at the next city councilwoman of Eagle Wyoming!"

"Really? You're sure?"

"I'm sure if you are Bell. I think you would be great. Now tell me how this works. Who pays for your campaign, do you need a political manager, figure out your platform…"

"Yes, all of that but I'm sure the people I met with have most of it figured out. I will give them a call first thing tomorrow and tell them I will accept the nomination!"

We talked about this new and exciting proposal, trying to figure out a few things. I knew it would be hard during the campaign for the boys and me, but Bell certainly deserved to give it a go. The only thing I was really concerned about was who she was going to be running against.

"You know, in the last election, Graham Stone didn't play fair," I said. "Plus as the incumbent, he might be tough to beat."

"I know," Bell said. "Last election he ran a pretty dirty campaign. Dug up some scandal involving his opponent. But I don't have any skeletons hiding in my closet. And neither do you."

"Well, I'm not sure he could find out about my involvement in the Under my Thumb gang and DeSade. But if he did and tried to use it, we will deal with it openly and honestly. I'm not worried about it, and I don't think you should be."

Just then, both boys came flying down the stairs and jumped on either side of us on the couch. I wondered if the boys only had two speeds, very slow or very fast. Maybe one day their feet would actually hit the steps.

"Homework's all done!" Bear called out.

"Geez Bear, do you have to yell?" Ben said.

"I wasn't yelling!" Bear yelled out, again.

"Okay you two, that's enough," I said. "Your mother has some news."

"What's up mom?" Ben asked.

"Yeah mom, what?" Bear joined in.

"I have been asked to run for city council."

"Wow Mom, that's awesome," Ben cried out.

Bear sat there, not saying anything.

"Aren't you excited for your mom, Bear?" I asked.

"Would it mean you wouldn't be here anymore, like when we get home from school and stuff?" Bear asked, looking down.

Bell pulled Bear onto her lap and told him, "You never have to worry about me being here for both of you and Dad. Nothing could ever stop me from taking care of you, watching your sports or anything else."

"Will you still be able to cook for us?" Bear asked. "Dad's cooking sucks!"

"My cooking sucks?!" I said. "Just for that, take this!" I yelled out and hit Bear with a pillow.

Next thing I knew, we all had grabbed pillows, and an all-out war had begun. It lasted a few minutes and then everyone fell on the floor laughing.

"Okay boys, time for bed," Bell called out as she tried to fix her mussed up hair.

"Okay Mom," Ben said and went up the stairs as fast as he had come down.

Bear headed up slowly and then turned back to us.

"I'm proud of you mom and I guess we can eat some of Dad's cooking, if we have to," Bear said with a smile.

I picked up a pillow and threw it at him. He took off and once again, I was sure his feet never touched the steps.

Bell and I fell back on the couch, smiling and laughing.

"Well I guess that settles it," I said. "Now you have both mine and the boys okay."

"Yup," Bell said. "Looks like my hat is in the ring. Now, do you think you can get your flabby self, up the stairs to the bedroom for a bit of a private celebration?"

I jumped up and ran for the steps, and said, "My feet won't even touch the steps!"

CHAPTER 10

I was lying in bed, stretching, and smiling, reliving last night's private celebration. Bell had gotten out of bed a few minutes ago, and I heard the shower running. I got up, and walked into the bathroom, naked. Slowly, I opened the sliding glass door and stepped in.

"Excuse me sir," Bell said, "do I know you?"

"Maybe not," I replied, "but I'm sure you can get to know me."

The next fifteen minutes came in a close second to the night before. Bell got out of the shower to get dressed and start breakfast. I stayed in the shower, thinking how lucky I was. I had a sexy, beautiful, loving wife, two great boys and a great job. And now, I was going to be the husband of a Councilwoman! Well, I thought, as long as she won.

I finished breakfast and told the boys goodbye before they headed off for school. Then I kissed Bell and wished her success in town today.

"As soon as I get home tonight," I said, "you will have to tell me all about the plans being made for your run."

"I'll tell you everything!" Bell said. "Be safe honey."

I headed down the mountain, not thinking about anything in particular, smiling and singing along to the radio, where an old Elvis Presley song was playing. I even thought I sounded a bit like the King of Rock and Roll as I belted out *Jailhouse Rock*. Everything was great and I was looking forward to whatever the day brought.

I pulled into my spot and immediately saw a huge man standing nearby. His back was to me, but I was sure it was Max Yellowfeather.

Max was an Eastern Shoshone Indian, about 40 years old, and most of the time he lived on the Wind River reservation. He had been arrested numerous times, mostly for public intoxication and it had become a game to him. Max was an excessively big man, maybe 6'5" or so and weighing in at about 280lbs. He wore his jet-black hair in two long braids, both tied with an eagle feather. It was against the law to harm an American eagle, but I was sure no cop had ever made it an issue. Max never got into any real trouble, even though he had been involved in a few altercations. And I knew Max always carried several knives on him, though he had never used them as far as I knew.

The first time I met him he had been sitting on the back of an ambulance. His cousin had stabbed him for some reason or another. She was never caught, disappearing back east, and Max never brought it up to me. When I asked him where he had been stabbed, he turned his back to me. There about halfway up was a knife, shoved all the way to the hilt. Max didn't seem to be in any pain, and it always amazed me every time I thought of it.

I stepped out of the car and Max saw me and walked over.

"*Tsaangu Beaichehku* Max," I said. If it had been someone else, Max might have thought I was condescending, saying good morning in his native language. He accepted it, coming from me.

"*Tsaangu Beaichehku,* Detective," He said in his deep baritone voice.

"What can I do for you Max?"

"Is there somewhere we can talk, privately, Detective?"

"Follow me."

I walked him in the back way and more than one officer stopped whatever he was doing or talking about as this mountain of a man walked by. Max was unperturbed, having dealt with people staring at him since he was a young man.

I opened up the door to a conference room, not in use. Max sat down and so did I.

"Can I get you anything Max?" I said.

"Nothing but *Tsaa*," he said, meaning thank you. "There is something I need to discuss with you. But you must agree to say nothing about it to anyone here in your police department."

"Well Max, the only thing I can promise is, I won't say anything to anyone, unless there has been a crime committed. Even then, I will try not to involve anyone else unless absolutely necessary. Okay?"

"You are a man of honor and so I will accept what you have said. A cousin of mine had her apartment broken into."

"If it was on the res..."

"It was here, in Eagle. She lives with her older brother on the west side of town."

"Okay. What are their names?"

"She is Maggie Bright Star, and her brother is Abel Bright Star."

"And the address?"

"They both live in the Charles Apartments, in 201."

"What was stolen?"

Max paused for a second and his hand went to his chest, holding onto something under his shirt. "I do not know if anything has been taken. Maggie came home and found the place... what do you call it?"

"Tossed?"

"Yes, tossed. She called the police and made a report, but when Abel got home, he told her she had made a mistake in calling them. They did not need help from the Eagle Police.

When an officer eventually responded, Abel would not let him in. He told the officer it was a mistake and there would be no further need of his services."

Max was holding onto the object under his shirt as he talked. It was not a big deal but being a detective I noticed it. Maybe it was just a habit. I knew Max never lied, even if it meant getting himself in some trouble. Maybe he didn't know if anything was stolen, but I wasn't sure. But I thought he had something in mind, or else he wouldn't be here.

"But nothing was taken?" I asked.

"I cannot say," Max said again. "My cousin would only say it was very serious."

I took a deep breath and said, "Do you want me to talk with your cousins?"

"No, you must not Detective. Abel spoke with me. He was very concerned about the burglary but said he could not reveal if anything had been taken. It was very strange and not like him at all."

"Let me get this straight. Your cousins apartment has been broken into. You can't or won't tell me what was stolen if anything. I am not allowed to talk with them, and you have told me all of this...why?"

"There may come a time when this will become clear. I wanted to... give you a heads up."

Max then stood and made to leave. His hand released whatever he had been holding.

"I'll walk you out Max. Since a report was made, I'm going to see what the Officer's report states. Is that okay with you?"

Max thought for a second and then said, "I suppose it would do no harm. If I can tell you anything further, I will. *Tsaa* Detective."

We went down the hall to the main lobby. I walked outside with Max just as Chuck was making his way in.

"Good morning Eric," he said. "Is there any trouble?"

"Not a thing Chuck."

"Okay then, I'll see you inside."

Chuck had some run-ins with Max also, and I think he was just a touch afraid of the big man.

"Remember Detective," Max said, "Say nothing to anyone."

Max walked away and I thought, what the hell would I tell anyone, since I had no idea what I had even been told.

Oh well, I guess if it ever came to finding out anything about what was stolen or not from Maggie and Abel Bright Star, I would deal with it then. I walked back into Police HQ and went straight to a meeting room. Lt. Will Tolliver always started the day with a meeting of the Investigation Squad. All were required to be there unless they were out working a case. Each Detective would give a small summary of any new cases they were working, or any new leads on older cases. Will would also go over any crimes which had occurred overnight.

As I sat down with a cup of coffee, I couldn't help but wonder why Max had come to see me. It was mysterious and he seemed to think it was serious. It was a puzzle, and no detective liked unsolved puzzles. It was in our blood to solve them. I decided after the meeting I would look up the Bright Star's and see the report or if they had a rap sheet. I wouldn't go and speak to them...yet. But if something popped, I would have to ignore Max's request and go to them.

Will began to speak, and I tried to stop thinking about the little info Max had told me. It was a losing battle.

CHAPTER 11

Eagle General Hospital, near the back where the morgue was located, Charlie Two Horse was being autopsied this morning. Although Bobby knew what had killed him, he still needed to attend the autopsy for a few reasons. One, it was his job. Two, he had to see everything for himself, it was the way he did his job. And finally, it was a matter of respect for Charlie's wife and family, and the respect he felt for any Shoshone who had passed on. He felt a Shoshone should be present out of respect for Charlie Two Horse.

He sighed and walked up to a pair of glass doors which opened as he stepped forward. In front of him was a long hallway, painted in an awful color of green. Why hospitals painted their halls in such ugly colors was a mystery to Bobby.

On his right was a desk with a young woman behind it. She was very young, no more than eighteen. Pretty in a white woman way, with yellow hair tied in a pony tail. There was too much makeup on her face, green on her eyelids and bright pink lipstick on her full lips. The top she wore could have been less close fitting, and buttoned higher but Bobby figured she wore it tight to show off her figure.

"Good morning," Bobby said. "I am here to observe the autopsy of Charlie Two Horse."

"Uh huh," she said, looking at some papers on a clipboard. "Your name?"

"I am Robert Black Bear, Lieutenant in charge of the Wind River Tribal Police."

"Ummm, I think the Doc is about to begin. You can go right back. Down the hall and third door on the right. Have a nice day," she said with a big smile, flashing overly white teeth.

Bobby thought maybe she didn't really know where she was or what was done down here. He sure hoped she was less enthusiastic and had some empathy if family members came here to view or identify loved ones. He nodded to her and walked down the hall.

As he got closer to door number three on his right, the strong smell of disinfectants, formaldehyde, alcohol, and death became more noticeable. He passed what was probably an office, and another room for autopsies before he got to room three. He paused, preparing for the sight of Charlie laid out on a cold metal table. He had been to many autopsies, but he never wanted to see them. But again, it was his job and responsibility.

Bobby entered and saw Jim McAddams, the County Coroner about to begin. He shuddered from either the cold temperature in the room, or the sight of Charlie Two Horse laid out on the table. Most simple autopsies were done by Doc McAddams, and if a body needed someone with more experience, they were taken down to Loveland, Colorado. There, a medical examiner would perform the autopsy.

Jim was in his lower sixties, with no signs of retiring, which was a good thing since he really knew his business. He was also one of the best doctors in Eagle and was always a very busy man. When the owner of the Senior Center, Carl Meadows was killed two years ago, Jim took over running the place with the help of some college kids. He had been a frugal man and had plenty of money, but he loved working.

Bobby knew Jim well and walked in saying, "Good morning Doc."

"Nice to see you Bobby," Jim said. "Of course, I would prefer other circumstances."

"Can't argue with you. I guess I'll stand by until you finish Doc."

"Sure, sure. I don't expect any surprises. Death was definitely caused by his head nearly being decapitated. But I might be able to give you an idea of the knife used. Well, let's get started."

It took almost an hour for the autopsy to be completed. When the Doc had finished, Charlie lay with his chest cut open in a typical Y cut. His head had been opened, his brain removed and weighed. Most of his internal organs had been removed and samples taken. There had been nothing else found out. Of course, Doc would send some samples for a toxicology screen, but there didn't appear to be anything else of value found.

Bobby had not gotten too close, but now as Doc sewed up Charlie Two Horse's chest, he noticed something just under his left nipple. Stepping closer he tried to see what it was.

"What's under his nipple Doc?" Bobby asked, pointing.

"Not sure," Doc replied. "Let me get a magnifying glass."

Doc rummaged through some drawers and then brought over a circular magnifying glass. He moved it up and down over the mark, trying to get it into focus.

"Well, now what is this?" Doc said. "Looks to be a small tattoo. I can't make it out with these old eyes. Maybe you can see what it is Bobby."

Bobby took the glass and moved closer to the table. It was a good thing it never bothered him to see a dead body, even one which had been cut open.

"It looks like...like...I'm not really sure."

"I wonder why Charlie would have a tattoo of something so small, it is almost impossible to see?"

"I don't know Doc, but I will need someone to take a good picture of it and then get it enlarged. Can you handle it, or should I call in someone?"

"I can get it for you. I have a great macro lens on my own digital camera. Gonna take me a bit though. I will have to set up some better lights, and get my tripod, and..."

"Great Doc," Bobby said, interrupting him. "Just let me know when you have it, and I'll come by."

"Just leave me your e-mail with Donna and I will send it to you as soon as I have it."

"Okay Doc, but make sure you keep a printed out copy for the record. Thanks Doc."

"See you around Bobby."

Bobby left his e-mail with Donna at the front desk. He explained how Doctor McAddams was going to forward something to him, and please give him the information. She looked a bit confused but took his info with another dazzling smile.

Bobby made his way back to his truck, wondering where Charlie had gotten such a tattoo, and why. Did it have a special meaning for him? And why get it so small no one would be able to see it, unless with a magnifier? Whoever had done it had some real talent, of that, Bobby was sure. He couldn't wait to see the image blown up. Maybe it would mean something to him once he saw it. He would also show it to Delores and ask her if she knew anything about it.

In any case, Bobby figured it had nothing to do with Charlie's murder. Still, he thought it was strange, and he wanted to find out more about it. He also needed to find whoever had killed Charlie. Unfortunately, he had no leads and thought the case might never be solved. But he would do anything he could to bring his killer to justice.

Bobby got into his truck and headed for the res. He needed to go over a few things at his headquarters. He wanted to talk to George to see if he had come up with any forensic evidence. He also wanted to look over all the pictures George would have taken. He wanted to talk to Dan again. Maybe he had thought of something Bobby had missed.

Most people didn't understand how an investigation really worked. It wasn't like on TV or in the movies. It was hard work with long hours, interviewing people, putting facts together and even then, there was no guarantee it would be solved. But the only way to solve a case was to get started. Bobby got into his truck and drove back to the reservation.

CHAPTER 12

Tuesday 12:10 pm

Bobby sat behind his desk in his small, cramped office with his boots up on it. His was the largest office in the Wind River Reservation Police Department, which wasn't saying much. On the walls were a few pictures of old Chiefs. He also had a copy of a treaty dating back to 1864, which had been signed by President Abraham Lincoln. He kept it to remind himself not to trust white people. He also had the torn picture of the Chief he had taken from Charlie Two Horse's home. He was going to get it repaired and give it back in a new frame to Delores.

He was reading over the two reports, one from Dan and the other from George. Neither gave him any leads or ideas of who could have committed the murder of Charlie Two Horse. He was feeling frustrated and knew this case might never be solved.

So many crimes committed on the res weren't solved. Young Shoshone and Arapahoe girls would go missing, many times more often than young girls who didn't live on the res. They usually were never found. Did they run away, or were they abducted and possibly raped and killed? It was a question which always angered Bobby every time some native woman would come in to report their daughter was gone. Once in a while, some bones would be found on the prairie or discovered in a shallow grave. More often than not, the bones would never be identified, and he would have to tell the mothers of missing girls their daughters were still missing.

There were other less serious crimes on the res, and Bobby and his officers solved a fair amount of them. But most of the people on the reservation were suspicious of the tribal police. They were often very close mouthed, keeping their opinions and information to themselves. It made Bobby's job difficult, but he knew someone had to do it.

He checked his phone for the tenth time, looking for an e-mail from Doc McAddams. The tattoo was curious, and he wanted to know what it was. He also had put together a list of names of natives who performed tattoos on the res. He wasn't sure which of them would have been able to do a tattoo so small, but at least it was something he could try to run down.

He was just getting up to start his patrol rounds when his sergeant knocked on his open door. Her name was Betty Slow River, and she had been with the department for ten years. She was short, not more than five feet tall, and looked to be a little plump. But Bobby knew she wasn't fat, she was all muscle and had black belts in several forms of martial arts. She wore her hair up and Bobby thought he had never seen her with it down. She didn't go in for makeup or jewelry, and she was respected by all of his officers.

"Just got a call from Tommy White Hair, Boss," she said. "He's out by the north end. He was doing his regular patrol when he was stopped by one of the elders. Ummm, Jim Longbow. He asked for you because he isn't sure what to do."

"Did he say what he wasn't sure about what it was he didn't know to do about?" Bobby asked.

"You want to say that again Boss?" Betty said with a smile.

"Never mind. I'll go out and see for myself. Hold the fort down Betty."

"The fort? Are sure you want me to hold, *the fort*, down?"

"Okay Betty, just make sure this building is here when I get back. Okay?"

"You got it Boss," she said with a giggle.

Bobby got into his truck and headed out to the north end of the reservation. He knew the area was sparsely populated, mostly by Shoshone who wanted to be left alone or were too old to move. The north end had many small mountains on the furthest part and knew many Shoshone and Arapahoe hunted there. The homes were small and in need of repair. Some trailers were here and there but mostly the homes were put together with different materials found by the owners. There was a small store, no name ever given it, for items which might be needed, but that was all. If someone needed something other than what the store held, or if they needed medical attention, they would have to drive or sometimes walk many miles to the more populated areas of the res.

Bobby finally arrived outside the trailer of Jim Longbow. It was tilting to one side and looked as if it had been there for a thousand years. There were small holes in the sides, and the stones it was settled on were broken and sinking into the dirt. The dust and dirt was so thick on the small windows it would be impossible to see into. Behind it was a medium sized mountain with large boulders here and there on it. Bobby wondered if any boulders ever came tumbling down onto the trailer.

Bobby knew Tommy White Hair was young and had only been a tribal police officer for three years, but he was sure he would have tried to find out what had happened. He wrote good reports and did his job well. He was around six foot tall, very strong with a great physique and wore his hair straight and long.

Bobby saw his officer and Jim sitting at a small table outside the trailer on two wooden benches. At Jim's feet was a large *sadee*, a dog, and Bobby couldn't tell what breed it was. But since his officer was sitting there and the dog didn't seem to mind him, Bobby got out of the truck.

Walking slowly up to them, Bobby was surprised how old Jim looked. He was sure just a few months ago Jim had not looked young, but not as ancient as he did now. His hair in braids was white, and his face was covered in deep wrinkles. He wore an old buckskin shirt and pants and on his feet were moccasins with holes in both of them. Bobby was saddened by the sight but knew there were many Shoshone and Arapahoe in the same or worse predicament.

As he approached, the dog got up and stood in front of him.

"Come here Geronimo," Jim said.

The dog immediately returned to Jim, settling at his feet.

"*Behne*," Bobby said. "Good name for him."

"*Tsaa*."

"Okay Tommy, you want to tell me what's going on?"

Tommy stood up and pulled Bobby a few feet away.

"It's kind of crazy," Tommy began. "I was just checking on a few of the older residents out here, when Jim flagged me down. I got out of my car and Jim started to tell me his home had been ransacked. I followed him in to it, and he wasn't kidding. It looked as if a tornado had hit it."

Bobby thought about Charlie's home and how it had been ransacked as well.

"What did he say was stolen?" Bobby asked.

"That's the crazy part. He said nothing was missing and he was sorry he flagged me down. He didn't want to make any report and wanted me to forget about it and leave. But I figured after reading the report on Two Horse, you would want to interview him and see for yourself."

"Good thinking Tommy. Let's go talk with him."

Tommy stood and Bobby sat down across from Jim.

"I know you don't want a report about this, and that's fine Jim," Bobby said. "But I still need to ask you a few questions, okay?"

"There is nothing to speak about," Jim said. "Nothing was taken. Probably just some kids."

"You are probably right Jim. But just a few questions. Where were you when this happened?"

"I was visiting a neighbor."

Bobby knew the closest neighbor was more than two miles away. He didn't see a vehicle, so he asked, "Did you walk there?"

"No other way to get around."

"When was this?"

"I left early in the morning to avoid the heat. Geronimo came with me. He is good company, and he likes to chase the groundhogs and snakes. I try to stop him from playing with the rattlesnakes, but he doesn't listen. I am not sure of the time because I do not have any clocks. But the sun had just risen. I wanted to make sure Soft Petal was doing okay."

Bobby knew he was talking about an elderly Shoshone who lived in a more broken down place than even Jim's. If the sun was just coming up, Jim had probably left around six that morning.

"How long were you at Soft Petal's place?"

"Not sure. We talked, I cleaned up a bit and made her some food to eat. I do not think she will be with us for too much longer. Neither will I."

"You have many years left Jim," Bobby said, even though he didn't believe it, judging by the way he looked. "And when you returned you saw what?"

"I went into the trailer and saw everything had been tossed around, broken pottery all over the floor. Then I came out and saw your officer and foolishly waved to him. It was a silly thing to do. I have nothing of value, and nothing was missing."

"Still, it's not right Jim. Whoever did this should be found."

"No! I mean... there is no need to find out. Nothing was taken and what they broke does not matter. Now I am tired, and I must feed Geronimo. Please go."

"At least let me contact your son. He could come out and help you. Maybe take you home with him."

"There is no need. He has forsaken our ways and lives in Eagle. Now, goodbye," Jim said, stood and walked slowly to the trailer with Geronimo following close behind.

"See what I mean Lieutenant?" Tommy said. "He doesn't want to make a report, but his place was wrecked by someone. And I don't know how he can say nothing was taken. He couldn't have had enough time to look through the place."

"I want you to make a report, at least whatever you know," Bobby said. "Then I want you to visit Soft Petal and check on her. Maybe bring her out some supplies, like food and clothing. You can get some money from Sgt. Slow River. Tell her I said it was okay."

"Okay Lt., anything else?"

"Not for now. I'm going to drive into Eagle and talk with Jim's son."

They both left and Bobby was disturbed about the break-in and destruction of Jim's trailer. He was sure Jim had nothing of value, but neither did Charlie Two Horse. At least other than what had been hidden in the floor of his bedroom. Bobby wondered if Jim had something hidden too. And what if Jim had come home while whoever was tossing his place? Would Jim be lying dead in his trailer the same way Charlie had been found?

Bobby decided he would get Jim's son to come out to his father no matter what. Maybe he could convince him to take Jim back with him. Jim needed some good food and a safe place to live in. The hard part would be convincing Jim to leave the res.

As he drove, Bobby wondered what was happening. Were the two burglaries connected or just a coincidence? Like most cops, Bobby didn't believe in coincidences. But who was doing these crimes, including murder? Bobby was determined to find out.

CHAPTER 13

I was sitting in my office, reading the report about the burglary at the Bright Star's apartment. It was less than half a page. It wasn't the officer's fault. Both Abel and Maggie had not been forthcoming with the incident. The question was, why wouldn't they want to make a report? They had obviously been broken into, and yet they refused for any investigation to take place.

I had promised Max I wouldn't look into it, but there was something wrong. I didn't like it. It smelled. I got up and walked down the hall to Chuck's office.

Knocking on the open door, I said, "Busy Chuck?"

"Just checking on my report for the sexual assault Eric," he said. "Come on in and take a load off."

"Thanks. Do you want me to look over your report?"

"Nah. Besides, when it gets filed you and the Lieutenant will get copies. What did you think about Jimmy during the interview?"

"He did some good work in there, and I think he learned a thing or two from you."

"Yeah, he's going to be a good detective, even though he has a bit more to learn."

"We all have more to learn Chuck."

"True, true. So what can I do for you?"

"Remember Max Yellowfeather being here this morning?"

"How could I forget. What did he want?"

"It's a bit strange Chuck. He wanted to tell me about a burglary which happened here in town. His cousins, Abel, and Maggie Bright Star's apartment had apparently been broken into. Maggie called the police, but when the officer showed up, her brother Abel wouldn't let the officer in. He also stated there was no need for a report."

"Okay, I admit it's strange. What did Max want you to do?"

"Nothing. He told me about it, said he didn't know if anything had actually been taken. Just wanted to give me a heads up."

"Well, if they don't want to make a report there really isn't anything we could do."

"Not officially."

"Okay. You want me to talk with this Abel or Maggie?"

"Since Maggie was the one who called the police, I think she might be more willing to talk. The only thing is you can't go knocking on her door."

"I can handle it Eric. Don't you worry about it."

"Thanks Chuck. Let me know as soon as you find out anything...if you find out anything."

I got up and made my way back to my office. I was sure Chuck would contact Maggie Bright Star. Whether or not he could get her to say anything about the burglary, I thought was a maybe.

I began going over some reports from the cases my detectives had been working on. There was a possible rape of a waitress from one of the restaurants in town. No witnesses had been found. The woman had done a rape kit, but the results were still pending. Unfortunately, like child assault cases, a confession was usually the only way to get a rapist off the streets. The report listed all the things the detective had done, and it looked as if she had a handle on it. Usually when someone claimed they were raped, I preferred one of two female detectives to handle it. They had better empathy, and the victim usually felt more at ease.

Next I read a report made by my old office partner, Frank Baxter. He handled mostly frauds, embezzlements, and forgery cases. Once he was on the paper trail, he wouldn't let up. He was working on a case where there had been several twenty dollar counterfeit bills found around town. He had called in the Secret Service, notifying them as was protocol. Most people thought the Secret Service only protected the President, but they investigated all counterfeit crimes as well. They had held off coming to Eagle and were waiting on Frank to investigate.

I looked through several more reports, but my mind kept returning to Max Yellowfeather and what he had told me. I knew Max was not a frivolous man. He would have only come to me if he was worried, and the burglary was serious. But not telling me any details and being mysterious, only made me want to find out more. I was hoping Chuck could find out something more than what I knew now, which was basically zero.

Looking up, I saw it was getting close to one. Maybe Will would be available for a quick lunch. I knew I was hungry and a big hamburger from Five Guys sounded just right.

CHAPTER 14

Bobby Black Bear had gone to the lumber yard where Jim Longbow's son, Harry, worked. When he got there, his boss informed him Harry had left for lunch a few minutes ago. There were plenty of places to eat in the area, and Bobby didn't feel like waiting around. He had asked Harry's boss where he liked to eat. There were two regular places, a small diner named Carol's Place and Five Guys hamburger joint.

Of course Bobby had looked in Carol's first. Not finding Harry, Bobby had made his way to Five Guys. Sitting in the corner, he saw Harry chowing down on two hamburgers and a ton of fries. He also had the largest drink he could get there. Before walking over, Bobby looked around the place. It was something all cops did, checking out the surroundings. He was surprised to see both Eric Logan and Will Tolliver at the opposite end from where Harry sat. He waved to them, and they asked him to join them.

"Maybe in a few minutes," Bobby said.

Bobby continued to Harry's table and Harry didn't even bother to look up. Bobby did a quick once over. Harry Longbow didn't dress like a Shoshone. His black hair was cut short, and he was dressed in a tee shirt and Levi's. He had a pair of dusty work boots on his feet. On his wrist was an old wristwatch. He wore no other jewelry. Bobby estimated his age at about forty or fifty, and he looked to be in good shape.

"*Behne*," Bobby said.

Harry looking up at Bobby and swallowing said, "I don't speak the language anymore, Lieutenant. And I don't live on the reservation either. So what do you want?"

"Can I sit?"

"Suit yourself."

Bobby pulled out the chair and took a seat.

"I'm here about your father."

"Oh yeah. Is he dead?"

Bobby was getting pissed about Harry's attitude but figured if he got angry it wouldn't help matters. He took a deep breath and tried again.

"I was out at your Dad's trailer earlier today. His place had been ransacked. He wasn't home when it happened. He stated nothing was missing and he wasn't hurt."

"Okay, so what do you want of me? He has disowned me for wanting a better life off the res."

"Well, he didn't look too good Harry. He is still your father. I was hoping maybe you could take him home with you for a little while. Put some good food into him, maybe get him checked out by a doctor. It would be good for him and maybe for you too."

"I don't think so. He has his life, and I have mine. Now if you will excuse me, I'd like to eat my lunch in peace. Goodbye."

Harry began eating again and Bobby felt like knocking him off his chair and shoving his food into his face. But he knew it would do no good. Bobby got up and walked over to where Eric and Will were sitting.

"Good afternoon guys," Bobby said.

"Take a seat Bobby," Will said.

I said, "*Behne.*"

For a second Bobby thought how this white man

had used his native language as a greeting, and a Shoshone had refused to use the simple word. He thought it was sad.

"*Behne* Eric," Bobby said and sat down.

"How about a burger?" Will asked.

"No thanks. I just had to come into town to speak with Harry Longbow."

"Didn't look as if he was too responsive to you," I said. "Is he in any trouble we should know about?"

"No, nothing like that. I was just trying to get him to take his father off the res for a bit. Maybe get him some good food, a doctor check-up, and a warm place to sleep. His father is Jim Longbow, and he doesn't look too good."

"I gather he didn't want to help his father?" Will asked.

"Not even a little bit. Harry said he has been disowned for leaving the res. I don't believe it but what I believe doesn't matter."

"That's too bad," I said. "So how are things out on the res Bobby?"

"Same as always. A few missing persons cases, which I sent flyers out to you guys. A couple of minor shoplifting cases, a burglary, and a murder."

"A murder? We haven't heard anything about a murder. Who was killed?"

"Charlie Two Horse was found with his throat slashed, lying in his living room."

A woman with a young child suddenly got up, gave Bobby the look of death and stormed out with her two children.

"Guess I was talking a bit too loud," Bobby said. "Anyway, there aren't too many leads, and I have a feeling it may never be solved. But you guys know it's not too unusual, especially on the res."

"If there is anything we can do to help Bobby, just say the word."

"Thanks. Guess I better head back. I'm going to get some food and warm clothing for Jim. If his son won't help out, I suppose I will."

"Take care Bobby and seriously, if there is anything we can do for you, just ask," Will said.

"*Tsaa.*"

Bobby left the restaurant and went in search of a thrift store. He couldn't afford brand new clothes but even some preowned ones would be better than nothing. He walked along the streets, comparing them to the streets of the res. He was saddened but there was nothing he could do to change things.

CHAPTER 15

Jim Longbow had been more upset about the break-in than he showed to Black Bear and his deputy. Someone had been looking for something no one should have known about. Jim had heard about Charlie Two Horse and how his home had been ransacked. Although he wasn't supposed to know about others who held the gift, he and Charlie had been friends. Each knew what the other had held. Jim wasn't positive about his assumption, but he wasn't going to take any chances.

He began straightening out his place, saddened by the destruction. Whoever had done this was extremely angry. There was no reason to be so destructive, breaking picture frames, pottery, and other Shoshone knick-knacks. Jim thought the person was more than looking for something, he desired it, which was a dangerous thing.

As Jim cleaned up, taking the broken items outside to a large trash bin, he made sure to look around. He studied the long way down the dusty road, and then the mountain behind his home. He was sure there wouldn't be anyone watching him, but he wasn't going to take a chance.

When he had the place reasonably clean, he sat down at a small wooden desk. One leg was broken, and it tilted slightly. Jim pulled out a clean piece of paper and an old pen. The pen didn't have too much ink left in it, but it would have to do.

Jim sat thinking about what he needed to write. He wasn't sure if he could or even should write the letter. His son was his only heir, and his ancestors demanded he follow the laws as set up by them. He would have to try to explain everything so Harry would understand. But what worried Jim the most was whether or not Harry would also obey his ancestors. Harry had left the res, given up his Shoshone ways. He had cut his hair and did not speak the language any longer. Why he had done this made no sense to Jim.

Maybe he could find another, although the law was clear. It had to be a son preferably or a daughter. No one outside the family was allowed. Jim's brother and sister had died several years ago, and so there was only Harry. Besides, there was no one Jim could think of to use instead of his only son.

Sighing, he began to write. Nothing of the past was to be written down, only told orally from one to another. But Jim didn't think he had any choice. After an hour he had filled both sides of the paper and took out another. He filled one more side and then he was done. He slowly read what he had written. It wasn't the best telling of the ancient story, but it would have to do. Jim got an envelope and closed the story within. Then he addressed the envelope to his son and placed it on his table. He would mail it first thing in the morning. After that, there was nothing else he could do. He could only hope his son would carry out his wishes, and the wishes of his people.

Jim ate a small meal made up of some old stale bread and a few pieces of meat. The meat was old and probably spoiled, but like most of his people, Jim wouldn't think of complaining. He had a few cans of dog food for Geronimo, and he opened two and dumped them into a large dog bowl. Then he replaced the water in another bowl with fresh water, or as fresh as it would get. Geronimo was probably eating better than him. He forced the last of his sandwich down. He washed it down with some water and then checked outside. It was getting a bit darker now, and he wanted to be sure he wouldn't be seen. Geronimo would stay here in the trailer. Patting his dog on the head, Jim then went out and into a small storage shed and came out with a flashlight and small shovel. On his waist was a knife he had worn as a young man. It still held its edge.

He slowly walked to the back of his trailer and began to climb the mountain, following an old trail. Every few steps he needed to rest, take a breath before climbing further. He knew the way even though he hadn't climbed this trail for over twenty years. Ever since he moved to this trailer at the base of the mountain. He had buried it here, right after his own father had died and passed it onto him.

He had to stop, sitting on some small rocks before continuing on the last few feet. Breathing heavily, he went off the trail, counting his steps as he went. Looking around a final time for anyone spying on him, Jim began to dig. Slowly the dirt was removed, and Jim had made a small hole. Where was it, he thought. He was sure he was at the right spot. Just as he was about to give up, and rethink where he buried it, Jim struck something. Bending down and clearing the dirt off, he pulled out a small tin box. He had found it.

CHAPTER 16

Nihoono biitooeeihii had hid behind some boulders up on the mountain. He was watching for the old man, Jim Longbow. What he wanted was not in the broken down trailer. At least, he was relatively sure. Something so small might have been hidden inside, but he didn't think so. He figured, the old man might have hidden it outside, somewhere either on the mountain or close by. He didn't care how long it took. He was willing to sit hidden in his spot, looking for the old man for as long as it would take. After seeing his home ransacked, he thought the old man would probably check on his treasure.

Nihoono biitooeeihii had been sitting here ever since the old man had waved down one of the Tribal Police officers. He had seen the Lieutenant; Bobby Black Bear arrive and question him. The old man hadn't said much and soon both of the police officers left. He watched as the old man and his large dog went into his broken down trailer. When he ransacked the old man's trailer he hadn't known of the dog. Luckily the old man had brought him when he had left earlier in the morning.

Soon, he had brought out some things which could not be repaired or he no longer wanted. He had put the broken things into a trash bin on the side of the trailer and then walked back inside. Perhaps he was eating or taking a nap. He certainly didn't think the old man was long for this world. He was old and frail, very close to dying. *Nihoono biitooeeihii* prayed he wouldn't die before revealing the object of his desire.

So he waited and waited. The hot day had started to cool as the sun slowly began to set. Still the old man had not come out of his trailer. *Nihoono biitooeeihii* was beginning to think it might be a good idea to go to him. Force him to give up his treasure as Charlie Two Horse had done. As he sat making up his mind, he saw the old man exit the trailer. He made his way to a small shed and exited with a small shovel in his hands and a flashlight.

Nihoono biitooeeihii waited, feeling his excitement grow. Soon he would have what he wanted, what he had killed for twice. He would kill again if he had to. He watched as the old man slowly made his way up an old trail on the side of the mountain. Soon he lost sight of him and had to move. He was silent as he moved in the old man's footsteps. It took a long time for the old man to make the climb, but finally he moved off the trail. It looked as if he was counting his steps.

When the old man began to dig, he could hardly contain his excitement. *Nihoono biitooeeihii* took a hood out of his pocket and slipped it on over his head. He didn't want to kill him, and as long as he gave him no trouble he would not. This way the old man couldn't identify him.

He waited nearby, silent and watched as the old man dug. It was hard for him, but he continued digging. Finally, the old man lifted a small box out of the ground. He opened it, looking into the box. Then he sat down on a small rock to rest. As he was resting, *Nihoono biitooeeihii* came up behind him.

He reached for the box, but the old man was quicker than he would have thought.

"No!" the old Indian said. "This is not for you to have!"

"Maybe not, old man, but I still will have it!" *Nihoono biitooeeihii* said.

He was amazed when the old man pulled a wicked looking knife from his waistband.

"If you try to take this, I will have to kill you," the old man said. He stood and took up a fighting position. The old man might have been a warrior and a man to be afraid of many years ago. But now he was too old for fighting and he wobbled on his feet. Still, he might get lucky and cause some damage.

Nihoono biitooeeihii said, "Okay old man. You can keep your box and whatever is in it. I do not wish to fight."

Then *Nihoono biitooeeihii* made to leave, but spun on his feet, driving his own knife deep into the old man's chest.

The old man began to fall, his eyes wide, as his blood began to seep from the wound.

Nihoono biitooeeihii tried to pull the box from the old man's dying hands, but the old man had a death grip on it. Looking around for a stone, he raised it up and hit the hand holding the box. It took a few times, hitting and breaking the old man's bones, but finally the box fell free. Lifting it up, he quickly looked inside and smiled. He had what he had come for.

As *Nihoono biitooeeihii* turned to walk away, he heard the old man try to speak. It was soft as a whisper, and he bent down to hear what he wanted to say as he died. Suddenly the old man lurched, his knife in his hand. But *Nihoono biitooeeihii* was quicker and easily knocked the knife away. Then he watched as the old man died.

CHAPTER 17

Tuesday 9:30 pm

The boys had gone up to their room and it was now time for Bell to tell me all about her day. It was a warm night and so we took our coffee's out on the patio. We sat close to each other, and I reached out, taking Bell's hand in mine. The stars were filling the sky and as we both sat contented and star gazing, I smiled.

"What are you smiling about?" Bell asked.

"Oh, I guess I'm just happy, right here, right now," I answered. "Who knows what tomorrow may hold for us. But tonight with our boys safe, and you next to me, your hand in mine, I'm happy."

"Well so am I. And I suppose you're right about not knowing what tomorrow might bring. My run for the city council begins tomorrow with a formal announcement in front of City Hall."

"That's great honey! Tell me all about your meeting today."

"I met with four men and two women. I'm sure you know them all. They are all wealthy and community minded. Together they have got enough money for me to start my campaign. Of course we will have to raise some funds too."

"Sounds terrific but let me hear who these mysterious benefactors are."

"Okay, but remember, they wish to stay in the background."

"Sounds a bit silly to me, but I will respect yours and their wishes. I won't say a thing to anyone. Now give."

"The men were Alan Cummings, the owner of the Eagle Trust and Loan, Brett Trask, owner of the Eagle Star, John Miller who runs and owns the lumber mill and..."

"And?"

"Imp."

"Imp as in Benedictus Angelo Carmelo Impeletti, the District Attorney and my best friend?"

"Yup. Now you see why they want to remain in the background. Each of them can offer a great deal, strategy wise. With the biggest bank, newspaper, and mill with so many employees, they will be a terrific asset. And Imp being the D.A. will also be a feather in my cap. They all agreed once I announce and the campaign has gathered some steam, they will come out on my side. In any case, the women were Sally Jacobs and Teresa Benton. Both wealthy widows and interested in my being elected."

"You were right about them all having money. Although I didn't know Imp was in their class. Then again, he never married and lives pretty frugally. Well I think, with their help, you will run a great campaign."

"Thank you sweetheart, but I have a great deal of work to do. I need to come up with a list of things I want to accomplish, a campaign manager and of course a motto."

"Hmmm, a motto. Have you got anything yet in mind?"

"Not yet. My mind is a blank. Also, I'm worried I won't have the time to be with Caroline, Paul, and the girls. They arrive in about six weeks, and I don't want to disappear on them while they are here.""

"I'm sure the girls will be kept busy by Ben and Bear. And Paul will be with me a lot, looking over the town and the police department. Maybe Caroline would like to help you with your campaign while she is here. So stop worrying and let me come up with a slam bang motto. Let me think a minute. How about, *Just as our forefathers rang the liberty bell for a change, you can ring Bell for a change today!*"

"Ummm, I think you better stick with solving crimes."

"Didn't like it?"

"A bit too long. It needs to be snappy and short, so it is easy to remember."

"I'll keep thinking, even though I might only be good at solving crimes."

"I think you are very good at solving crimes Eric, and maybe a few more things. I'm thinking we could go to bed and give you a chance to show off your skills, if you want to."

Bell stood and went inside. I watched her move toward the stairs, swinging her hips just to get my attention. It worked. I stood up and followed her up the stairs. I had better have my A game tonight, since I wanted to prove my skills were more than just good.

CHAPTER 18

Bobby gathered up the things he had bought at the thrift store to bring to Jim Longbow. He was still angry at Harry Longbow for the way he spoke and neglected his own father. The Shoshone way was to revere the elders of the tribe. Obviously Harry had forgotten everything about the Shoshone way of life.

He got into his truck and made a stop at the office. Of course Betty was on duty, even this early in the morning. She was standing with Tommy who had just finished up his midnight tour. Getting ready for his patrol was Dan Red Shirt. Dan looked as if he had dropped some weight, and his normally short hair looked like he was starting to let it grow out. Walking in, Bobby said hello and went directly to his office. There he found a few reports from the day before. Nothing too serious, so he put them down and headed back out.

"Here pretty early, Lt," Tommy said.

"Yeah, well I spoke to Jim Longbow's son yesterday," Bobby said. "I was hoping he could take Jim to town, get him some medical attention and a warm, safe place for a while. But Harry is basically worthless when it comes to his father or being a Shoshone."

"So what are you going to do?" Betty asked.

"I got some things from the thrift store in Eagle. Figured I would bring them up to Jim."

"You know he won't accept charity Bobby."

"Well, all I can do is bring them to him. It will be up to him if he takes them or tosses them. Either way it is something I should do."

"Want some company Lt?" Tommy asked. "I brought some things out to Soft Petal early last night."

"Aren't you tired? You just finished a midnight tour. Dan can come with me."

"I would Lt. if I could, but I have that talk at the school this morning," Dan said. "You know, advising the kids with summer coming, how not to get into trouble."

"I wish all of the kids would take the advice but I'm sure we are in for another summer of petty thievery and graffiti," Bobby said.

Tommy said, "I'm not really tired and I figure checking up on Jim is my responsibility too. I was the one he flagged down and maybe he will be willing to talk about what really happened at his trailer. I don't believe it was a bunch of kids."

"Neither do I Tommy. Okay, let's get going."

It took a bit of time to drive all the way back to where Jim lived, and on the trip Bobby decided he would get to know his deputy. They talked the entire ride, all about the plans they wanted to carry out. Bobby only wanted to continue to work and retire many years from now. Tommy wanted to find a wife, have a bunch of kids, and become head of the Wind River Tribal Police. Of course, after Bobby retired. Bobby had given Tommy a look and then said, "Of course after I retire."

They pulled up in front of Jim's trailer, the dust settling behind them. They got out and Tommy grabbed the box full of clothes and supplies for Jim. Bobby walked up to the trailer door and knocked. Immediately he heard Geronimo inside, wailing. Bobby tried the door, and it was unlocked. He slowly entered and as he did, Geronimo came flying out, launching himself straight at Tommy.

Geronimo nearly knocked Tommy over and headed behind the trailer.

"Probably had to relieve himself," Tommy said.

"I don't think so," Bobby replied. "Why wouldn't Jim have let him out? Go see where he went, and I will go look to see where Jim is."

"Okay Lieutenant."

Bobby stepped into the trailer and saw Jim had cleaned the place up. There were no broken things on the floor and the place looked clean. Well, as clean as possible. He walked slowly through the trailer, calling out Jim's name. Coming back into the living room, Bobby saw an envelope on the table. Picking it up, he saw it was addressed to Harry. Now why was Jim writing a letter to Harry when just yesterday he didn't even want to speak with him? Putting the envelope back down, he went back outside.

Now where could Jim be? Maybe he had gone back to Soft Petal earlier this morning. But why wouldn't he take Geronimo? He doubted he would leave his dog behind, and even if he did, he would have let the dog out. Bobby was stumped and walked toward the back of the trailer.

As he turned the corner, Tommy came running up to him.

"Geronimo ran straight up an old trail, Lt." Tommy said. "I began to follow but he was too fast."

"Okay Tommy, let's see where Geronimo ran off to." Bobby said and began to follow Tommy up the mountain.

They had climbed about halfway up the mountain when they both heard Geronimo. Moving off the trail, they found Geronimo standing by a pile of rocks. As they approached him, Geronimo bared his teeth and let loose with a low growl.

Tommy moved slowly forward, holding out his hand and talking low.

"Be careful Tommy," Bobby said.

"I'm good with dogs Lt." Tommy replied.

Tommy got closer, murmuring soft words, and smiling.

"It's okay Geronimo, good boy, good boy."

Tommy was soon able to pet him and pulled him by his collar away from the rocks. He moved Geronimo away and took some rope from his pocket and tied him to a small tree stump.

"You always carry rope with you Tommy?" Bobby asked.

"Never know what you will need when out on patrol," he answered. "I try to think ahead."

"I'm glad you do. Now, what do you think is under all those rocks?"

"I'm thinking it might be Jim Longbow."

"Me too."

Bobby and Tommy began to move the rocks aside until they revealed the face of Jim Longbow.

"Damn!" Bobby said. "We better not move anymore of these rocks right now Tommy."

"Doesn't look like a rock slide," Tommy said.

"No it doesn't. I think whoever trashed Jim's trailer came back. He or she didn't find what they were looking for. But the question is, did Jim come up here under his own steam or was he forced up here? And why up here?"

"I have no idea."

"Well, I want you to head back down and take Geronimo with you. Get in touch with George and call Doc McAddams. Ask the Doc if he is willing to come up here. If not, we will bring Jim's body to him."

"Okay, got it. But what are you going to do?"

"I'm going to look for a reason Jim had climbed all the way up here."

Tommy grabbed the makeshift leash and began to leave when Bobby called out.

"Take the dog to the station, not the shelter Tommy," Bobby said. "And go into the trailer. On the living room table you will see an envelope. No need to bag it for evidence but I want you to put it on my desk. Without opening it."

"Got it."

Bobby began to look for any sign of where Jim might have been. He walked a bit higher up the mountain and then came back down. On his way down, he saw some footprints moving off to the east side. He carefully followed, making sure to not disturb them. It looked as if two set of prints went one way. Then only one came back. The one's coming back were deeper in the earth than when they went the other way. Bobby thought whoever they belonged to was carrying something heavy. Something like Jim Longbow.

Bobby followed the steps and found a flashlight and shovel near a small hole in the ground. It reminded him of the secret spot Charlie Two Horse had hidden something. Bobby sat down on a small rock and thought about what had happened.

Bobby figured the shovel and flashlight belonged to Jim. They would be checked for fingerprints, but Bobby was sure only Jim's would be on them. So Jim had probably come up here to retrieve something buried. He was taken by surprise and killed. Then the killer had taken whatever had been dug up, carried Jim away from this spot, and covered Jim's body with rocks. If it weren't for Geronimo, his body may never have been found.

Bobby took another look around to see if he had missed anything. As he looked, a glint of light shone off of something a few feet away. Bobby walked over and found a long knife on the ground. It didn't appear to have any blood on it. Bobby didn't want to move it, but he got down on his hands and knees to get closer. On the hilt, which was wrapped in colorful cloth, Bobby saw what looked to be a bow. It was the mark of Jim Longbow. So this knife belonged to Jim. Bobby wondered if Jim had been able to at least wound his assailant.

Bobby made a few notes in his notepad and began the climb down. He would have to wait here for George and Doc McAddams if he was going to come out. He didn't mind the wait; it gave him time to think about the two killings. Whatever the killer was after must be very valuable. But both Charlie Two Horse and Jim Longbow were relatively poor. Neither would have had anything of monetary value. Therefore, whatever these things were, had value of a different kind. But what?

Bobby decided he would get some shade to sit in while he waited. The sun was up, and the day was going to be another scorcher. Bobby sighed, wondering what was going on here on the res. He was sworn to not only solve the killings, but to protect both the Shoshone and Arapaho who lived on it. So far, he wasn't doing a great job doing either one.

CHAPTER 19

Chuck Blackwell was known around the department as being a bit of a gruff bulldog. If Chuck got on your scent, there wasn't anything he wouldn't do to catch you. In the past two years, it was Chuck's doggedness which had solved many cases and also saved a few cop's lives, including Eric Logan's.

After Eric had asked him to look into the burglary report made by Abel and Maggie Bright Star, he had done just that. Unfortunately the report had about two lines written down. The officer had not been able to investigate or get any real information. Earlier this morning, Chuck had located the officer, a rookie named Greg Harper.

Harper had looked at his notes, sparse as they were, and told Chuck how Abel had appeared angry. Maggie on the other hand had looked frightened about something. Harper had gotten a quick look in the apartment before the door had been slammed in his face. The place had looked as if a tornado had hit it.

Chuck had thanked Harper and gone to think things over in his office. Neither Abel or Maggie had ever had any run ins with the law. Both were law abiding citizens. They had rented their apartment three years ago. He had gotten that info from the manager at the Charles Apartments. Why they had left the res was a mystery.

Chuck had done some digging in some of the city offices and found out Abel worked at the lumber yard, where several Shoshone who lived in town worked. Chuck knew they were one of the bigger companies in town, supplying lumber to both commercial and residential properties.

Maggie Bright Star worked in the mall at one of the boutiques. Chuck decided he would get nowhere with Abel, and Maggie might be more forthcoming. Chuck knew Eric had asked him not to pursue anything without talking to him first. But Chuck decided just talking with Maggie wouldn't be a big deal.

After the morning meeting, Chuck left police headquarters and drove over to the mall. The mall had fallen on some hard times. Many of the spots inside were empty. Everyone blamed the economy, but Chuck knew the owner of the property was charging too high on the rent. Many store owners had packed up and moved into some strip malls around the town. No one could afford to stay there, pay the rent and still make any profit. Those who could pay, were barely eking out a living. In fact, the food court now only held one place. Chuck was friends with the owner, a Chinese man named something Chuck couldn't pronounce. Which was why he and everyone else called him Buddy. His Chinese food was good, hot, and served fast.

Chuck decided he would stop by and get an eggroll. He would also ask Buddy if he knew Maggie Bright Star, and what she was like.

Bobby walked into the mall and went directly to Buddy's place. Buddy still had a strong accent and some- times it was hard to understand him. He also tended to speak in a sing-song way, which only complicated matters.

"How's it going Buddy?" Chuck asked.

"Okay, I guess Detective," Buddy answered. "It going sometimes good, sometimes not so good."

"Yeah I suppose the crowds have disappeared, what with half the stores empty."

"That true but I heard a rumor just yesterday. Someone new buying the mall. Gonna try to get more stores in and also in food court."

"I suppose even though there would be more places to get food, if the spaces were filled, there would be a lot more people. I sure hope so."

"Me too Detective, Now what can Buddy get for you?"

Although Chuck had only wanted an eggroll, once he saw and smelled the food cooking, he changed his mind.

"Ummm, how about some General Tso's chicken, some Lo Mein, maybe a bit of the Beef and Broccoli, two eggrolls and a diet coke Buddy."

"You feeling okay Detective? "Kind of a light lunch," Buddy said and laughed.

Chuck laughed too and then asked, "By the way Buddy, do you know a woman who works here in the mall...name of Maggie Bright Star?"

"I think I do not know many people working here. But might be a pretty native girl, maybe thirty or so. Always with a smile. I think she works at Delightful Debbie's. Silly name for a store."

"Okay, thanks Buddy,"

Chuck took his mountain of food and sat down at one of the tables. He dug in and while he ate, he thought of the best way to approach Maggie. He didn't want to upset her or spook her so she would talk to her brother Abel. As he was thinking about it, a very pretty Native American woman came walking up to Buddy's place. Chuck looked her over. She was about 5'5, maybe 120 lbs., with long black hair tied into two braids. The braids were adorned with small feathers of different colors. She had on turquoise cowboy boots and wore a turquoise pendant around her neck. Her legs were bare and looked toned and smooth. She was wearing a short dress, showing off everything inside of it.

Chuck was stunned momentarily and began choking on something he had swallowed without chewing. He stood up, coughing and turning red. Finally he got himself under control and felt like a fool in front of this beautiful woman, who Chuck was sure was Maggie Bright Star.

She got her food and as she passed by his table, she asked, "Are you okay?"

Bobby thought her voice was as beautiful as she was.

"Ummm, yeah," Chuck replied. "Guess it just went down the wrong way. Ummm if you are going to eat that now, how about a little company?"

Maggie looked him over and then sat down, saying, "Why not?"

""I'm Chuck."

"Maggie."

"I guess you work here in the mall?"

"I do. At Delightful Debbie's. Silly name but she does a good business. And what do you do?"

Chuck was going to lie, but somehow he couldn't bring himself to do so.

"I'm a detective with the Eagle Police Department."

"A detective? Wow, I don't think I have ever met a detective before. Your job must be very exciting."

"Uhhh, not really. Listen Maggie, I have to tell you something."

"Okay. What?"

"I was sitting here and if you hadn't walked over, I was going to find you."

"Find me? Why would you be looking for me?"

"I'll explain everything, but I have to ask you something first. I want you to give me an answer before I explain why I was looking for you. Because after I explain you might change your answer, or maybe not, or ...I don't know."

Maggie smiled and said, "You seem a bit flustered Detective. But go ahead and ask your question."

"Will you have dinner with me tonight?"

Maggie looked directly into Chuck's eyes. Then she tilted her head, first one way and then the other. Finally she nodded.

"Yes?"

"Yes Detective, but I think you better tell me now why you were here."

Chuck began to explain, and Maggie listened carefully for a few minutes.

Then she said, "I have to get back to work. Maybe we can discuss this further tonight, over dinner. I assume you know where I live, being a detective, so pick me up at seven."

Then Maggie got up and walked away. Chuck couldn't take his eyes off of her. He was thinking if she looked back it would be a good sign. Maggie turned the corner without looking back, and Chuck was disappointed. Just as he was about to get back to his food, she reappeared from around the corner and gave him a wink.

Chuck felt as if he had just won the lottery!

From behind the counter, Buddy smiling said, "Me think you falling in love Detective!"

"Awww, knock it off Buddy!" Chuck said.

Then as he started eating again, Chuck thought somehow Buddy might just be right.

CHAPTER 20

Wednesday 12:15 pm

Bobby had waited outside of Jim Longbow's trailer under a small tree. It offered little shade but was better than nothing. He would have stayed in his truck with the AC running, but he had no idea how long it would be till Tommy, George and Doc McAddams arrived. He didn't want to run the old truck and possibly run out of gas.

As he waited, he picked up a large stick lying on the ground and began to whittle. He tried to make some sense out of the two killings. He knew both men had been killed for something they were hiding. He also knew whatever it was, it wasn't very big and probably had no monetary value. But what could have no monetary value and yet, still be worth killing two men for?

Bobby thought both men had been elders and he wondered if that was an important fact. Maybe George would be able to find some kind of evidence up on the mountain or on the body of Jim Longbow. He sure hoped so or else it was possible there might be another body soon. Bobby was sure whoever had killed the two elders wasn't done yet.

Bobby looked up as three vehicles came up the road. The dust flew up from the first vehicle, coating the back two with dust and dirt. George was in the first car, followed by Tommy and then Doc McAddams. They pulled up near Bobby, and he took off his cowboy hat and waved the dust away from his face.

Tommy got out first and said, "I placed that envelope on your desk Lieutenant. Doc McAddams wanted to come out to see the body as it lay. I figured I better come back in case you needed some help in getting Jim down the mountain."

"I appreciate it Tommy, but aren't you a bit tired?" Bobby asked.

"I'm okay. Plus I'm off the next three days."

"Okay then. Good afternoon Doc, George. You guys ready for a climb?"

"Lead on McDuff," Doc said.

"Who's McDuff?" Tommy asked.

"Read a book Tommy," Bobby said. "Do you think we should try to bring a stretcher up the mountain Doc?"

"It would be pretty tough, so let's see what we can do when we get up there," Doc replied.

"So who's this McDuff guy?" Tommy asked again, and Bobby, George and Doc shook their heads and laughed.

Bobby, George, and Doc began to move toward the trail leading up the mountain, with Tommy feeling dumb, but not knowing why.

As they climbed slowly, Bobby asked what Tommy had done with Geronimo.

"Betty took to that dog and Geronimo to her," Tommy replied. "When I left, Geronimo was sitting under her desk, barely, with his big head resting on her lap. I think she might take him home with her. Or maybe keep him in the office."

"Oh no, not in the office," Bobby said.

They continued climbing until they came to the rock pile where Jim was buried.

"George, Tommy and Doc can uncover Jim, so let me show you a secondary site which needs to be processed," Bobby said. "I want pics of everything, and I can show you a knife I want processed as well. There is also a shovel and flashlight. Do the whole area as best as you can. We need to find something. You guys wait a second for me to show George the other area."

Bobby walked further off the trail till he came to the shovel, flashlight, and the small hole in the ground. Then he showed George where the knife was. Bobby left George to do his work and returned to the body.

"Okay, Doc, how do you want to do this?" Bobby asked.

"Let's start at the head and slowly remove the stones," Doc stated. "Wear gloves even though I doubt we can get anything from the stones themselves. We can pile them up together over there, by the tree stump. If you see any stones with blood or stains, keep them separate from the others."

Together they began to remove the stones, one by one. Once Jim Longbow's chest had been uncovered, Doc stopped them.

Doc got close to the body, examining it where there was a large blood stain.

"Looks like he was stabbed once," Doc said. "He was so thin; it looks as if it might have gone almost clear through him. Lot of force used, maybe anger or rage. Maybe not. Either way I think the killer was very strong. He probably died immediately. I'll know more when I do the autopsy. Let's clear some more but be careful not to disturb the body yet."

It took another hour to slowly remove the stones. Then all the stones smeared with blood were gathered into a small pile. They were small enough to be placed into a bag

Tommy had brought with him. The body was now clear of all the stones and Doc McAddams was examining it.

"Bobby," Doc McAddams said, "come over here and look at this."

Bobby walked over and looked at Jim's left wrist. There was a small tattoo there, and it looked similar to the one Charlie Two Horse had on his chest. Being so small and not being able to get a good look at it, Bobby was not positive it was the same.

"What do you think Doc?" Bobby asked.

"I'm not sure if it is the same, but once I get back to the office with him, I will take a picture," Doc said. "Okay Bobby, I don't think there is much more I can do here. Now, how are we going to get his body down the mountain?"

"Tommy and I will make a travois," Bobby said. "We can tie together some branches and sticks and then place Jim's body on it. One of us will take the feet and the other the head and carry and slide him slowly down. Is that okay with you Doc?"

"As long as you don't drop him or injure yourselves," Doc answered. "I will follow behind you."

As they were building the travois, George came back. He was carrying several evidence bags and his equipment.

"George check out the body before we move it. There might be some fibers or something we can use. And better bag his hands to check under his nails later. You get everything up at the hole George," Bobby asked.

"Yup, but I don't think I can carry all of this down in one trip," George answered.

"I can carry some of it," Doc said.

"You sure Doc?" Bobby asked.

"Listen here youngster, I'm not too old yet where I can't carry a few bags. Now how about you get building that thingamajig, and we can get started down."

"Yes sir," Bobby said with a salute.

Twenty minutes later after George had examined the body and bagged the hands, they put Jim's body on the travois fashioned from sticks and branches. Bobby took hold of the front and Tommy the back. Then Doc was next in line with George bringing up the rear. It took a long time to get down the trail, but they finally arrived back at the trailer and their vehicles.

Tommy and Bobby placed the body on a stretcher and loaded him into Doc's vehicle. Doc left and the other three stood around talking for a minute.

"Do you want me to look for anything in the trailer Bobby?" George asked.

"Nah, I don't think there would be anything to find," Bobby answered. "You both did great work today and I appreciate it. Tommy, you head in and write up a quick report. You can do a more thorough one when you get back to work. Get some rest, and thanks for your help today."

"No problem Lt., I wanted to help," Tommy replied.

George loaded up his equipment and evidence bags, and then he and Tommy took off. The sun was slowly setting, and Bobby didn't feel like leaving just yet.

Bobby sat down at the table he, Tommy and Jim had been sitting at just yesterday. Once again, he took up his knife and stick and began to whittle. He thought about Harry, and how he would react to his father being murdered. Would he feel guilty for not coming to take care of him? Would he care at all? Bobby wasn't sure. Maybe the letter addressed to Harry would give Bobby a lead. He sighed, thinking he really had nothing else.

Then he thought about the tattoo on Jim, similar to the one on Charlie. What could it mean? If they were the same, Bobby wondered how many others might have the tattoo as well.

Slowly he stood, feeling the weight of the two murders on him, pushing him down. He shook it off, looked to the sky and promised both Charlie Two Horse and Jim Longbow he would find their killer. He would arrest him if possible, but if he couldn't, he would have no problem sending him to his own well deserved death. The thought of it being a woman was now gone in Bobby's mind. Whoever had killed the two men appeared to be very strong.

Bobby got into his truck and began the slow drive back to the Tribal Police building. He was not a man who usually reacted with anger or any emotion. At least not to others, but Bobby was angry. Very angry and saddened by the death of two men who never hurt another soul. It took a long time, but Bobby finally got himself back under control as he pulled up in front, and slowly got out of his truck. He took a deep breath and entered the building.

CHAPTER 21

It had taken Chuck two hours to prepare himself for dinner with Maggie Bright Star. He had put on at least ten different shirts, finally deciding on a button down shirt with pearl snaps, and a design which included some turquoise coloring. He figured Maggie would like it. Black pants, and boots, along with a big buckle on his belt, and a black cowboy hat finished his look. He had stared into the mirror, not sure if he looked good enough to eat dinner with such a beautiful woman.

He pulled up and parked outside of her building fifteen minutes early. He wasn't sure if he should go up to the apartment or wait outside. Finally, he got up the nerve and climbed the stairs to Apartment 201. He was hoping Maggie's brother wouldn't be home. He knocked on the door and was unhappy to see a large Shoshone Indian standing there. He was looking at him like he was something you wiped off your shoe.

"Ummm, good evening Mr. Bright Star," Chuck said. He tried to smile but wasn't having any luck. Hesitantly, he continued, "My name is Chuck…Ummm… Charles Blackwell. I'm here to take Maggie, ummm I mean your sister to dinner."

In a deep baritone, he said, "Come in."

Chuck walked into a small foyer and stood with his hat in his hands.

"Sit," the man said, pointing to a chair in the small but neat living room.

Chuck sat and quickly looked around. He saw some pictures of past Shoshone Indian Chiefs on the walls.

There were also some more recent ones which he assumed were their parents. No other pictures but there were some small pottery items. The shelves on the walls were sparse and Chuck figured some things had been broken in the burglary. He saw a few places where shelves had been ripped down, leaving some broken plaster and holes.

"I am Abel Bright Star," the man finally said, identifying himself. "My sister says you are a Detective with the Eagle Police Department."

"Yes I am," Chuck said, and then, "do you want to see my badge?"

"Yes."

Chuck couldn't believe he actually wanted to see his badge, but as he began to reach for it, Maggie stepped into the room. He nearly lost his breath at the sight of her. Her hair was no longer in braids, and it hung straight down well over her shoulders. It was black as midnight and had a luster to it. She had on a simple dress, pale blue in color, that fit perfectly in all the right places. On her feet were simple black flats and Bobby couldn't stop staring at her. Her face had a little makeup on it, and her eyes were black, but were sparkling.

"Now Abel, I'm sure we can believe Chuck when he says he is a detective," Maggie said.

Abel's answer was a simple, "Hmmph,"

"Shall we go Detective?" Maggie asked.

Chuck jumped up, nearly knocking over a small table next to his chair.

"Yes?" he said. "Ummm, definitely yes. Nice meeting you Abel, ummm Mr. Bright Star.

Maggie tried to hide her smile, took Chuck's arm, and walked out of the apartment. As they got to the stairs, they heard Abel call out.

"You have her home by eleven, no ten!" Abel said.

Starting down the stairs, Maggie yelled out, "Maybe I will be home in the morning!"

They heard Abel slam the door.

"You think it was a good idea to get your brother angry?" Chuck asked.

"He thinks he is my father and yes, once in a while I need to put him in his place," Maggie said with a smile.

Chuck saw her teeth were white and perfect.

They got into Chuck's car and Maggie asked, "So where are you taking me Detective?"

"You can call me Chuck, Miss Bright Star," Chuck said.

"I kind of like Detective for now. But please call me Maggie."

"Okay... Maggie. I have reservations at Johnny Q's." Realizing what he had just said, Chuck said, "Not reservations, I mean, you know, I had them, umm, keep a table for us."

"Relax Detective, I haven't scalped a white man in at least ten years."

They looked at each other and laughed.

Soon they pulled up in front of Johnny Q's, and a valet took Chuck's keys. Chuck opened Maggie's door and escorted her into the restaurant.

Johnny Q's was well lit with plush carpeting throughout. There was a place to check your coat and hat, with a young girl behind the half door. Chuck gave her his hat and pocketed the ticket stub. Most of the tables in the main area were filled. Johnny Q's was a great steakhouse run by a congenial older couple named Scott and Barbara Mills. They always greeted their guests and made the rounds around the tables.

Scott had the duty at the front door this night, and when Chuck and Maggie walked in, he put out his hand to shake with Chuck.

"Good evening Detective!" Scott stated with enthusiasm. "Always a pleasure to have one of Eagle's finest. And who is this beautiful woman on your arm?"

"This is Maggie Bright Star Scott," Chuck replied. "Is our table ready?"

"Of course! Of course! Right this way."

Scott led them through the restaurant to a table near the back. It was in a private area, and Chuck was surprised. He didn't want to offend or make Maggie uncomfortable.

"Is this okay with you Maggie?" Chuck asked.

Smiling and sliding into the semi-circle booth made just for two, Maggie said, "I think this is perfect."

Chuck , who had never tipped Scott before, pulled out a twenty dollar bill and thanked him. Scott smiled and left the couple. They had just began to talk when a waiter came up to their table.

"Good evening," he said. "My name is Maurice, and it will be my pleasure to serve you two beautiful people. Is tonight a special occasion?"

Maggie answered, "It is perhaps the beginning of something special."

Chuck's heart was beating hard within his chest. Perhaps Maggie liked him as much as he did her. Tonight was definitely going to be one to remember.

"Can I start you off with something to drink?" Maurice asked.

"Perhaps a bottle of wine, maybe a nice Moscato?" Maggie said.

"At once!"

Maurice soon arrived with a bottle, poured out two glasses and stood by. Chuck and Maggie took small sips.

"Mmmmmm, delicious," Maggie said. "Could we wait to order for a few minutes?"

"Of course, I will bring you our menus and come back in a small while," Maurice said and actually bowed.

"Now Detective, I think it would be the right time to tell me about yourself, and then I will do the same," Maggie said with a smile. "This way we will no longer be strangers, and we can begin to know each other. Does that sound good to you?"

"Anything you say, Maggie," Chuck answered.

The evening passed with great food, good wine and many smiles and laughter. It was close to two am when Chuck pulled up in front of Maggie's apartment. They had spent over two hours walking around a park after their dinner. By the time they had left it, they were holding hands.

Chuck walked Maggie up to her apartment, and standing outside her door, said, "I had an amazing time Maggie. Can I see you again?"

"I would like that, Detective," Maggie said.

"I hope getting in so late won't get you into trouble with Abel."

"Don't worry about Abel. He likes to roar but he's really just a small pussy cat."

Some cat, Chuck thought.

Then she leaned in lightly kissing Chuck on his lips. It was quick and Chuck felt a bolt of lightning go through him. Then she opened her door and with a coy smile, closed it.

Chuck wasn't sure what had just happened, but he was sure he would do everything possible for it to happen again. Skipping down the stairs, Chuck made his way outside, looked up at the stars and gave out a loud, "Yeeha!"

Someone on the third floor of the building opened a window and yelled out, "What the hell is wrong with you! People are trying to sleep!"

Chuck bowed and saluted. Then he got into his car and drove home, slowly. Running the entire night over in his mind, with a huge smile on his face.

CHAPTER 22

Nihoono biitooeeihii walked around his small living room. He was thinking about his plan and what he had to do next. Once he started obtaining the objects, he stopped calling himself by his given name in private. Now he only thought of himself as *Nihoono biitooeeihii*, the One True Chief. To everyone else he was still known by his given name.

He had discovered three of the items he wanted, no, not merely wanted, what he desired and needed to get at all costs. One from Charlie Two Horse, one from Jim Longbow and one from the old shaman, *Tatakix Tangwe*, Walks in Wind. Walks in Wind had been the first and most important one.

Nihoono biitooeeihii thought back to the night he had been walking around the res in the cool night air. He heard some voices and discovered the old shaman talking with his son. The old shaman still lived like his ancestors, in a large teepee. *Nihoono biitooeeihii* had been walking by it when he heard the two men arguing. *Nihoono biitooeeihii* had stopped and kneeled near the opening. It was dark without a moon in the sky, and he hadn't thought anyone would see him.

The old shaman was talking about a great responsibility, something which had been handed down for centuries. The son, who had given up his name for a white man's, and renamed himself Matt Jones, had said how he didn't care. It was a foolish legend, made up by people who

"

didn't know anything but their superstitions. Matt didn't want anything to do with it and his father was turning into an old woman.

Walks in Wind had been angry, telling his son if he did not accept the gift and the responsibility, the shaman would disown him! Then what would happen to the gift! He must accept the gift and pass it down.

The son had said, he was not living in the ancient past. He was a modern man, one who did not follow some old superstitions. "Disown me if you want," the son had said, and then stormed out. Luckily, *Nihoono biitooeeihii* had heard the son getting up and had moved to the side of the teepee away from the opening..

Nihoono biitooeeihii then moved away from the teepee, into some woods nearby. He needed to think about what he had heard. There was a gift, something very old if the old shaman was to be believed. Many centuries old. Now what could it be?

He was not sure how to proceed and then a thought struck him. The shaman was an old man. He could be easily overpowered, made to talk. Perhaps he should slip into the teepee and see if he could get the gift without being heard or seen. Maybe he should wait till the shaman was gone. But if he confronted him now, he could get whatever this gift was. Even if he had to kill the old man. He had never taken a life before, but he sensed this gift was of great value. He could make his death look like a natural one. Afterall, the shaman was closing in on one hundred years old.

Nihoono biitooeeihii had waited until the old man was asleep. Then, he silently made his way into the teepee. Even in the dark *Nihoono biitooeeihii* could see the form of the old man, sleeping on some old furs, snoring lightly. He began to search, but not knowing what he was looking for, the search was fruitless. He decided he would wake and tie the old man up. Gag him so he couldn't alert anyone.

Nihoono biitooeeihii moved quickly to his truck, removing some rope, and a rag to use as a gag. Then checking no one was in the area to see him, he returned to the teepee.

Nihoono biitooeeihii grabbed the sleeping man, surprising the old shaman, and tying him up in just a few seconds, pushing the rag into his mouth. Then he placed his flashlight, shining into the old man's face.

Nihoono biitooeeihii had said, "Listen to me carefully old man. I may let you live, or I may not, it will be up to you. Perhaps your life no longer has meaning. But your son, Matt Jones has three small children and a wife. If you do not tell me what I want to know, I will kill them all. But first I will rape the oldest girl. She is about sixteen, right? In any case, look into my eyes and believe me in what I am telling you. Any hesitation, and I kill you, rape the oldest girl, rape your son's wife, maybe even the young one. Then I will kill them as well. Nod if you understand."

After *Nihoono biitooeeihii* moved the light out of the old shaman's eyes, he saw Walks in Wind nod. He removed the gag. The old man had not yelled out.

Walks in Wind stared into the eyes of the man holding him. He softly asked him what he wanted.

"The gift you were going to give your son," *Nihoono biitooeeihii* said.

"Never!" Walks in Wind yelled out, struggling to free himself.

Nihoono biitooeeihii hit him in the face and then gagged him once again.

Nihoono biitooeeihii said, "That was a mistake old man. Now I will have to hide you somewhere. Then I will visit your son. I wonder if your granddaughter will enjoy or hate what I will do to her? Maybe I will kill the others and keep her alive for a while. I will rape her every day, and every night. When I am tired of her, I will kill her. And all because of you refusing to give me a simple gift. One last time old man. Will you give it to me!"

Walks in Wind had no choice. He would have to give this beast what he wanted. He could give him the gift, but the tale written on many sheets of parchment must stay hidden. It was the only written thing concerning the responsibility he had been born to. Somehow, he would have to give the gift and keep the parchment from being seen.

Walks in Wind nodded, and the gag was removed. He told *Nihoono biitooeeihii* it was not within this teepee. It was hidden in the woods, within a hollow tree. He would take him to the tree and give him the gift. But he must promise not to kill his family. *Nihoono biitooeeihii* had agreed and soon the two of them were walking deep into the woods.

When they got to the hollow tree, Walks in Wind said there were traps within the tree, and he must get the gift. If he didn't do it himself, the man might die or be seriously injured.

"Okay old man," *Nihoono biitooeeihii* had said, and watched the old man carefully.

Walks in Wind had reached in, seeming to move things around, perhaps disarming the traps within, and soon removed a small box. He handed it to *Nihoono bi-itooeeihii* and told him it had no value.

Nihoono biitooeeihii smiled wickedly, and had said, "I think you might be lying to me old man. And if the tree had traps in it, traps that might kill me, why wouldn't you have let me reach in there? Because you old fool, there are no traps! Now, what else do you have hidden in there?"

When *Nihoono biitooeeihii* reached into the tree, Walks in Wind threw himself at him. He tried to stop him, but *Nihoono biitooeeihii* was too strong. *Nihoono biitooeeihii* knocked Walks in Wind down and forced his face into the dirt. He held him there, till the old man stopped struggling. He was dead.

Then *Nihoono biitooeeihii* reached into the hollow tree. He felt something deep down, and struggling to reach it, finally pulled it out. It was parchment, several sheets tied with a ribbon. He did not open the parchment to read there. He wanted to do so in his own home. But he also did not want Walks in Wind to be found here in case anyone else knew about the gift and parchment.

He turned him over and wiped all the dirt from the old shaman's face. Even reaching into his mouth to scoop out any dirt. Clearing the dirt from around his eyes, brushing his hair clean as well. Then he carried Walks in Wind back to his teepee, placed him on his furs and left. He knew everyone would think the old man had simply died in his sleep.

Then *Nihoono biitooeeihii* had returned to his home, spending hours reading the parchments, over and over again. Then he had decided on a plan. He began writing down names and places. He decided on a schedule and would begin the very next day.

Now as he stood in his living room, he thought about the next step in his plan. He had failed to find the gift the first time in the apartment off the res in Eagle. It would be too soon to return there. The next time, he would have to get the better of the big Shoshone. Perhaps he could use his sister to make him reveal the gift.

Now he sat looking at the parchment, looking at the names he had written down and where they all lived. Most were on the res, but there were two who lived in Eagle. He had visited one and found nothing. Maybe tomorrow, he would visit the other home of the Shoshone living in Eagle.

He looked at the clock on the wall, seeing it was close to one. The next Shoshone with the gift was old, living in a trailer just within the city limits. On top of being old, the next victim was a woman. *Nihoono biitooeeihii* didn't want to kill an old woman, but he would do whatever was necessary.

He gathered up some tools to break into the trailer, two knives and some rags and rope. Before he left, he thought about what he could threaten the old woman with. He knew she only had one daughter, and she was married to a white man. It would make things more difficult if he had to get ahold of her daughter, possibly the white man too. Maybe just the threat would work. He smiled and left his home. He would be at the trailer within an hour and would have more of the gift a short time after that.

CHAPTER 23

I was sitting in my office going over some reports I would have to discuss with Will, when Chuck bounced into my office and took a seat. He had a big smile on his face and couldn't sit still. I had never seen him like this.

"Okay, give," I said. "What has you so happy Chuck?"

"Eric, I'm going to tell you, but first you have to promise not to get angry," Chuck said. "Well, at least not too angry."

"I suppose if I don't agree you won't tell me so, okay, I promise."

"I think I'm in love!"

"In love? Who have you fallen in love with?"

"Ummm, who is why you can't get angry."

"Okay already, who?!"

"Maggie Bright Star."

"Maggie...do you mean the woman whose apartment was broken into? The woman who I told you to stay away from. Chuck, I made a promise to Max and now you broke it."

"I know Eric, but see I wasn't planning on falling in love and taking her out to dinner and..."

"You took her out to dinner? I suppose you also spoke with her brother Abel."

"Ummm, not about the burglary. I did ask Maggie about it over dinner, but I didn't press her. Really Eric, it was just a fluke. I went to the mall where I knew she worked. I was sitting having some Chinese food from

Buddy and she ordered food right after me. When I saw her, my heart stopped. You know how that feels Eric, at least you told me it was what happened when you saw Bell."

"Yeah, I know," I said, "but what made you go see her at the mall? Did you find something you needed to pursue?"

"Not really, it was more like curiosity about the burglary. But once she sat down with me, we began to talk, one thing led to another, and I asked her out to dinner."

"Well the bell can't be unrung, so you might as well tell me the rest of it."

"We had a great dinner at Johnny Q's and…"

"Not about your date Chuck. About the burglary."

"Oh yeah, right. Maggie said both her and Abel had been at work. She had gotten home first and saw everything in the apartment had been turned over, broken, or smashed. All the drawers in the bedroom had been dumped out. The kitchen cabinets had been opened and some dishes thrown to the floor where they broke. She had been scared and had walked out of the apartment and went to a neighbor. Then she called 911. Before Officer Greg Harper had gotten there, Abel had come home. When she told him she had called 911, he had gotten very angry and told her they were not going to make a report.

Maggie said she had never seen her brother so angry and was a bit frightened and confused. When Harper showed up, her brother wouldn't let him in the apartment and sent him away. I spoke with Harper, but he didn't have much useful info."

"Very suspicious and concerning. Obviously whoever burgled the apartment was looking for something in particular. You don't tear the place apart if you are just looking for something of value to steal. Max said he didn't think anything had been taken. Very strange indeed."

"You're not upset about me talking with Maggie?"

"Nah, especially not if you really have fallen in love. A bit quick though."

"I know. But Eric, she is the most beautiful, kind, intelligent funny woman I have ever met!"

"What about her? Do you think she has fallen in love with you?"

"I don't know for sure, but when she kissed me goodnight, I felt as if a thousand volts had passed through my body."

"Well I hope it is the real thing Chuck. About time you settled down with a good woman, had a bunch of kids..."

"Kids! Slow it down friend!"

"When are you seeing her again?"

"Tonight, unless something comes up. We are going to take a drive to Casper and eat at Bosco's. She said she loves Italian food."

"Sounds great, but..."

Just then an officer knocked on my door and entered.

"Sorry to disturb you Sergeant," Officer Mike Satchell said. "There's been a homicide over on the north side. Old Shoshone woman named Sarah Tall Tree. Figured you would want to know right away."

"Who is over there right now?" I asked.

"Bobby Kincaid Sarge."

I was happy Bobby Kincaid was on the scene. He was a great cop. On the job over twenty-five years. He had never wanted rank and spent all his time on the job on patrol. He had probably seen everything there was to see. In fact, he said working patrol was like watching reruns on television. Nothing really new ever happened.

"Sorry Chuck about your date tonight but being in charge of person's crimes means this case is yours. If you miss your date because of it, you can always go another time. Plus it might be a good idea for your new girlfriend to see what a life with a detective would be like. Make sure you get Jimmy over to the scene. I'm going over too."

Chuck left to get Jimmy, and I went to Will to tell him about the homicide. Then I headed out and drove over to the north side of town. The north side of Eagle housed mostly the poorer people of Eagle. But even though the people living there were poor, their pride in their small homes was easy to see. Of course, there were lowlifes and drug dealers mixed in, but on the whole the people were poor, not criminals.

As I drove, I thought about who and why someone would kill Sarah Tall Tree. I knew her from my years on patrol and knew she had no enemies or anything worth killing her for. I also had heard from her how she could trace her family back several centuries. I knew her daughter Cindy Walker, formerly Tall Tree, would have to be notified.

And as always, I tried to promise myself whoever had done this would be caught.

CHAPTER 24

Bobby had driven into Eagle early in order to tell Harry Longbow about his father's murder. He also wanted to give him the letter he had found, addressed to him. Maybe something in the letter would be a clue as to why someone had killed Jim Longbow.

Bobby didn't have too much time to talk with Harry because Doc McAddams was doing the autopsy on Jim Longbow at 8:30 this morning. Bobby wanted to be there to see if there were any other findings besides the knife which had been plunged into Jim's chest. He also was hoping Doc had gotten enlargements of the two tattoo's.

Bobby pulled up at the lumber yard where Harry worked. He parked his truck and walked into the work area. He stopped one of the workers and asked where Harry Longbow was. Pointing to an area in the back, Bobby saw Harry cutting some large pieces of wood in half.

Bobby walked over and tried calling out Harry's name, but the buzzsaw drowned out his words. Finally, he tapped him on the shoulder and Harry turned around, with an angry look on his face.

"Don't you know not to touch someone when they are operating dangerous machinery!" Harry yelled out.

"I'm sorry Harry," Bobby yelled. "Think you can turn that thing off?"

Harry turned it off and immediately the noise level lowered.

"What do you want now, Black Bear?" Harry asked, removing his goggles and gloves.

"I'm sorry Harry, but your father is dead."

"Dead? Heart attack?"

"I'm afraid not Harry. Your father was murdered. He was found up on the mountain behind his trailer. Someone stabbed him and covered his body with stones."

"Who did it?" Harry asked with a hint of anger. Bobby realized it was the first emotion he had shown.

"I don't know Harry, yet, but I promise I will do everything I can to find out and bring him to justice. Your father is being autopsied…"

"Autopsied? You know he would not have wanted that!"

"Sorry but we have to do it when someone is murdered. If you want you can come with me over to the morgue to see him. Also, there is one other thing."

"Yeah what?"

"I found a sealed envelope addressed to you in the trailer."

"I suppose you opened it."

"No, I didn't," Bobby said and handed it to him.

"I guess I should thank you, Black Bear. I will go see my father later today, after the Doc is through cutting him open."

"Okay Harry. One other thing. I have no idea why your father was killed, or why he was up on the mountain. We found a shovel, flashlight, and his knife off the trail. There was also a small hole dug. If you know why he was there, or if the letter explains anything, I would appreciate you letting me read it."

"If the letter clears up anything, I will think about giving it to you. When can I get his knife?"

"Right now it is evidence, but as soon as I can, I will get it to you."

"*Tsaa* Bobby Black Bear," Harry said and began to walk away.

"One other thing Harry."

"What?"

"Your father's dog Geronimo is the one who led us to your father's body. Geronimo must have loved your father a great deal. Right now I have him at the Tribal Police office. If you want him, he's yours."

"I'll think about it. Again...*Tsaa*."

Bobby was surprised Harry had used the Shoshone word for thank you. Maybe his father's death affected him more than he was showing. Bobby hoped Harry would take the dog. Bobby thought owning a dog and having its unconditional love and loyalty, sometimes made a person better. Looking at the time, he saw he would be late for the autopsy. He got into his truck and headed over to the morgue.

CHAPTER 25

While Bobby was with Doc McAddams at the morgue, watching him cut up Jim Longbow, Eric, Chuck, and Jimmy were looking down at the body of Sarah Tall Tree. Standing next to them was Bobby Kincaid, who had been first on the scene.

"As I was saying," Kincaid said, "I was on patrol when I was flagged down by Ruth Nabors. She was trying to get into Sarah's trailer to deliver some food from the Eagle Food Bank. The trailer door was locked, and she told me Sarah rarely went out. Plus she said, the trailer was never locked.

I went to the door and checked it out. No signs of anything, so I went to a window and looked in. I saw a body sitting in a chair, facing away from me. It appeared she was tied up and she was naked. I told Ruth to wait by my car. Then I forced my way in and found Sarah dead.

Definitely a homicide by the cut across her throat. Plus there were multiple small cuts all over her body. There were also some cigarette burns as well. Her hands had been tied behind her back and her two legs tied to the chair you see her in. Someone tortured this old woman. That's about all I have Eric."

"Looks like you have everything covered Bobby," I said. "Call Dispatch and ask them to get Doc McAddams to please come over. Also get a statement from Nabors and make sure she is okay. Get our CSI guys out as well. Then you can resume patrol and write up your report later. And thanks Bobby for your good work, as always."

Bobby left the trailer, and we all began to look around. There wasn't anything broken or tossed around, so I didn't think it was a burglary. Then, as I was looking in the bedroom, I noticed a panel from the drop ceiling pulled out of place. Grabbing a small stool, I stood on it and looked into the space. There was nothing in it, but I was wondering if there might have been something hidden there. Maybe we would get lucky, and our evidence guys would get some DNA, fibers, or a fingerprint, but I wasn't holding my breath.

"Find anything?" I asked Chuck and Jimmy.

"Not a thing," Chuck replied. "Maybe our CSI guys will get lucky."

"I was thinking the same thing. Let's go outside and get some fresh air. We can wait for Doc and our guys to show up. I had Bobby Kincaid call them and tell them to come over."

The three of us found a table and two benches under a tree near the trailer. We sat there waiting for our people to arrive.

"Looks like you might make your date after all, Chuck," I said.

"Date?" Jimmy asked. "I'm your partner and you never told me you were dating someone. Who is she? Wait a second, is it a female?"

Chuck turned a little red and said, "Yes, it's a she! I mean, she's a she, a female!"

"So give, what's her name, how long are you dating, is it serious..."

"Is this an interrogation!"

"Calm down Chuck," I said. "Jimmy is your partner and should know about your new girlfriend."

"Yeah okay," Chuck said. "I met her at the mall, and we had one dinner. Her name is Maggie Bright Star, and we are supposed to go out tonight. Anything else Mr. Nosy?"

"Arapahoe or Shoshone?" Jimmy asked.

"What's the difference?"

"Well the Shoshone have different traditions and..."

"No idiot, what's the difference to me which one she is? And just for your notes, if you are taking any, she is a Shoshone."

"That's enough you two, here comes Doc," I said, "and it looks like he has a passenger."

Doc pulled up in front of us and he and Bobby Black Bear got out.

"*Behne*, Bobby, Doc. What are you doing here?"

"*Behne* Eric," Bobby said. "I was with Doc at the morgue getting ready to autopsy Jim Longbow, when the call came in. Figured I would tag along and see how the big city guys work."

"Jim Longbow? Isn't he the father of Harry Longbow?"

"One and the same. You have trouble with Harry?"

"Drunk and disorderly sometimes when he goes to Kelly's Bar. Nothing more than that. What happened to his father?"

"How about you guys get some tea and cookies and have a nice long chat," Doc said. "I have lots to do and I'd like to see the victim please."

"Okay Doc, sorry," I said. "Right this way."

The five of us made our way back into the trailer. Jimmy and Bobby hung back a bit. Doc got down on his knees to examine Sarah.

"Who is this?" Doc asked.

"Sarah Tall Tree Doc," Chuck said. "Found by Bobby Kincaid a few hours ago."

"Kincaid? Good, at least I will get a good report from him. She died after some torture. Looks like she doesn't have anything under her fingernails. I'll get a better idea when I get her back to the morgue. I'd say time of death was probably about one or two in the morning."

Doc stood up and we were talking to him when Bobby got closer to Sarah. He was looking very carefully at the back of her neck.

"Hey Doc, come and look at this?" Bobby said.

As Doc walked over, Chuck said, "What do you see Lieutenant?"

Doc was looking and then he stood up, shaking his head.

"Come take a look Chuck," Bobby said.

Chuck looked at the back of her neck and then I did too. What I saw was a very small tattoo. Too small to really see what it was.

"I think we had better talk Eric," Bobby said. "And maybe you guys should come back to the morgue with us so we can show you something."

"Feel like filling us in Lieutenant?" Chuck asked.

"I think you will get a better idea when you come back with us."

"Okay Bobby," I said. "Jimmy, you wait here for CSI and when they are done with the body, get a couple of guys to help bring her to the morgue. Doc, we can ride over in my car, and you can leave yours for the body transport."

"Okay Eric, I'm sure it will be fine," Doc said.

Myself, Bobby, Doc, and Chuck piled into my car, and we headed over to the morgue. What Bobby wanted to talk about was a mystery for now, and I hated mysteries. At least without a solution. But soon I would know what he was being so mysterious about.

As we pulled up to the morgue and got out, something told me I wasn't going to be so happy about whatever Bobby was going to show us. A feeling of dread was hanging over me and through the years I knew not to ignore it.

Something bad was going on and I wasn't looking forward to finding out. But there was nothing to do about it until I knew what it was. I looked over to Chuck and he seemed to be feeling the same way. Chuck and I followed Doc and Bobby past the receptionist and instead of going into one of the examination rooms, Doc led us into a small conference room.

"You guys can wait here," Doc said. "I have to get a few things and set them up."

"What's going on Doc?"

"Never mind, just wait a few minutes."

Doc walked out with Bobby and the door closed behind them.

"What do think is going on Eric?" Chuck asked.

"I have no idea, but I am sure they aren't wasting our time," I answered. "Let's just wait for them to tell us what they are up to. But I don't think I am going to be very happy about it, whatever it is."

The door opened and Doc walked in with a small box and Bobby was carrying a slide projector. He set it on the table and then pulled down a screen which was hanging on the wall.

As Doc was setting up, he said, "I know this is a bit old fashioned, but so am I."

Doc fiddled with the projector and then turned the lights out. He then hit a button and a picture of what looked to be some kind of object, with some kind of stream of material behind it. I couldn't quite make it out.

"Looks like a meteor," Chuck said.

"You got it Chuck," Doc said. "Now here is another view of it."

A second picture appeared and then Doc turned on the lights.

"Okay guys, I'm a bit intrigued, but what does this have to do with Sarah Tall Tree?"

Doc said, "Why don't you tell them Bobby?"

Bobby took a deep breath and then said, "In the past few days, Charlie Two Horse and Jim Longbow have been murdered. Those pictures of a meteor were small tattoos found on both of them."

I looked at Chuck and he said, "You mean like the tattoo on Sarah's neck?"

"I won't know till I take a pic and blow it up," Doc said, "but I have a good idea it will be the same as these two."

Chuck and I looked stunned.

"I think we better sit down and talk about everything you know Bobby," I said.

He just nodded.

CHAPTER 26

Bell sat down at the large conference table in the Eagle Star's building. A meeting had been called to discuss her run for councilwoman. Sitting around the table was Alan Cummings, Brett Trask, John Miller, Sally Jacobs, and Teresa Benton. The only one not there was the District Attorney, Benedictus Impeletti, or Imp as Bell thought of him.

On the table was an assortment of donuts, bagels, butter, juice, and cream cheese, and two large pots of steaming coffee. There were utensils and cups, plates, and napkins. The only one not eating anything was Bell. She was too nervous and thought she might spill something with her hands slightly shaking.

"Okay, let's get this meeting started," Brett Trask said. "You ready Belinda?"

"I am Mr. Trask," Bell said.

"No need to be so formal Belinda, first names will do."

"Okay then, please call me Bell."

"We have been working on your campaign and we think we have a pretty good platform. We have gone over some of the major problems concerning our city and tried to come up with some answers which make sense. Of course, we want you to read over all of the items we have discussed and add any to the list you feel are important."

"I have been thinking of a few things. Like..."

"Maybe it would be better to hold off on your thoughts for the moment Bell," Alan Cummings said. "We have a full printout of our ideas. After you read them we can all get together once again to discuss them and ummm, any ideas you might have. Okay?"

"Okay Alan, sure," Bell answered.

"Fine. What we want to discuss here today is your opponent, Graham Stone."

"I know he will be tough to beat."

"Normally, he would be Bell. But we have uncovered some interesting things about Graham."

"What do you mean?"

"If you remember the last election, Graham and his people smeared his opponent with accusations and lies. He ran a dirty campaign. This time around, we don't think he will be able to find any skeletons in your closet. So we figured, we should strike first, just in case."

"A smear campaign?" Bell asked.

"Now Bell," Trask said, "not a smear campaign, just some strategic leaks. We understand your hesitation. But the difference between Graham and us is we will only use true facts. No lies or made up accusations. Graham has been involved in some shady business and the people of Eagle should be informed. You see that, don't you?"

"I'm not sure if I want to run based on my opponents possible shady dealings, as you called them Brett. I want to run on my abilities and the things I want to do to make Eagle a better place to live."

"That's a bit naïve Bell," John Miller said. "In today's world anyone campaigning must use whatever is available to them. Look at the campaigns for President in the past few years. All of them from Clinton to Obama, to Trump and Biden have used any dirt they could dig up. And of course, your character, ideas and wants for Eagle will play a major part in your campaign."

"I will have to think about it," Bell said. "I think I need to do some...some soul searching about this. I'm sorry if I am disappointing you all. I will look over what you have written so far and then I will call with my decision. I know you all have worked hard on this, and I don't want to waste your time. Now, if you will excuse me."

"We understand Bell but let me say one more thing before you leave," Trask said. "This city is growing every day, and we all need someone who is honest, has a head on her shoulders and only wants what is best for Eagle. You are that person Bell. You can make Eagle great. Now, we will be waiting on your decision, only don't take too long. On behalf of all of us, thank you for being here today."

Bell stood, took the folder with their ideas, and walked out of the conference room. As she closed the door, she paused for one minute to listen.

"I thought you said she will be easy to control!" she heard John Miller yell.

"Be quiet you fool," Trask had replied.

"Well I think she is right," one of the women said, Bell not sure which one.

"Who cares what you think!" Trask said. "You are here because you are rich, and no other reason. Now, let's figure out what we are going to do!"

Bell felt a tear run down her cheek and quickly walked away. She was devastated at what she had overheard. There would be no public announcement today, not until she decided if she was running or not. She needed to talk with Eric but there was one other person she could talk with first. She wiped her face and headed out of the building. She was only a few blocks from Imp's offices and decided she would walk. On the way she would get her mind clear and think of what she would say to him.

CHAPTER 27

Thursday 1:00 pm

We had been sitting in Doc's conference room, discussing the cases which seemed to be connected. Other than the tattoos and the way each victim had been killed, we didn't have much. We didn't know what the killer was looking for, or why each of the victims had a tattoo. We didn't have a clue as to who might be killing these people, and it didn't look like any of our questions were going to be answered anytime soon.

As we sat thinking, each of us silent, the receptionist came in with a few bags in her hand.

"Your food is here," she said.

"Did you get something for yourself?" Doc Addams asked.

"Sure did sir and thank you."

She put the bags on the table and then left.

"I don't know about you guys, but I'm starving," Chuck said.

He then proceeded to take everything out of the bags, finally finding the chicken parmigiana plate with rigatoni pasta in a meat sauce he had ordered.

The rest of us had gotten sandwiches.

"Good thing all of this is coming out of the PD's pocket," Doc McAddams said, as he unwrapped his sandwich.

"No kidding," I answered after taking a bite out of my meatball sub. "Knowing how Chuck eats, I always get as big a budget as I can."

"Hey, I can't help it if I like to eat," Chuck said as he wiped his mouth.

"You better think twice about eating like that Chuck," Bobby said. "What will Maggie Bright Star say if you get fat!"

"You guys have been telling secrets behind my back!"

"Calm down Chuck, you should know nothing is off limits when it comes to cops."

"I suppose so. So, do you know Maggie?"

"I do know her and her brother," Bobby said as he swallowed some food. "Both are good people, good Shoshone. They left the res when their father died a few years back. But they both still come to the res for celebrations and other events."

"And what do you think about a white man dating her?"

"It is not for me to say. I only wish whatever you two do, brings happiness and honor to both your houses."

"Good enough for me," Chuck said with a smile.

The receptionist knocked on the door and entered again.

"Doc, Detective Bridges has arrived with Sarah Tall Tree's body," she said. "which examination room do you want her in?"

Getting up, Doc said, "Let's bring her to room 2. I'll help you and Detective Bridges. Do you want to be in the room Bobby?"

"Yes Doc, I will be there to give her the respect she deserves, even though she is gone. *Tsaa* Doc."

"Once Chuck is finished eating his large meal, I think we will head back to the PD," I said.

"It's not large!" Chuck answered and began to finish it off.

"I need to go over this with Lieutenant Tolliver, and maybe the Chief. Doc, can you send over a report to me as soon as possible?"

"Of course," Doc said.

"Bobby, it appears our cases are tied together. Would it be okay for Chuck, Jimmy, and I to come out to the reservation? I'd like to see the places where the victims were killed."

Of course," Bobby said. "Why don't you all come out first thing tomorrow. I will take you. Then maybe we can discuss all of this again. Maybe a night with some sleep will clear away some of the shadows in front of us."

"Okay, we will meet you at Tribal Police headquarters Bobby. Thanks for your help."

"It is I who is grateful for your help Eric. Till tomorrow,"

Doc and Bobby left to do and watch over the autopsy on Sarah Tall Tree. I needed to find her daughter, Cindy Walker. I knew she had married a white man named Carl Walker and lived on one of the tree streets. The tree streets, like Elm, Maple, Spruce had been named for trees being planted all along them many years ago. They now towered over the large houses which were built in that area.

"Let's head back Chuck," I said. "We need to look up where Cindy Walker lives. She needs to be told of her mother's death, plus we might be able to get some information from her. Maybe she will know what Sarah Tall Tree had been hiding."

"Damn, I hate death notifications," Chuck said.

"We all do Chuck, but it is something we have to do. Get Jimmy and we all can go to give her the bad news."

As Chuck went to find Jimmy, I thought about everything we had found out so far. Someone was killing Shoshone natives. They seemed to all be elders and they all had a mysterious tattoo. Two had been killed on the res, and one here in Eagle. Which meant, the killer didn't care about where he killed. I wondered who else might have the tattoo. Did any Arapahoe have it as well, or only Shoshone?

Then the burglary at Abel and Maggie Bright Star's came to mind. Could our killer have been the one to toss their home, maybe looking for something specific there? And if so, were Abel and Maggie in any danger? I would have to discuss this with Chuck. The only thing I was really sure of, was somewhere living within Eagle or the Wind River Reservation, was a serial killer. Now all I had to do was catch him, hopefully before he killed anyone else.

CHAPTER 29

Before Bell went to Imp's office, she found a quiet spot to stop and think about the meeting. She wasn't so naïve as to believe airing out an opponent's dirty laundry wasn't the norm. In fact she knew if Stone had any dirt on her, he wouldn't hesitate to use it. Still, she was having a hard time accepting this fact of running for office.

She then thought back to what she had overheard through the door. Some of them obviously thought she was a weak minded woman, easy to control. They were using her as a figurehead only. She was getting angrier with each passing second, and finally took a deep breath and cleared her mind.

First thing she needed to do was to get herself completely under control, now and whenever she was out in public or in a meeting. She knew who she was and what she wanted to accomplish. Now she would have to show her backers what she was made of. Next, she needed to see what ideas they had developed. If they went against her beliefs, then she would either have to drop them or the race. Then she needed to talk with Imp. She didn't believe he thought of her the way some of those men did, but she needed to be sure. And finally, she would talk to the one person who truly mattered, Eric.

Bell opened up the folder the backers had prepared for her. On the first page was a numbered list of different projects. As she glanced at them, she didn't see anything she disagreed with, except for a bridge on the east side of town which they wanted to replace. The bridge was definitely old, but she drove over it every time she visited her friend Barbara. It seemed to her it was still in great shape, but then again, did she really know? She wasn't an engineer, she thought. So maybe it did need replacing.

A few of her own ideas had not been addressed, such as either building or acquiring a bigger building for the offices of the Police Department and the District Attorney. She knew her opponent Stone had been fighting the proposal for the past few years. Her husband being a member of the department had nothing to do with her desire to get a new place for them. But she also was sure Stone would imply her only reason for wanting it was because of Eric. She would need to express her reasons for backing it, and she would not shy away from mentioning her husband in any debates.

Bell closed the folder and walked the few blocks to the law enforcement building. On the way in she saw several officers she knew and waved hello. Then she made her way to the elevator to go up to see Imp. When she stepped off the elevator, she walked up to a window where a receptionist sat. She knew the woman from some of her activities.

"Hello Charlene," Bell said. "Is it possible to see Imp, I mean District Attorney Impeletti?"

Laughing, Charlene said, "We all call him Imp, Bell. Let me see if he is in."

Charlene dialed and then spoke into the phone.

"He says you can go right in Bell."

"Thanks Charlene. We need to get together for a girls night out soon."

"Definitely," Charlene said, and buzzed Bell in through the door.

Bell walked down a hallway and then came out into a large office space. There were several small offices along the walls, which Bell knew belonged to some of the Assistant District attorneys. In the middle were about six secretaries and paralegals. The place was very busy, with people walking around, stopping to talk or drop off folders. Bell waved to a few of the people she knew, and then walked up to Imp's personal secretary. Theresa Knowles was Eric's aunt, and I knew from the many times Eric had visited Imp, if Theresa didn't want you to see Imp, you didn't get in.

Theresa had worked for the last three District Attorneys, and although she was not a lawyer, probably knew more about the law than some of the ADA's. She also knew where all the bodies were buried, all the judges and most of the defense attorneys in town.

Bell remembered how Eric told her if he didn't address her as Aunt Theresa, she would glare at him, folding her arms and tapping her foot.

Therefore, Bell said, "Good afternoon Aunt Theresa. You are looking very pretty today."

Theresa smiled and said, "Well good afternoon to you to Belinda. It's been awhile since I have seen you."

Bell knew she was implying how Eric and she hadn't had her out to dinner in a long time.

"I know Aunt Theresa, but Eric and I were just talking this morning about having you out for a barbecue on Sunday. I hope you are available."

"You tell me the time and I will be there."

"Let's say about noon?"

"Perfect. Now, you can go in to see his majesty," Theresa said with a chuckle.

"Thank you Theresa, I mean Aunt Theresa."

Whew, that was a close one Bell thought. She walked past Theresa's desk into a large office. There was a large oak desk at the far end. Connected to it in the front, was a long conference table. It was covered with law books and folders, some spilling their contents in a pile. Bell was sure Theresa knew where every single file was located, even if Imp didn't. As she got closer to the desk, she saw Imp furiously typing on a laptop. She watched him for a few minutes and then coughed to get his attention.

Looking up, Imp said, "Bell! How long have you been standing there. Why didn't anyone tell me you were coming up?"

Bell thought Charlene must have called the keeper of the gate, Aunt Theresa, and not Imp himself.

"I hope I'm not disturbing anything Imp." Bell asked.

"Of course not. I just came from court, and I wanted to get some thoughts on the trial going on. But it can wait. Let's sit over on the couch."

Imp moved around his desk and walked over to a large leather couch in front of a window. Looking down at it, he saw it was covered with books and folders, the same way his desk and table were. He picked everything up in a few handfuls and placed them on top of the table. Some of them threatened to fall over onto the floor, and Imp fixed them.

Sighing and letting Bell sit first, Imp said, "What can I do for my best friend's wife and future council-woman?"

"That's just it, Imp," Bell said. "I just came from a meeting with all the other backers. They said some things which disturbed me and since I know you are also one of my backers, and thank you for that, I figured I could talk with you."

"All I have done so far is put up some money. I haven't really done anything else as far as your campaign. But why don't you explain what is bothering you."

Bell recapped the meeting with her backers, leaving out nothing, including what she overheard through the door. When she finished, she was visibly shaking and angry.

"Take a breath Bell. How about some water or a shot of some 18 year old scotch?"

"I'll take a water please."

Imp got up and walked to a small refrigerator in the corner. He returned with a bottle of water, opened it, and handed it to Bell. She took a sip, and then a longer one. She had calmed down and was feeling better.

"First of all," Imp said, "no one is going to be controlling you. Once you are elected, if you still want to be, you are your own woman. You are bright, honest and a caring person, which is why I am putting money into your campaign."

"But those men will want favors for helping me!"

"No doubt, but there is a difference in wanting favors and demanding them. I'm sure there will be some favors asked of you, but I also know you will never do anything wrong for the city or its people. So don't worry about that. Now, have you looked at some of their ideas?"

"Yes and to be honest, most of them are ones I had thought about. A few I disagree with, but on the whole I think I have a good beginning for a platform. But the whole thing about Graham Stone bothers me."

"When I first ran for District Attorney, I had to bring up some dirty things about my opponent. I didn't want to sling mud, but there were things I thought the people should know. As long as nothing is made up and not too personal, I think it's the way you need to run a campaign."

"I'm still not sure. I don't even know what they were talking about."

"I have an idea. How about if I meet with some of them and see what they have in mind? Then I can get back to you and you will have a better idea if you want to run or not."

"Really Imp? That would be great and just what I need to make up my mind. Thank you so much!"

"Don't be silly Bell. Now one other thing."

"Yes?"

"There are only five people alive who know about DeSade and the Under my Thumb gang. Me, you, Eric, Danny Brown...oh and of course his wife, and Michelle Carlyle. Michelle is in prison for life, but Danny and his wife still live here in Eagle. I don't believe Danny, or his wife would tell the story, and Michelle certainly can't. But if it should come out, it might destroy your run."

"Eric and I have discussed it, and if it does come out, we will have to deal with it then. But neither you or Eric really did anything so bad."

"You mean like setting a cabin on fire with someone inside?"

"You were a kid and trying to help your best friend. But I suppose we should just wait and see. I better get going Imp but thank you. I'll be waiting for your call.

"No problem Bell."

Imp kissed her on her cheek and Bell turned to go. Then she suddenly stopped and said, "By the way. We are having a barbecue at noon on Sunday. Theresa, I mean Aunt Theresa will be there, so why don't you come too?"

"Sounds good. By then I will have some info for you. See you then."

Bell walked out, reminding Aunt Theresa about the barbecue and took the elevator down. Normally she would stop to see Eric, but she had too much to think about. Tonight would be soon enough to discuss her day with him. She trusted his judgement and knew he would be able to look at everything with a clear and open mind.

CHAPTER 30

Thursday 5:10 pm

Nihoono biitooeeihii entered his small house on the res and immediately took a shower. It had been a long dusty day, and he needed to wash all of the dirt from his skin and hair. He let the steaming water stream over his hard, toned body, not thinking about anything, letting the steaming water wash away the dirt and relax his strong muscles.

After a half hour, the water began to cool off and he shut it off. Stepping out he grabbed a robe made by his mother, a long time ago. It had the traditional colors of his tribe, and it was the only thing he kept from his childhood. His childhood had been as good as could be expected. His mother had raised him by herself, his father leaving the reservation and Wyoming when he had been only ten. Still, his mother had provided a shelter, food and teaching him about his ancestors. He had also learned the language of both the Shoshone and Arapahoe. He was never abused, did well in school and loved his mother. He laughed thinking about how all of that would fit in with a profile from the FBI.

He made himself a dinner made of jerky, some raw vegetables, and a beer. He had to think about his plan. Originally he had planned on gathering all the gifts from the gods in one week. But all of that changed when he had failed with Abel Bright Star. Still, he had obtained four and he knew where the others were.

The problem was, because he needed more time, it allowed the police more time to find him. He didn't think they had the slightest clue as to what he was doing or why, or who was left on his list. He worried one of the children of his victims knew what he knew and would eventually go to the police. He couldn't kill them all, and so he knew he had to do a better job and move faster.

He went to his bedroom and pushed an old oak dresser aside. He took out his knife and pushed the tip into a small slot in the floor. He had gotten the idea where to hide the gifts and the parchment letters from Charlie Two Horse. Prying up a piece of the floor, *Nihoono biitooeei-hii* smiled. There, lying wrapped in a piece of cloth were the gifts and the letters.

He reached in to feel the gifts, momentarily holding them in his hand. They did not feel special or like any gift he had ever had. But he knew once he had all the gifts and they were together, their special powers would be revealed to him. Placing them back in the secret space, he removed the parchment letters.

He brought them to his living room and began to read from the beginning. He knew the story by heart now, having read the story over and over again. He read the story of *Kettaa Piatukkuppiccyh, Kettaa Ciwox Huu-Pin,* and *Kwipuntahkanten Nymypoai.* He read of the night when the gift had struck the side of *Tahna Pia Na-Nankha.* Then he read of how *Kettaa Piatukkuppiccyh* and the shaman, *Pi-a Taikwawoppih* had decided what to do with the gift from the sky.

The gifts had been handed down from father to son, sometimes to a daughter or brother if there had been no male child to hand it down to, for more than four hundred years. One of the elders would write down who had the gifts, when they were passed down and to whom. Now *Nihoono biitooeeihii* reread the last part of the list of names. He decided he could not go after the gift Abel Bright Star still kept. Now was not the time and so he would have to have patience and wait for the moment to be right.

He saw the next victim's name and thought about how he would get the gift. This one might not be so easy. He knew Lewis Deep Water was a very strong man, even though he was approaching 55 years of age. In fact, he was the champion wrestler whenever the games were held on the reservation. He was a tall man, standing nearly 6'6, with a large barrel chest and arms and legs toned with hard muscles. He worked in Eagle in the lumberyard, hauling heavy sleds of logs, moving equipment, and wielding an axe whenever one was needed.

Nihoono biitooeeihii knew he would have to make sure the plan he came up with would work. If it did not, there was a good chance he would either be turned over to the police or possibly killed. But in his mind, he knew there was a solution, a way to get the gift from Deep Water. He would just have to make sure the plan was foolproof.

He sat on his sofa, drinking his beer and planning. The hours passed and still he sat. He had thought up several plans and just as quickly dismissed them. Somewhere around 3:00am, he believed he finally had it. Yes, he thought as he went to bed to catch a few hours' sleep, he would soon have the fifth gift.

CHAPTER 31

Bell had wanted to tell Eric about her day. She needed to get his opinion on her continuing to run for the City Council. But the boys had asked to watch a new movie which had just come out on HBO Max, and Eric and she had relented. The movie had been pretty good, even though she had missed most of it thinking about the campaign. Finally it had ended, and the boys had gone off to bed. Now, as they lay in bed, she was trying to explain everything which had been said.

"Okay honey, tell me what has been on your mind since I got home," I said.

"That obvious, huh," Bell said.

"Even if I wasn't a detective, I think I would know when you are concentrating on something other than me, the kids and a movie."

"Okay, you're right. Let me start at the beginning and don't say anything till I'm done. Then you can ask me anything and give me your best advice. Okay?"

"Okay."

Bell began with the meeting with her backers. How they wanted to play dirty, and how she had overheard them talking about her as if she was going to be a puppet. Next she went over the platform she had read while sitting on the bench. Then, how she had walked over to Imp's office, talked with Aunt Theresa, and invited her for a barbecue on Sunday. She ended with her discussion with Imp, including her concern the acts by Eric and Imp more than twenty years ago might be uncovered.

"Wow," I said. "Seems like you had a very upsetting day. Why didn't you stop in to see me when you finished with Imp?"

"I needed to sort through it all before I told you," Bell said. "Plus, I didn't want to bother you if you were involved in something. I figured it would be better to go over it all with you here at home, just the two of us. So, what do you think?"

"I think a barbecue is a great idea."

Bell smacked him lightly and said, "No you silly man, about the campaign."

"Oh, that. Well, I'm not really surprised about them wanting to play dirty. I don't think there has been one election in the last thirty years, whether here in Eagle, or in the state or in the country where someone didn't play dirty. It's the way it's done nowadays. As for them thinking they are going to control you, I know it will never happen. You are too strong minded and honest to allow them to make you do anything you think is wrong."

"Okay, and what about the facts about DeSade coming out?"

"I really don't believe it will, but even if it does come out, I think between Imp and I, we could explain it. There might be some angry people or even some determined to not only see you lose, but to get rid of Imp and me. We can cross that bridge when it comes up...if it ever comes up."

"Pretty much what Imp told me. Still, if I don't run we can be pretty certain it will never be revealed."

"Honey, Imp, and I have lived with it hanging over our heads for a very long time. I stopped worrying about it when Carlyle was caught and sent to prison."

"You think I should still run?"

"I do. Wait and see what Imp can find out about this dirt on Stone. Then you can decide if it should be revealed. Maybe it is something illegal or something the people of Eagle should know about. If you think it's a lie or made up, then you can decide the best thing to do. But until then, I suggest you take the platform they wrote up and add your own ideas to it."

Bell leaned over and gave me a big kiss. Then she lay her head down on my shoulder and I held her.

"How did I ever get so lucky to marry such a smart man?" Bell asked.

"Don't forget brave and handsome," I said. "Oh, and a great detective. And a terrific father and..."

"Come here you brave, smart, handsome, terrific father," Bell said and kissed me deeply. I thought I had been pretty lucky to have her as well.

CHAPTER 32

Friday 8:20 am

I had met Chuck at the department at 7:00 and then the two of us had met with Lt. Will Tolliver. We outlined everything we had so far, which he had said wasn't too much. I knew he was right, and I also knew he wasn't the type to micromanage his department. He told us to keep on it, and he would brief the Chief. If the Chief wanted to talk with us, he would let me know.

Before we walked out of Will's office, he asked me to hang back.

"What's up Will?' I asked.

"Eric," he began, "Do you know how long I have been a cop with the Eagle Police Department?"

"I guess you must have your twenty in by now."

"More like thirty."

"Really? I didn't realize it. So?"

"So I'm thinking it's about time to retire."

"Retire? Are you nuts! You have at least another five years in you. Maybe even ten."

"Eric, I'm tired. Not the kind of tired where a good night's sleep will help. I am finding it harder and harder to keep getting up in the morning and coming to work. The cases are beginning to get to me. I don't think I can go on much more. And that's why I wanted to talk with you."

"You know I will support anything you decide, but please, think it over carefully."

"I appreciate you saying that Eric. Now, if and when I retire, I want you to take over Investigations. I will talk to the Chief about making you a lieutenant. What do you think?"

"I think I've only been a sergeant for a short period of time Will."

"You can do the job Eric, and you deserve it. Give it some thought. I'm not biting the bullet for a while, so just think about it for me."

"I will, but I still think you are still the right man for the job. And thanks for thinking of me and having faith in my abilities."

"Better use those abilities to catch this murderer. Get back to work Sergeant."

"Yes sir, Lieutenant."

I walked out thinking about what Will had told me. Head of Investigations? Wow. But now I needed to get my head back in the game. I searched for Jimmy Bridges first.

I found Jimmy and gave him an assignment to try and locate Max Yellowfeather. It was time to find out what if anything he knew about these burglaries and killings. He was also going to talk with Abel Bright Star. Both Max and Abel had to know more than what they were telling us. Since Chuck was becoming involved with Maggie Bright Star, I figured he should not be the one to interview or interrogate Abel. Chuck had agreed, telling me he didn't want to be the one to interview his future brother-in-law either. That statement had stopped me in my tracks. All I could do was stare at him and shake my head.

As we drove out to the res to meet with Bobby, I said, "Future brother-in-law?"

"I know, it seems really fast to be saying things like that, but it's how I feel," Chuck answered. "I've never felt anything like this Eric. I mean just thinking about Maggie gets my heart racing."

"Okay, I get this is new for you, but..."

"Yeah, yeah. I need to take it slow and make sure she is right for me."

"You might want to make sure you are right for her."

"How would anything else even be possible?"

We both had a good laugh and then talked about the case. After a while, we pulled up on the res in front of the Tribal Police building. We got out of the car and walked in. Sitting at the front desk was Sgt. Betty Slow River, and by her feet was a large dog.. I knew her well and had worked with her over the years when cases brought me out to the res.

"*Behne* Betty," I said, and Chuck said good morning. "You starting a K-9 department?"

"*Behne* Eric," she replied. "This was Jim Longbow's dog, Geronimo. We are waiting to see if his son will be taking him. If not, I want to keep him here, but Bobby is against it. How have you been? And who is this with you?"

"Betty, this is Detective Chuck Blackwell. He has been my partner and now is in charge of Person Crimes."

"Nice to meet you Detective. I thought Person Crimes was your baby Eric?"

"Well, since Will made Lieutenant, and I made Sergeant..."

"Sergeant? Well now, I'm going to have to make Lieutenant just to stay your superior," she said with a laugh.

"Betty, I could never think of myself as your equal. Now, where is Bobby?"

"Go back through the hall and you will find him in our spacious conference room."

"Thanks Betty."

Chuck and I went down the hall and found Bobby sitting at the head of the conference room table, with some papers spread out. He was so absorbed in his work; he didn't notice us. Well, actually, he couldn't be sitting at the head of the table since it was round and could only seat four people. The spacious conference room was smaller than my office.

We walked in and Chuck said, "Bonnie Bobby."

Bobby stood and said, "I think you mean *Behne*, good morning Chuck. But thank you for trying."

"Ummm, yeah," Chuck said and sat down.

"*Behne* Bobby," I said with a smile. Bobby repeated it to me. "So, do you have anything new?"

"Got a report from Doc McAddams concerning the small tattoo on Sarah Tall Tree," Bobby said. "It looks very much like the ones found on Charlie Two Horse and Jim Longbow. Maybe slightly different but still depicting what looks like a meteor in the sky."

Sitting down I said, "Any ideas what it represents?"

"Not a clue. I thought about putting out a request for anyone with a similar tattoo to come forward. But then I figured since it is so small, maybe whoever has one wants to remain anonymous. I think the people with the tattoo have it for a very good reason, a secretive one."

"I agree. How about finding the person who did the tattoo?"

"Yeah," Chuck said. "There can't be too many people on the res who could do a tattoo like the one these people had."

"Actually, there are about twenty tattoo artists I know of here on the res," Bobby said. "Fifteen who are

Shoshone and five Arapahoe. I have their names and locations where they work right here. I would say we could split them, but I'm not sure if they would talk to two white devils."

"Uh huh," I said. "Okay then Lieutenant, shall we get started?"

We left the building, getting into Bobby's truck. I sat next to him, and Chuck sat in back. He wasn't too happy about it.

"What the hell is in these sacks, Bobby?" Chuck said, starting to push them over.

"Better be gentle Chuck," Bobby said, "those are a few rattlers I picked up on the way in this morning."

"Rattlers? You mean I'm sitting next to some snakes!?"

"They won't bother you if you don't bother them Chuck. When we get a bit further out, I will let them go. Snakes are believed to be old Indian Gods, taking the shape of a snake to fool people and observe them."

"Uh huh. How about we get them out of here as soon as possible!"

"Are you afraid of snakes Bobby?" I asked.

"Let's just say I never met one I liked."

Bobby and I laughed and soon we were in an area which was uninhabited. Bobby got out and opened the back door. Lifting the sack up, he moved to the side of the road where there was some brush and opened the top of the sack. Then he placed it down and with the tip of his boot, nudged the snakes out. Three large rattlers, each about five feet long, slithered out and disappeared away.

"Next time Eric, you sit in the back with the snakes!" Chuck said.

We got back in the truck and the first stop was at a small store, in a small strip mall with only three other businesses. The front of the one we stood in front of, had a sign nailed to the spot above the door. It read, *Tuakah,* which I assumed meant, tattoo. Bobby led the way in, and Chuck and I followed.

Inside, there was a small front reception desk with a middle aged woman seated behind it. Looking up, she saw it was the tribal police and two white men. She lowered her eyes and did not acknowledge us. I figured Bobby would talk with her.

Bobby said a few words and the woman continued to ignore him. He then said something, which made her instantly look up and point to a back area behind a dusty curtain. Bobby went through it and motioned for us to follow.

Behind the curtain was a small room, set up with a few chairs, a cushioned table, another table with ink bottles of every color and some art on the walls. Most of the art were tattoos of animals and words, all in the Shoshone language. The chairs and the tables looked to have seen better days, and nothing looked to be too sterile. Dust was thick on everything, except for a small area where an older Shoshone was working on a man, approximately in his twenties.

Bobby greeted him in his native language, speaking for a good five minutes. The man doing the tattoo appeared not to have heard him at first, and then got up and took down a small jar. He rubbed some ointment on the tattoo he had been working on and said something to the young man. He got up, said something to Bobby and walked out. The tattoo artist then walked to the back of the room and opened a door. He stepped outside. Bobby motioned for us to follow.

Outside was a small area of shade under a tree. There, the tattoo artist sat with a drink in one hand and a hand rolled cigarette in the other. As we sat down on two benches near him, Chuck and I immediately smelled the burning weed. I gave a small shake of the head to Chuck to make no mention of it.

Bobby said, "This is Tom Rising Wind. I have told him we need to ask him some questions. I also told him we will be speaking English. To speak in our native tongue with two white men listening, would be very rude. He has agreed to speak with us and to answer any of your questions, as well as mine."

"Speak," Tom said. "I have to finish the tattoo for Lone Deer."

Bobby began by taking one of the enlargements of the meteor out of a folder.

"Look at this and tell me about it," Bobby said, as he passed the picture over to Tom.

"How big is the original?" Tom asked.

Bobby pulled out another picture of the tattoo at the original size, with a ruler next to it.

Tom raised his eyebrows and handed the two pictures back to Bobby.

"Well, what can you tell me about the tattoo?"

"I only know of two other artists who can do such work," Tom said. "It takes a very special skill to do such detail in so small a tattoo."

"What about you, could you do it?"

"No, I could not. My hands do not have the skill. I can give you their names, but I doubt they will talk with you."

"And why is that," I asked.

Looking me in the eye, Tom said, "They hate white men, and they hate police even more. Even our good lieutenant here."

Bobby said, " Tell me their names. Then, forget all about this conversation. You know I can make trouble for you Tom."

Tom looked angry but stood and went back inside. He wrote down the two names on a scrap of paper and then came out back once again. Bobby, Chuck, and I left and got back in the truck. Before he started the truck, Bobby handed the paper to me.

I read the two names out loud.

"Billy One Arm and Painting Chief," I said. "Interesting names. Do you know them Bobby?"

"I know them, and Tom was probably right," Bobby said as he drove. "They will not talk to us, at least not right away. But I will get them to talk. Billy One Arm was not his original name. He served in the military and his convoy had been attacked after running over an IED. He lost his left arm and renamed himself. As for Painting Chief, he is an old man but still does tattoos. And both of them do hate the police and white men."

"Hey Bobby," Chuck said, "what did you say to the woman in the front of the store? She looked like she wanted to slit your throat."

"I told her if she didn't tell me where Tom was, I would let the two white devils do as they wished with her."

Chuck looked astonished and all I could do was laugh.

"Well that ought to make her love white people and cops!" Chuck said.

"It will take aboufifteen minutes to get to One Arm," Bobby said. "Maybe we will get lucky, and he will cooperate. But don't make any bets on it."

CHAPTER 33

Harry Longbow was on a break at work, in the lumberyard. He was alone in the break room, and he took out the letter his father had written him. He reread it for about the hundredth time. He still couldn't believe what it said.

His father had written down an old tale, more than likely passed down by some illiterate and scared shamans. They always made up tales about gods and demons, things to explain many different things. If the snows came early, they prayed to their gods to take away the evil spirits. If the crops were good and the weather calm, they thanked the gods. A baby was born, thank the gods. A child died, pray for forgiveness from them. Harry didn't believe in any of it.

When Harry told his father he was leaving the res, his father had been angry. Harry had left the res, cut his hair, and forsaken the Shoshone way of life. At eighteen, he had joined the military, the Marines, and left. After serving four years, he had been honorably discharged and came back to Wyoming. But there was no way he would go back to the res. His father had pleaded with him, threatening to disown him, but none of it mattered to Harry. All that mattered to Harry was to get a job, an apartment and live his life in peace. Money was not too important to him, so he took a job at the lumberyard in Eagle. He had been working there for a long time, and up till now, had been satisfied with his life.

Then Bobby had brought the news of his father's murder and delivered the letter. Harry was very upset about his father's death, but he refused to show it like a hysterical woman. Right before closing, he had gone to the morgue. Doc McAddams had allowed him in to see his father for the last time. When he had looked down upon his father's face, he was hit by many memories. His father teaching him how to use a bow and arrow, how to read sign on the ground and other Shoshone traditions. He remembered the times he had taken a sweat with his father, and some of the other Shoshone warriors. He smiled thinking how even today, the trials to become a man and warrior went on. He wondered if his father thought of him as a warrior, having been in combat. He didn't know. Harry was surprised to feel a tear slide down his cheek. He had wiped it away and said goodbye to his father. Harry didn't need to make a funeral; his father had seen to it.

Now, as he sipped on some coffee, he reread the letter once again. The tale or legend was an old one. It had something to do with a meteor which had struck the old sacred mountain over four hundred years ago. There was some type of a gift from the gods and these gifts had been handed down from father to son, or daughter. No one knew who had the gifts, each family keeping it secret from anyone else.

Harry thought how ridiculous it all seemed, now in the twenty-first century. Secret gifts, promises to be kept for over four hundred years. Harry folded the letter, putting it back in his pocket.

He was about to go back to work when he remembered how Bobby Black Bear wanted to see the letter. But Harry couldn't believe this ancient myth could've had anything to do with his father's murder. It wasn't possible. Still, there really wasn't any reason for Harry not to show it to Bobby. He decided he would think about it and then decide. For now, his break was over, and he had to get back to work.

CHAPTER 34

They had found Billy One Arm in a dilapidated home. According to Bobby, he had one room set up to do his tattoos and the rest of the house for everyday living. It looked as if a strong wind might blow it down, and outside the home, was a broken down car which would never run again. When they got out of the car, Bobby had indicated for me and Chuck to wait outside. I wanted to be in on the interview, but figured Bobby knew what was best.

Chuck and I had found a large tree, offering some shade, and sat down to wait. Bobby had walked inside the home without even knocking.

"So, do you think Bobby will get this One Arm guy to talk?" Chuck asked.

"I hope so because I am sure he wouldn't talk to us," I answered.

"By the way, I heard a rumor Bell was thinking of running for the city council."

"She is thinking about it, but there are some issues."

"Well she would get my vote for sure."

"Great, along with me and her, that makes three votes."

"Nah, she would win by a landslide Eric. She's smart, a great mother and wife and easy on the eyes."

"Hey now, you have your own woman who is easy on the eyes," I said and laughed.

We continued to talk about the case, Bell running, and I wasn't sure if I should let Chuck in on Will's possibly retiring. Before I could make up my mind, Bobby came walking out of the house. Chuck and I got to our feet and met him at the truck.

"How did it go Lieutenant?" Chuck asked.

"Please Chuck, call me Bobby," he said. "And it didn't go too well."

"He wouldn't talk to you?" I asked.

"Oh he talked. He talked about pink elephants, and being a warrior back in time and every other ludicrous thing he could think of. Unfortunately, Billy was high as a kite. Looking at his remaining arm, I saw tracks. Billy is using heroin."

"Damn, but I guess I can understand why."

"Yeah Eric. Once we get back to the department I will send out one of my men to get him to a hospital, at least until he comes down. Then I will try to get him into a rehabilitation center in Lander. Whether or not he stays and gets clean will be up to him."

"Not much more you can do Bobby," Chuck said.

"What now Bobby," I said. "Do we try to find Painter Chief or not?"

"I have a good idea where we can find him, so I think we might as well try," Bobby said.

We got back into the truck and headed west. We traveled along a dirt road for the better part of an hour. Finally, we pulled into a small area with a few buildings and one very large traditional teepee.

"You want us to hang back," I asked.

"No, I think Painter Chief will be willing to talk to us," Bobby said. "But maybe you both should let me lead the discussion."

"You got it Bobby," Chuck said.

We let Bobby enter first, heard him say something in Shoshone and then followed him in. The teepee was decorated on the inside with drawings of animals, flowers, and Shoshone words. They must have been there for customers to pick out to be tattooed. There wasn't any type of table or chair to sit on. I figured Painter Chief must have had his customers lie down on some skins spread around.

I saw a very old Shoshone Native sitting on some skins. He looked to be 100 years old, but I knew that wasn't likely. His face was covered in deep wrinkles, and his skin had a yellowish tint. I thought he might have jaundice. He was dressed in traditional clothes and his hair was very long and gray. He was smoking a hand rolled cigarette, but this time all I smelled was tobacco.

Bobby motioned for us to sit down with him, on some of the skins. Bobby crossed his legs as he sat, and Chuck and I attempted to do the same. We finally got as close to crossing our legs as we ever would.

Bobby began to speak in his native tongue, and Chuck and I just listened. Painter Chief made no indication he was hearing anything Bobby had said. Bobby stopped speaking and sat there waiting. Close to ten minutes passed before Painter Chief spoke.

His voice was surprisingly strong, and he spoke for a long time. When he was finished, he closed his eyes and didn't say anything further. He once again looked like a statue.

Bobby said something to him and then stood. I shakily stood and gave Chuck a hand to get him up. Bobby went out and Chuck and I hobbled behind him.

Bobby moved to a picnic table with two benches and sat down. I sat opposite him.

"I think I'll just stand to get some blood into my legs," Chuck said.

"It seemed to me Painter Chief had a great deal to say to you Bobby," I said.

"He did," Bobby said, "but unfortunately everything he said to me had absolutely nothing to do with our case."

"So what was he talking about?"

"Painter Chief stated he has seen 106 winters."

"He's 106 years old?" Chuck said.

"He is. He stated the way of the Shoshone is coming to an end. The children no longer learn the language. They do not learn the old ways or the traditions. More and more are leaving the reservation. Even here in his own teepee, two white men have come."

"Did he say anything about the tattoos?" I asked.

"He admitted he had done the tattoos of the meteor. He said there wasn't anyone here on the reservation who would be doing anymore. He said like the Shoshone, the sacred tattoos will no longer be made."

"Sacred tattoos? Did he say who else might have them?"

"He said he would not reveal anyone else. He had taken a sacred vow and would not break it. That's all he said."

"Damn! Looks like we are back to square one. I can't think of any other way to find out who else might have these tattoos, or what they mean, or why someone is killing the people with them."

"Unfortunately, I agree. Let's head back and get some food and drink. Then we can maybe figure out what we need to do next. Hopefully we will figure out something before another Shoshone is killed."

The ride back was quiet, each of us thinking about the killings, the tattoos and what could possibly be the things the killer had been searching for.

CHAPTER 35

Friday 2:00 pm

Chuck and I got back to the Eagle Police Department feeling a bit angry and frustrated. Driving around the res in the dirt and heat had left us both feeling exhausted.

"Hey Eric," Chuck said, "if it is okay with you, I'm going to call it a day. I have a date with Maggie tonight and I need to get some rest."

"No problem Chuck," I replied, "and I suggest you change your clothes and take a shower."

"No kidding. I feel like I have half the dirt of the res on my body. See you on Monday unless something breaks before then."

"What are you bringing her?"

"Ummm, bringing her?"

"Come on Chuck. You should know you should bring her something for your second date. Maybe some flowers?"

"Yeah, flowers. Good idea Eric. Thanks!"

I watched Chuck leave and wondered if this new romance would go anywhere. Chuck seemed to have fallen hard for Maggie Bright Star. The question was, did she fall just as hard for him? Oh well, I thought, it would all work itself out, for better or worse sooner or later.

I turned on my computer and began to type up the notes from the past few days. Paperwork was something which was always there. No matter what happened, sooner or later a report or two would have to be written.

I was as dusty as Chuck, but I wanted to get it done. I had promised my son's to take them fishing out at

Tranquility Lake on Saturday. We always went to what used to be my secret place back when I was a teenager. And Bell had made plans for a barbecue on Sunday. Maybe I should've invited Chuck? I still had tomorrow to give him an invite. I would call him up and invite both him and Maggie. Bell would love to observe Chuck and Maggie together. By the end of the day she would either say they would be getting married, or they would be breaking up. Many times in the past my wife had been on the nose when it came to relationships.

I was just about to finish up for the day when Jimmy Bridges walked in.

"How's it going Jimmy?" I asked. "Were you able to find Abel and Max?"

"I struck out finding Max," Jimmy said. "I finally gave up about ten minutes ago. I searched for Max everywhere I could think of. I went to Kelly's Bar, and a few others. I spoke to so many Shoshone I was feeling like Custer."

"Did you talk to Liz Butler?"

Liz was the town hooker; and she wasn't much of a drunk. She probably knew almost everyone in the city, at least the men between 18 and 75. Liz was about thirty-five but looked closer to forty-five. At one time, she had been quite the looker and had grown up in a nice home on the east side of Eagle. Her mom was a teacher, and her dad had been a banker. She had gotten pregnant in her junior year of high school. Her dad threw her out of the house and her mom didn't try to stop him. She never had the baby, suffering a miscarriage, but the damage had been done. First from her mom and dad, and then from the boy she had slept with. He had started a rumor, saying how

Liz had screwed all the boys in the junior class...and some of the girls. She was also one of Max Yellowfeather's friends. She would probably know where to find Max.

"Well, I thought about asking her, but the bartender at Kelly's said she had picked up some stranger and had probably gone back to her place or a hotel. I didn't want to spend all day trying to find her."

"Okay, no problem. We will look for him again on Monday. So what did Abel have to say?"

"He was as tightlipped as a statue. He said he had nothing to say about the burglary and knew nothing about any tattoos."

"Did you tell him how Charlie Two Horse, Jim Longbow and Sarah Tall Tree had all been murdered?"

"I did and for a second I thought I saw something in his eyes. Maybe something which spooked him. I figured he might talk after telling him about them, but he still refused to say anything. Guess I might need some more experience in interviewing."

"Nah. You know what you are doing Jimmy. I doubt Abel would have said anything to any of us. Maybe we will try again on Monday."

"I did have an idea Eric."

"Always willing to hear any ideas. What do you have in mind?"

"Since all three victims had those tattoos, and Abel's place was obviously tossed, maybe we could get a search warrant to see if he and maybe Max have the same tattoo?"

I thought about the possibility of a judge signing a warrant like that. I wasn't sure if we had enough. Afterall, just because Max had spoken to me and Abel and Maggie's place had been burgled, didn't mean they should be suspected of having the tattoos.

"Not a terrible idea Jimmy, but I don't think we have enough right now."

"Would it hurt to give it a try?" Jimmy asked.

"Ummm, I'm not sure. Sometimes our judges remember warrant requests which don't meet probable cause. I would hate for any of them to put you in that category. Better to wait on it for now. But it wasn't a bad idea Jimmy. Keep thinking. Now get out of here and have a good weekend."

"Thanks Eric. You too. If anything breaks, please get in touch with me."

"Count on it Jimmy."

I sat there thinking about Jimmy's idea. He wouldn't be able to get a judge to sign off on a search for a tattoo. Of course, either I or Will might be able to convince a judge. Nah, I thought, we really couldn't point the finger at Max or Abel based on what little we had. We would just have to come up with something else. Hopefully something would break before another body was found.

I closed up my office, stopped by to say goodbye to Will and invite him out Sunday. His office was dark. He must've left a bit earlier. I would give him a call once I got home.

I started the drive home and hoped no other killings would occur over the weekend. I had my fingers crossed, made a quick wish, but somehow felt like it was a meaningless. I and no one else had any control over what this maniac would do. I would just have to wait and see.

CHAPTER 36

Chuck had taken Eric's advice and bought a huge bouquet of flowers for Maggie. It had cost him a hundred bucks, but he didn't mind. If they stayed together he would be willing to bring her flowers every day of the week! Well, maybe not every day but at least once a week.

He knocked on the door of her apartment and was greeted by Abel. He didn't look so happy to see him, but he did say to come in.

Chuck sat down on a chair in the living room, and Abel sat on a sofa. They sat there staring at each other and then Abel finally spoke.

"Why are you dating my sister?" Abel asked.

"Well, I suppose because I have never met a woman so beautiful, smart and funny," Chuck answered.

"It is tradition for a man to ask to date a Shoshone woman's father first for permission, and in this case her older brother. Me."

"If I had known I would have asked you...Abel. But I can still follow your tradition by asking you now."

"Too late but I suppose it wouldn't hurt. Go ahead."

Chuck was unsure of what to say. What if Abel told him no, he didn't have his permission? Would Maggie stop dating him? Would she go against her brother's wishes?"

Chuck took a deep breath and said, "Abel, your sister is someone I have come to care deeply about. I think she is my soulmate, the woman I am meant to be with. I will never cause her any pain, and I will honor her every day, I am lucky enough to have her in my life. I promise not to ignore the Shoshone ways or traditions. If we should marry and have children, they will be raised with both the white man's ways and the Shoshone ways. This I promise to you and to her."

Abel sat there quietly, staring at Chuck, and saying nothing. Finally he stood and Chuck stood as well. He walked over and stood directly in front of Chuck. He towered over him, and for a second Chuck thought he might knock him down. Then Abel put out his hand and Chuck took it.

"You speak well for a white man," Abel said. "You have my permission to date my sister. You will still have to earn my blessing."

"Hey, what's going on here?" Maggie said as she came out of her bedroom into the living room.

Chuck and Abel turned to see her. She was wearing a turquoise dress, cut low showing off her cleavage, and short, showing off her legs. Seeing them looking at her, Maggie did a little spin. Chuck thought she might be pissing off Abel on purpose.

"Not a thing *Nammi*," Abel said, "your white man and I were just discussing something."

"He has a name *Padzits*. His name is Detective Charles Blackwell, but you should call him Chuck."

"Hmph, we will see *Nammi*, for now I shall call him, Detective."

"Ummm, that would be great Abel," Chuck said. "Come on Maggie, let's get going."

Abel said something to her in Shoshone and then Chuck and Maggie left. When they got to the car and were on their way, Chuck asked her what Abel had said.

Maggie laughed and said, "Well first *Nammi* means sister and *Padzits* means brother."

"Okay," Chuck said, "I'll try to remember that. I suppose it would be a good idea to learn some Shoshone words."

"Oh, are you planning to stick around?"

"As long as you will let me."

Maggie smiled and then said, "Abel warned me not to fall for any white man tricks. He also told me...well he told me to basically keep my legs closed."

"He said that!"

"He did."

"What did you answer him?"

"I told him it would depend on how the evening went."

Chuck looked at her, his eyes wide and she had to tell him to put his eyes back on the road.

"Ummm, well, ummm," was all Chuck could say.

Maggie smiled and said, "How about telling me where we are going?"

"Right. I know a great Italian restaurant in Casper. It will take an hour or so and I figured we can talk and get to know each other better on the drive. Is that okay with you?"

"Yes Chuck it is," Maggie said and leaned over giving him a light kiss on his lips.

They enjoyed a good meal, some wine, and some little Italian powdered donuts called zeppole's dipped in raspberry sauce. Feeling as if they had eaten way too much, they left the restaurant and headed back to Eagle. As they were driving back, Chuck asked her, "I hope you enjoyed the meal."

"It was delicious Chuck," Maggie said. "I hope you enjoyed it as well."

"Oh yeah, I mean yes, it was great."

"The only thing is, even though we had dessert, I'm still in the mood for some more."

"I'm sorry Maggie, would you like to stop for some ice cream or pie somewhere when we get back to Eagle?"

"Actually, I was thinking of a totally different type of dessert."

"Anything you want."

"Then let's head to your place."

Chuck looked at her, smiled and put his foot down on the gas pedal, moving as fast as he could toward his home.

CHAPTER 37

Nihoono biitooeeihii sat in his car outside the home of Lewis Deep Water, keeping his eye on the front door. He needed to figure out the best way to confront him. Deep Water was a very big man and powerful, and *Nihoono biitooeeihii* had no intentions of getting hurt or worse when he finally attacked him. *Nihoono biitooeeihii* thought Deep Water might have a hobby or something he would do on the weekend when he wasn't working. He knew he couldn't possibly attack him in his home or at work. That meant he would need to get him alone somewhere else, a place where he would be able to subdue the big man.

As he sat watching, he saw Deep Water exit his home with some fishing gear. *Nihoono biitooeeihii* thought it might be the answer. If Deep Water went to fish at a secluded spot, *Nihoono biitooeeihii* would be able to get him under his control. Then he could collect another of the gifts.

Deep Water got into his old pickup truck and headed out of town. *Nihoono biitooeeihii* followed, but not too closely. There were only a few nearby lakes he would be going to, and *Nihoono biitooeeihii* would be able to tell where shortly. He followed him for a few miles, until Deep Water turned into the road leading around Tranquility Lake.

There were many quiet spots along the road, and soon, Deep Water pulled into a small area which appeared to be sealed off from view. *Nihoono biitooeeihii* kept driving and stopped about a quarter mile further on. Then he slowly walked back to the spot Deep Water had pulled into. He used all of his Native American training to leave no footprint or sign of him being there. He moved slowly, taking close to a half hour to get close enough to see Deep Water, standing at the water's edge.

Nihoono biitooeeihii saw him place two rods into holders on the shore, their fishing lines disappearing into the blue water. He had a third rod in his hands, and he would slowly reel the line in and then throw it out again. *Nihoono biitooeeihii* watched a few more minutes and silently backed up and started walking down the road back to his car.

As *Nihoono biitooeeihii* began the drive back to town and then to the res, he thought about what he had seen. The little secluded spot was perfect. It was out of view and *Nihoono biitooeeihii* believed he would be able to sneak up on the big man and knock him out. Then he would be able to get him to tell him where the gift was. Even if he had to torture him, *Nihoono biitooeeihii* thought no one would hear his screams.

Of course there was no way of knowing if Deep Water did this every Saturday, or only once a month. Maybe he wouldn't return to this spot for many months. There was only one thing to do. *Nihoono biitooeeihii* would prepare as if Deep Water was going to fish again the following week. If he did, *Nihoono biitooeeihii* would strike. If Deep Water did not go fishing, *Nihoono biitooeeihii* would have to come up with another plan. Either way, he was sure he would come up with something. It was his destiny to gather all the gifts together, and then gain the power they would bestow on him.

He drove to the res, thinking of an excuse he could give for being late to work. Soon he would never have to work again. The thought made him smile and he decided to listen to some white man music. Most of the new music he couldn't tolerate, so he tuned in a station which only played old time country music. Coming through his speakers was an old John Denver song, *Country Roads*. *Nihoono biitooeeihii* knew the song and sang along. 'Country roads, take me home, to the place, I was born.'

Yes, *Nihoono biitooeeihii* thought. Soon he would be taken back to the place where he was born, but he would now have the power to change everything. He smiled thinking how soon all the Shoshone and Arapahoe on the reservation would revere him. Make him their one true Chief and he would lead them all back to their rightful lands. He would be like a god to them, and rightfully so.

Perhaps in time other tribes would fall under his rule. And why not? It was his destiny.

Nihoono biitooeeihii sang along and smiled. It wouldn't be too long now.

CHAPTER 38

Eric, Ben, and Bear had gotten to his special spot at Tranquility Lake early in the morning. Up until the capture of DeSade's adopted daughter, Carlyle, he thought he would never come back to the spot. Afterall, it was here where he first met DeSade, and his summer of hell had begun. But now he realized just how beautiful and quiet this spot was.

When they got there, they had laid out all their equipment, including some fly's, and bait they had stopped for. Ben was excited about fishing with his dad, but Bear was being a bit quiet.

Bear had never really taken to fishing, not being able to sit quietly for a few hours just to catch a fish. Most of the time, if they ever did catch any fish, his dad would throw them back. Only if they were big enough would they take them home. His mom would cook them, and he never had gotten to like fish very much. Still, being here with his dad at his secret spot did make Bear feel happy. He had sat quietly for the first few minutes, and then got into the spirit of the day. He actually had been the first to catch a fish, and it was a whopper. His dad had kept it, and Bear had looked at his brother, sticking his tongue out at him.

"Don't worry Bear," Ben said, "I'm sure I will catch one soon and it will be twice the size of yours!"

"Yeah right!" Bear replied.

"Okay boys," I said. "If you two don't stop yelling at each other, none of us will catch another fish."

"Sorry Dad," Bear and Ben said, and soon they were concentrating on their lines.

I sat back, feeling great about being able to take my boys fishing. It was something we all enjoyed, well, at least Bear almost enjoyed. I loved just being with them, telling stories and having some alone time with them. I was sure it wouldn't be long till neither one would want to go fishing with their old man. They were growing up fast. Thinking of that, I thought about Paul and Caroline coming out soon. Ben certainly had his eye on their oldest daughter Tara. Bear on the other hand just about allowed Abigail, who was the same age, to tag along with him. They had met last summer when we had been at Bell's father's ranch in Whispering Rock, Montana.

With Will retiring and me possibly taking over Investigations, I thought Paul coming out couldn't be better timing. If he decided to take my offer of staying in Eagle and becoming a detective, it would certainly help our numbers. Beside Will leaving, I knew one of the other detectives was planning on retiring as well. Plus, one of my men would have to be promoted to Sergeant, to be my second in command. Basically, even with Paul coming onboard, I would still be down by at least one man. I thought about who I would recommend as my sergeant? Chuck would definitely be in the running, but the position would have to be opened up to the whole department. Civil service wouldn't let it go any other way. At least I didn't think it would.

Then again our Chief, Todd Lewis, did things his own way. He had over thirty years with the Eagle Police Department and had moved up through the ranks. Most of the men and women on the job not only respected him but liked him as well. If he wanted someone in particular for the job of sergeant, I figured somehow he would get his way.

As we were casting out our lines, I looked across to a nearby spot similar to my favorite one. Someone was fishing with what looked like three rods. I wondered if he was having good luck like we were having. We had two large fish caught and soon we would reach our limit.

I thought I recognized him, due to his huge size. The only other Shoshone I knew who was almost as big, was Max Yellowfeather. This had to be Lewis Deep Water. I had seen him around town and knew he was the champion wrestler on the res. He also worked at the lumberyard in town.

Thinking about the lumberyard, I remembered Harry Longbow also worked there. I wondered if they were possibly friends. Maybe I should go talk with him and see if he knew anything about the murders.

Looking at my boys casting their lines, I decided it could wait. If I wanted to speak with him, I could always go over to his work. Then I could speak to both of them.

We continued to fish for another couple of hours and had four large fish to bring home. Of course both boys argued over who had caught the largest one. I didn't have the heart to tell them it had been me.

We loaded up the car and headed back to town and up the mountain to our home. The boys and I would clean the fish, and Bell would cook them for our dinner tonight. My stomach was grumbling just thinking about the delicious meal we would have tonight.

When we got home, I would call Chuck and Bobby, inviting them both to our home for the barbeque. I'm sure Chuck would be there along with Maggie. Bobby on the other hand had never been to my home, and I wasn't sure he would come. Still, I thought our friendship was growing, especially with us both working on the homicide investigation. Whether or not he would bring anyone was something I was unsure of. In fact, I didn't even know if he was married or had any kids. Will had agreed to come as well.

Tomorrow would be a great day, I was sure. Having friends over to the house, eating, drinking a bit, and having great conversations was something Bell and I loved.

CHAPTER 39

Bobby got up off the ground and dusted off his pants. He had been playing an old traditional Shoshone game with a bunch of young kids. Danny had not joined in, being an Arapahoe sometimes left him feeling out. Bobby had tried to get him to play, but Danny decided he would sit and talk to some of the older men sitting nearby in the shade. Perhaps, Bobby thought, it was a good idea for Danny to keep in touch with the men on the res. Maybe he would learn something about the murders from them. Bobby didn't keep his hopes up. Both the Shoshone and Arapahoe didn't like the tribal police, and they often kept their mouths shut tight.

Walking back to his truck, he waved for Danny to join him. They had been out on patrol together since earlier in the day. Bobby liked to ride around the res on Saturdays, interacting with anyone he saw. It kept him aware of some of the things happening on the res. Today he had decided to take Danny Red Shirt with him. He wanted to get him used to doing the same thing whenever he was on patrol by himself.

They had driven all around the res, stopping for short periods of time with both men and women. So far, he hadn't heard anything about the murders, except for some of the men stating they were angry and worried. Bobby had tried to reassure them all, but it probably had been a losing cause. Most Shoshone and Arapahoe still believed in evil spirits and angering the gods. None of them felt safe for themselves, their women, or their children.

Earlier in the day, Bobby and Danny had come across Matt Jones at Walks in Wind's teepee. He had been carrying some things out to his truck, and Bobby figured he would stop to say hello. Bobby knew he was another who had given up the old ways and moved off the res. He had even changed his name from his traditional Shoshone name to a white man's. Bobby was disheartened by the number of young people moving off the res, but he knew there was nothing he could do. He knew it was just the way things were.

Exiting the truck, Bobby had said, *"Behne."*

"Good morning to you too Lieutenant," Matt had said, probably refusing to use the Shoshone word. "Hello Danny."

Danny said, "Hello Matt. What are you up to?"

"Maybe you didn't hear, but my father, Walks in Wind passed on a few weeks ago."

"I hadn't heard, and I am sorry for your loss," Danny said.

"My condolences Matt," Bobby had said. "How old was your father?"

"He was almost 95 years old and had lived a good life Lieutenant," Matt said.

"Please Matt, call me Bobby."

"As you wish Bobby."

"If you don't mind me asking, how did he die?"

"I suppose his heart just gave out. The night before his death, he and I had been arguing about some old superstitious nonsense. He had gotten very angry, and I am ashamed to say I walked away. The next morning he was found by a friend. He was found lying peacefully on his skins. I only hoped he did not suffer."

"Was there an autopsy?"

"No, there was no reason for one Bobby. Afterall, he was 95 years old."

"What superstitious nonsense were you two arguing about?"

"It doesn't matter Bobby and now if you will excuse me, I have to empty out this teepee before I take it down."

"You know Matt, there are several poor men and women on the res who might be better off living in your father's teepee than in the broken down trailers and houses they live in now. How about not tearing it down for now and allowing me to maybe find someone. I'm sure they will pay you, although it might not be too much."

"It's all yours Bobby, and I don't need any money. I know my father would be pleased to know his home was being used for shelter by another Shoshone. Or Arapahoe Danny."

Bobby had thanked Matt and he and Danny had continued their patrol. Bobby had asked Danny if he knew of anyone who would want to live in Walks in Wind's teepee. Danny couldn't think of anyone offhand but said he would ask around. Bobby had told him to hold off for a day or so. He had an idea he might know one or two who would like to change their living conditions.

Bobby and Danny continued on their patrol and were pulling in to headquarters when Bobby's phone rang. Danny went inside to write up the meetings they had had while on patrol. Bobby had sat down under the shade of a tree and answered his phone.

"Hello, this is Lieutenant Black Bear," Bobby said.

"Hi Bobby, it's Eric."

"Hello Eric, has something happened?"

"So far nothing new has happened or come to light."

"Good. I'm not sure I'm up for another homicide. So what's up?"

"My wife and I are having a barbecue at my house tomorrow. I would like to invite you and ummm anyone you might want to bring with you."

"That is very thoughtful, and I would be very pleased. Is it okay to bring my wife and children?"

"Of course! Chuck will be there with Maggie Bright Star, and District Attorney Impeletti, his secretary, who is my Aunt Theresa, Will Tolliver and anyone else my wife might have invited."

"Sounds like a big party. Thank you Eric. What time shall we be there?"

"About noon will be great. I'll text you my address. And Bobby, there is no need to bring anything."

"Uh huh. You are married aren't you Eric?"

"I understand," I said laughing. "Bring whatever you like, or I should say, whatever your wife likes."

Bobby laughed and said, "I suppose in both our families we must keep our wives happy. See you tomorrow Eric."

Bobby hung up and thought about Eric Logan. He was a good man, a good detective and he thought, someone he would like to know better. Maybe the only good thing about these murders was he and Eric had been thrown together. Bobby decided he was going to look forward to the barbecue. He hoped Eric and his wife wouldn't be too overwhelmed by his family. Afterall, he had six children.

CHAPTER 40

Saturday 11:30 pm

Nihoono biitooeeihii came out of his shower, drying off and thinking about his plans. He knew what he had to do to prepare for his possible meeting out at the lake with Deep Water. He was not troubled by it, except for the fact he couldn't be sure Deep Water would return to the lake next Saturday. No, something else had been bothering him.

Was it possible some of the families of the people he had killed knew about the gifts? According to the parchments he had read, only when someone was close to dying would the legend be revealed. But who knew when they were close to dying? Of course sometimes due to illness or old age, a person would know they didn't have long to live. But otherwise, did anyone really know?

He was sure some of the victims had told the legend to their offspring. And if they had, was it possible the police might be informed of it? *Nihoono biitooeeihii* decided it was not only a possibility, but it was also something which eventually would come out. But what to do about it?

Of course, he might be able to kill off the few relatives of his victims. The only thing was, with more deaths there would be a greater chance of him being caught before he could get all the gifts. And that was something he could not risk.

He thought about who the victims had been and their families. Charlie Two Horse had a daughter, and he had been in good health. He was sure TwoHorse had not revealed the legend to her yet. Next was Jim Longbow. *Ni-*

hoono biitooeeihii knew Longbow's son had left the res and he was sure his father had not been pleased. Jim Longbow probably had never said anything to his son. Sarah Tall Tree had a daughter and again, *Nihoono biitooeeihii* didn't believe she would have told her about the gifts yet. That left only the son of Walks in Wind. Matt Jones had left the res and given up on the old ways, but he had overheard Walks in Wind talking to his son. It was the night he had recovered his first gift and the parchment. *Nihoono biitooeeihii* knew he had told his son. *Nihoono biitooeeihii* needed to be sure the story went no further.

Nihoono biitooeeihii made his mind up. The son of Walks in Wind would have to die. But at the moment, he did not know where Matt Jones lived. He would have to find out and then somehow kill him before he could tell anyone about the gifts.

Perhaps he would try to make Matt Jones' death look like an accident. He certainly didn't want Bobby Black Bear or Sergeant Logan to suspect anything, and possibly link the murder to all the others. But how could he do it? *Nihoono biitooeeihii* decided he would have to give this some thought. It would have to be foolproof and not lead the police back to him.

Perhaps a car accident, or a fall? Maybe a run in with a rattlesnake. *Nihoono biitooeeihii* wasn't sure what he was going to do at the moment, but he knew he would come up with something. Afterall, he thought, he was destined to have all the gifts and the power which came with them. It was his destiny to lead his people off the res, back to their rightful lands and for him to be their Chief.

Nihoono biitooeeihii sat on his sofa and thought about his next victim. Since Matt Jones had left the old ways and moved off of the res, *Nihoono biitooeeihii* didn't think twice about his death. All who didn't follow the old ways, would never follow him. And because of that, he thought of the people who had abandoned their true life, had abandoned the old ways and gods, did not deserve to even live. Perhaps when he had the power, he would kill them all. He smiled at the thought, and soon he was filling the room with maniacal laughter. He continued laughing long into the night.

CHAPTER 41

As usual, Bell had put out a huge spread of food for the barbeque. There was the usual hot dogs, hamburgers, and all kinds of smaller things to eat. Cole Slaw, potato salad, macaroni salad and, well, salad. She had gotten some nice steaks from the butcher in town and even had made some sandwiches made of tuna, egg salad and turkey. I thought looking at it all, we could feed a small army. But I knew Bell would never allow anyone at our home to go hungry.

I was setting up some tables for the feast when Aunt Theresa and Imp walked in.

"Hello, you two," I said.

"Morning Eric," Imp replied, "let me give you a hand with that."

"Morning Eric," Aunt Theresa said. "I think I will help Bell inside."

"You know she wants to be with Bell so she can pump her for all the local gossip," Imp said.

"More than likely Imp," I answered. "It's good to see you. What do you think about Bell's concerns regarding her backers?"

"I think Bell can handle anything those backers throw at her. Plus I think she would do a great job. This city needs some more good people leading the way, and Bell is a good one."

"You better tell her. Maybe she will believe you. Right now, I think she is fifty-fifty on running."

"I'll find some time later on to sit down with her. But for now, do you want me to fire up the grill?"

"Are you trying to say I can't cook?"

"Now Eric, you know you can't so just let me be the chef today."

Laughing, I said, "Okay Imp, the job is yours!"

Next to arrive was Chuck and Maggie Bright Star. Chuck had on some jeans and a tee shirt, and Maggie was wearing a button down top, a skirt and cowboy boots. I saw why Chuck was in love or maybe it was in lust. She was definitely a beauty. Looking at the way Chuck was smiling from ear to ear, and the way Maggie was holding on to him, she and Chuck might have fallen in love. Or at least into bed I thought.

Chuck walked up to me and said, "Eric, this is Miss Maggie Bright Star."

"Nice to meet you Miss Bright Star," I said and shook her hand.

"Please call me Maggie Sergeant," Maggie said.

"It's Eric and welcome to our home. Did you meet my wife Bell yet?"

"Not yet but I would love to."

"Okay but first, this is the District Attorney, Benedictus..."

"Just call me Imp, Maggie," he said.

I brought Maggie into meet Bell and Theresa and then went back outside. I had just opened a beer when Bobby Black Bear walked in with a lovely woman, carrying a large dish, and five, no six kids trailing behind him.

"Welcome Bobby," I said. "Is this your younger sister?"

"Cute Eric," Bobby said. "This is my wife *Aiukli*, which means beautiful."

"Well you certainly live up to your name, *Aiukli*."

She blushed a little and then Bobby introduced me to his kids.

"They all have Shoshone names Eric, but they also have English names for when they are in school. It makes life easier."

Bobby introduced his children and gave me their ages. There was the oldest Dave, then came Billy, Esther, Gloria, Sally and finally the youngest, Ted. They ranged from 16 all the way down to five.

"Nice to meet you all," I said. "Why don't you all come with me to the game room. My sons Ben and Bear are down there playing video games. We'll call you up when it is time to eat."

"Is it okay Father?" Dave asked.

"Yes, all of you go and have a good time." Bobby said.

Next to arrive was Will by himself. He had brought a red and white wine.

Introductions were made all around and I was happy to see everyone was mingling and talking and laughing and having a good time. About an hour later, Imp was cooking at the grill and soon we were all sitting down to some great food. I had to admit it, Imp knew how to grill.

I noticed Bell watching Chuck and Maggie and I knew, after everyone left I would get a full report. The kids had come out and ate mostly hot dogs and hamburgers, and then Ben had asked if they could go to the park. They wanted to play soccer.

"Fine with me but you better ask the Lieutenant and *Aiukli*," I said.

"Can we go sir?" Ben asked.

"I don't see why not, but be back in an hour." Bobby said.

"Sure! Hey, if you are a Lieutenant, you outrank my dad! Just like Lieutenant Tolliver."

"Ummm, I guess you are right Ben. Now go have some fun!"

All the kids ran off and I said to Bobby, "Would you care for another steak, *SIR*?"

We all had a laugh and again everyone dug into their food and drink. The dish *Aiukli* had brought was a traditional Shoshone recipe and although I had no idea what was in it, I had three helpings. None of us wanted to talk shop and instead we decided to each tell a story from our lives. Imp went first, then Theresa and then Chuck. Aiukli told a short story of her childhood as an only child. She said that was probably why she and Bobby had six children. Bell told about growing up in Montana, on her father's ranch. Will spoke of his years on the job and I thought I detected a little sadness as he told his stories. Then it was Maggie's turn.

Maggie began softly, "I grew up with two brothers and a sister on the reservation. My father was a carpenter, and he tried to help out as many Shoshone with their homes as possible. I knew he rarely took money if the family was poor. Most times they were. But my Mother had a good job off the res, and she provided most of our money.

It was a good childhood until the day my mother, father and two of my siblings had gone into Eagle. A drunk driver had crossed over into their lane. He was driving a big semi, and they were all killed instantly. I was only fourteen and my brother Abel was twenty-two. He took care of me since that day. Then later on, we both moved into Eagle. And we are still there."

No one said anything for a few minutes and then Maggie said, "I am sorry. I have ruined the party."

"No way," I said. "We all have happy and sad stories. Sometimes we can learn more about someone with a sad story. Now I know more about you and so does everyone here. Let's make a toast to the memory of your family."

We all raised our glasses and toasted. Then the party picked up where it left off. Somehow we began a tag football game on the grass. Everyone was laughing and having a great time. I stopped to catch my breath and thought about how lucky Bell, and I were to have some great old friends, and some new ones too.

Then I got back in the game.

CHAPTER 42

The barbeque had ended around eight, but not before Bobby, Chuck, Imp, and I had moved off to get some privacy. Will had left earlier and I was concerned he was upset after talking about his time on the Eagle PD. The women were sitting by themselves, obviously talking about us, judging by the looks and laughter. All the kids were down in the basement where we had set up a playroom with all types of games, a big screen TV and video games.

We talked about the murders, once again going over everything we knew up to this point. Then we decided on a plan for the next few days, if nothing else happened.

Bobby would stay on the res, trying to get anyone to talk among the Shoshone or Arapahoe. He wasn't too confident, but there wasn't much else for him to do. Since he was going to stay on the res, Chuck or I would meet with Harry Longbow concerning the letter his father had left him.

Imp wasn't going to be doing anything concerning the investigation, but he wanted to be kept in the loop.

Chuck and Jimmy would try to locate Max Yellowfeather again. I would meet with Abel Bright Star, hopefully with the help of Maggie. Chuck would talk to her about setting up a meeting. If nothing else happened, we decided we would all get together in Eagle at the department on Thursday morning.

I had gotten to the department early, wanting to go over all the reports concerning the murders. Then Will had the usual morning meeting with all of the detectives in the

Investigations unit. For once, everyone was there and we didn't break until 10:30, having to let everyone talk about what they were doing.

After the meeting, I met with Will for a minute and then we made our way to Chief Todd Lewis' office. It was time I personally briefed him on what had been going on. Of course he knew about the murders, but he hadn't been formerly told by me yet. Before we went to see the Chief, I asked Will if he was okay, and if he was reconsidering retiring. He had assured me he was fine and yes; he was still retiring soon. Then we went to see the Chief.

Will and I entered his office, and the Chief directed us over to a small round table where coffee and donuts had been set up. We sat, poured out the coffee, took donuts and then the Chief was first to speak.

"There are a few things we need to discuss this morning, but I would like to start with the murders," the Chief said.

"So far," I began, "we are sure of three murders and the possibility of one other person targeted. Charlie Two Horse was killed at his home. The place had been torn apart and Charlie's throat had been slit. Also, when Bobby Black Bear had searched the place, he had found a hidden space under the bed in the floor."

"Any indication of what had been hidden in the space?"

"No sir. Next was Jim Longbow killed halfway up the mountain behind his trailer. What was very interesting was Longbow had waved down one of the tribal police officers because someone had searched his trailer. His place had been torn apart. Longbow didn't want to make a formal report, even after Lt. Bobby Black Bear and another officer had shown up. Longbow said he had no idea why someone had tossed his place because he had nothing of value."

"Are we sure this is related to Charlie Two..."

"Two Horse Chief, and yes. Longbow was found the next day with the help of his dog Geronimo. The dog led Lt. Black Bear and his Deputy, Tommy White Hair, up the mountain where they found Jim Longbow buried under a pile of rocks. If Geronimo hadn't led them up, they never would have found him."

"Okay, I understand what you are saying so far, but where is the connection to Two Horse?"

"Besides both of their homes being searched, after Lt. Black Bear had sent Tommy for Doc McAddams and their CSU guy, Lt. Black Bear had continued searching. He found further off the path, a shovel, flashlight, Longbow's knife, and a hole in the ground. It was obvious Longbow had been digging something up when he had been attacked."

"Okay, I'm seeing the connection now. Who else?"

"Sarah Tall Tree had been killed as well, but here in town. That's when we got involved. Her place had been searched and she had been tortured. Whatever the killer was after, he had found."

"I see. Any other connections?"

"Actually, there is a very strange one. Each of the victims had a small tattoo. When enlarged by Doc McAddams, they were almost exactly the same. They appeared to be a meteor streaking through the sky."

"A meteor? Do you have any idea what it means or who else might have a tattoo?"

"Not yet sir, but before Tall Tree had been murdered, another Shoshone living here in Eagle, was burglarized."

"Just burglarized? Not attacked?"

"He hadn't been home when the burglary occurred. His sister, Maggie Bright Star had come home first, seen the place torn apart, and called us. Her brother had gotten home before our Officer had a chance to look in the apartment. The brother, Abel Bright Star had acted strangely, telling our officer there was no need for him to enter the apartment or to make a report. Of course our officer still made a report."

"I suppose you believe Abel Bright Star was hiding something. The same something the killer was after?"

"We think so Chief. Ummm, now, Detective Blackwell decided to follow up by talking with Maggie Bright Star."

"Why the hesitation, Sergeant."

"Ummmm..."

"It seems Detective Blackwell and Miss Bright Star, hit it off Chief," Will said.

"Hit it off?" Chief Lewis asked. "You mean, they liked each other?"

"Yes Chief," I replied. "They are actually dating now. But I can assure you Detective Blackwell will not let this relationship interfere with the investigation. In fact, it might be of help. As we speak, Chuck, I mean, Detective Blackwell is arranging through Maggie Bright Star a meeting with myself and her brother Abel."

"Hmmm, not sure I completely approve but I'm sure you know your squad Sergeant. Let's discuss something else."

I sat there for a second wondering what we would be discussing, and then remembered Will was planning to retire.

The Chief began slowly, saying, "As you probably know, Lieutenant Tolliver is planning to retire soon. In preparation, I have decided when he does retire, you will be promoted to Lieutenant. Of course, you will have to pass the civil service exam."

"Thank you Chief, but what about the position being opened to all sergeants?" I asked.

"They will take the exam, but as you know, I decide out of the top five or six who I want. So you better score in that group Sergeant."

"Yes sir."

"Of course, you will need a second in command. Once again it will be an open test for the entire department. You will choose who makes sergeant out of the top six. I personally would prefer someone with experience in Investigations, but it will be your choice. Are we clear?"

"Yes sir. Ummm, do we have any timeline for this?" I said, looking at Will.

"I will not retire until September, which will give you about three months to prepare for the test. Also, it will give the rest of the department time to study as well."

"Okay then, I think we are all caught up," Chief Lewis said, rising out of his chair.

Will and I stood, but before we left, Chief Lewis said, "Keep me apprised of any further developments. I'm counting on you to catch this killer. And Sergeant?"

"Yes sir?" I asked.

"Sooner would be better than later."

"Yes sir."

Will and I returned to his office to discuss a few things. I was still upset about his retiring, but I only wanted good things for him. We shook hands when I left, and I began to think about the studying I would need to do. Then I thought about who I would promote to my second in command. I wanted it to be one of two people, but they would need to score well for me to consider them.

I went into my office and called Chuck. He and Jimmy were out searching for Max and as of yet, they hadn't found him. Their next stop was going to be to find Liz Butler. She might know where Max had disappeared to. Finally before I left, I gave Bell a call. She was meeting with all of her backers, and I wanted to wish her luck. I also wanted to remind her who she was, and how strong a person she could be. After hanging up, I left the department and headed over to the lumber yard to speak with Harry Longbow.

CHAPTER 43

Bell entered the large home belonging to Teresa Benton for this meeting. The home was very large and had a fantastic view of Eagle. She knew Benton along with her husband had raised four children in this house. Her husband had passed a few years ago and all of her children had moved away. Bell thought she would be devastated if her children moved away.

This time she walked in with her head held high, and confidence in her step. Her backers in the room seemed to notice the difference right away.

Bell pulled out a chair and sat down, placing a folder on the table before her. Only Alan Cummings, Brett Trask, John Miller, and of course, Teresa Benton were present. Bell figured the men and Teresa were the bigger players in this game. She wasn't surprised by the others being missing.

"Good morning," Bell said.

They all replied the same and then Alan Cummings began to speak.

He said, "Well Bell, have you..."

"I have," Bell replied. "I have gone over your ideas and many of them I agree with. Some of them I don't. Now, the..."

"Excuse me Bell," Brett Trask started to say until Bell cut him off.

"I think it would be best if you all let me say what I came here to say first. Then we can discuss things. As I was saying, some of your ideas are good. Some not. I also have several of my own ideas to present to the people of Eagle. As for my opponent Graham Stone, I will not allow any dirt to be spread about him."

Both Trask and Cummings began to stand, and Bell saw a sly smile out of the corner of her eye on Teresa Benton's face. Maybe she was in Bell's corner.

"Please sit down gentlemen," Bell said. "As I was saying, I will not tolerate any dirty acts against Stone. If I cannot win using my character and the things I want to do for the people of Eagle, then I shouldn't win. I believe I can defeat Stone with your help. But if you do not accept my terms here and now, I will have to find some other backers. I realize the others who aren't present need to be told about my plans as soon as possible. But in the next ten minutes, I would like you four to make up your minds. I will step out onto the patio and let you discuss this among yourselves."

Bell stepped out of the room and the three men erupted.

"Just who the hell does she think she is!" Trask spat out.

"Giving us an ultimatum!" Miller added.

"Let's quiet down gentlemen," Teresa Benton said. "I have the most capital of this entire group, and it is I who will back Bell Logan if you three want to drop out."

"Terry, please..." Cummings started to say.

"Listen to me. We finally have a prospective candidate with some balls, even though she is a woman. A strong woman who speaks her mind. We know she has an impeccable past. Her family has never been involved in any scandal. Her husband is an excellent detective and a fine member of the community. If she thinks she can win against Stone, I am willing to let her try. I think you should all agree, but if not, don't let the door hit you in the ass!"

The men were shocked and spoke quietly among themselves. Finally, they seemed to come to a decision. They didn't say anything to Teresa, waiting for Bell to return.

Finally, after exactly ten minutes, Bell returned.

"I hope you all will stay on the team, but I will still run with or without you," she said.

"Ahem," Trask said. "We have decided you are still the best candidate to win against Stone. Therefore, with your approval, we would all like to remain on the team. How about we shake hands and then we can discuss your ideas?"

Bell smiled and shook hands with them all, leaving Teresa for last. As she shook her hand, Teresa gave her a smile and a wink. Bell sat as did all the others, and she opened her folder.

"First, I think..."

CHAPTER 44

Bobby had been driving around the res all morning. He had attempted to get anyone to talk about the murders or the tattoos. So far, no one had said more than good morning and goodbye to him. He was becoming disheartened with his people. Didn't they know he was there to protect them, to help them in any way he could? Didn't they understand without talking to him, he might as well sit in his office and wait for the next victim to die?

Bobby forgot about the case for a minute as he pulled up to a dilapidated home, made of every material possible. The roof was made from rusted steel sheets found at some junkyard. The walls were painted in different colors, probably with whatever paint could be found. There were no windows with glass. Instead the openings were closed off with tarp. The front door wasn't square and had no door. Again, tarp was hung to cover it. In the yard were toys strewn about, a line holding some clothes and a rusted out washing machine. It probably wouldn't have worked because Bobby didn't think they had any electricity. Bobby knew there was a husband, a wife and two children living in this wreck. He hoped they would consider moving into Walks in Wind's teepee. It wouldn't be a great improvement, but they wouldn't have to pay any rent on it. Maybe they could save some money. Also it was clean and out of the elements. Bobby also had a plan in mind for the man of the house.

Bobby saw the children playing on the side of the house, throwing a ball back and forth. They waved to him as he exited his car. Bobby waved back. In the front yard, a woman sat on a chair, putting together some Native jewelry to sell at the flea market many white people visited. They all wanted some authentic Shoshone trinkets.

Bobby approached and said, "*Behne*, Little White Dove."

Little White Dove replied, "*Behne*."

"Ummm, I'm looking for your husband."

Little White Dove merely pointed to inside the ramshackle home.

Bobby said thank you and entered the home through the tarp. Inside it was dimly lit and Bobby thought there was about the same amount of dirt inside as out. He knew Running Bear worked around the res doing odd jobs and didn't make too much money. Bobby thought he might have a solution for that if the man would speak with him. Bobby knew the Shoshone were proud and didn't like charity. So he had to word his offer carefully.

He found Running Bear sitting at a table, tinkering with a radio.

"*Behne*, Running Bear," Bobby said.

"Uh huh," was the only reply.

May I sit?" Bobby asked.

"Sit."

"I am here to ask for your help Running Bear."

"What help could I possibly give you?"

"I am in need of someone to work at the department, at Tribal Police Headquarters."

"What type of work?"

"I only have so many deputies and there are many things which need to be done every day."

"Like what?"

"Well, for instance, all of our vehicles need to be gassed and serviced regularly. They may need some repairs or cleaning. Also there is a need for a mechanic in the building as well. Some things are always broken. I have heard from many others; you have a talent to fix things."

"It is true. I can fix most anything. But it is a far distance to your headquarters. I have no car."

"There would be no need for you to travel very far. Do you know Walks in Wind?"

"I know of him."

"Do you know of his large teepee, a Chief's teepee?"

"I have seen it. It is very large and sturdy. But why?"

"Sadly Walks in Wind has passed, and his son is allowing me to let anyone I wish, to live in his father's teepee. It is close to my headquarters, and it could serve you and your family well."

Running Bear appeared to be deep in thought. Bobby figured it would be best to let him decide.

"What if there is nothing to fix? Do I still get paid?"

"If times are slow, I thought you might study to become a police officer. It is good pay and very important. I believe you would make a good officer Running Bear. You would soon be able to get a better home for your family, but in the meantime, there would be no rent to pay. What you make at first could be saved. What do you think?"

"I never thought about being a police officer. Do you really think I could become one?"

"Yes I do. I will arrange for you to be paid $350.00 a week to start."

Running Bear's eyes opened wide and then he said, "I agree. When can we move?"

"I will send one of my deputies out in two days. This will give you time to gather what you need. There will be food sent to your new home as well as beds, blankets, and storage bins for clothes. If you are still in the teepee when the weather changes, I will get you a free standing stove and wood. If you save your money and do well, you will be able to get a better house very shortly. I am happy you have agreed."

Running Bear stood and shook Bobby's hand. Then Bobby left and as he was driving away, he saw Little White Dove grab her husband. Then her children were called over and they all started to dance.

For the first time in a long time, Bobby felt good about himself. Now all he would have to do is figure out a way to pay Running Bear's salary. He would have to find a way to get it from the federal government. In the meantime, he would go into Eagle to get some things for the family. He knew they would need a large cooler, three beds and some other things. He would pay for it all himself and he wasn't concerned about the cost. They needed his money more than he did right now. Bobby started driving to Eagle and never noticed the huge smile he had on his face.

CHAPTER 45

Monday 1:10 pm

I entered the lumber yard to speak with Harry Longbow. I had waited till after the lunch hour, figuring I would be able to speak with him then. I didn't see him around and so I went into the office to see the manager. I knew the manager was a good man, never in any trouble and well-liked by his employees.

"Good afternoon, Sam," I said.

Sam Gooding rose from behind his desk and shook my hand.

"What brings you here Eric?" Sam said.

"No trouble Sam," I said. "I wanted to talk with Harry Longbow for a minute, but I didn't see him anywhere."

"I'm afraid you're out of luck. Harry took the week off to go and see his younger sister in Arizona."

"I didn't know he had a sister."

"Neither did I until he asked for the time off. I don't even know her name."

"Did he say anything about his trip?"

"You know it's funny. He said he had to show his sister a letter from their father. He wanted to discuss it with her."

"So he will be back on Monday?"

"Should be. If he calls or is delayed, I will let you know."

"Thanks Sam, I appreciate it."

"By the way, I heard a rumor your wife Belinda is going to run against Graham Stone for City Council. Is it true?"

"Well, she is definitely thinking about it."

"She has my vote Eric, and you can tell her, there are a lot of folks not happy with Stone."

"I'll tell her Sam, and thanks again."

I exited the office thinking about Harry and the letter. I couldn't help but think something important had been written by Jim Longbow. Important enough for Harry to take a week off and travel to Arizona, to show his sister. Bobby or I would have to get Harry to show us the letter. If he refused, I think I could make a case for obstruction. I wasn't sure if a judge would agree, but possibly just the threat would work.

I stood by the office, wondering what I should do now. Then I saw Abel Bright Star working a lathe near the back. I decided I would try and talk with him. I knew Chuck was trying to get Maggie to arrange a meeting, but there was no time like the present. Especially with people getting murdered here in Eagle and on the reservation.

I walked over and waited until he had shut off the machine. He turned and saw me, and it appeared as if he was expecting me.

"Hello Abel," I said.

"Sergeant," was his reply.

"Is there somewhere we can talk?"

"Follow me."

We walked out the back to a small area where I supposed the men came to smoke and take their breaks. He sat down and so did I.

"I have been expecting you, or Bobby Black Bear," he said.

"Well I hope you are not disappointed it is me," I replied.

"You want to know about the burglary, right?"

"I do but before you tell me anything, let me tell you about some things going on here and on the res, okay?"

"Okay Sergeant."

"Please call me Eric. Now, I am not sure if you have heard about the murders."

"I have not."

I watched Abel for any reactions as I began telling him of the murders.

"First, Charlie Two Horse was killed in his home. Something was taken by his killer. Something small which had been hidden under the floor in his bedroom. Next, Jim Longbow's house had been tossed and the next day, he was also murdered. Again, something had been taken from a spot on the mountain behind Jim's trailer. There was a small hole he had dug up right before he was murdered."

"I knew them both. They were good men. Good Shoshone. I will say a prayer for them tonight. But what does this have to do with me?"

"Abel, I think you know, but there was another murder, here in town. Sara Tall Tree..."

"Sara has been murdered?" Abel said, and he looked very upset. "Who would kill her? She was a sweet old lady. She could name ancestors going back many centuries, even to a Chief."

"As to who, that is why I am talking with you. I'm sorry to say she had been tortured and her place was searched. It looked as if her killer had been searching for something, and probably found it. So Abel, do you want to say anything to me?"

Abel seemed to be in deep thought and then he said, "When you became a police officer, did you take an oath?"

"Of course."

"And you swore to serve and protect, to follow the laws of your people, the city and this country, correct?"

"Yes."

"Would you break that oath?"

"That's not a question which is easily answered. I wouldn't break it for almost any reason. But, if my family was in some sort of danger, and I had to do something to save them, to protect them, and the only way was to break my oath...I would."

"You seem to be a good man Eric. I know you are only looking to catch this murderer before he has a chance to kill again. But I too am sworn to an oath. I do not know if keeping my oath will end up hurting more people or not. I will have to think about it, meditate on the answer. But I will seek you out, whatever my decision may be. Can you allow me to do so?"

I really wanted to somehow make Abel tell me what he was hiding right there and then, but I didn't think he would. It was better to agree and let him think about it. I only hoped nothing else would happen between now and when he made his decision.

"I understand Abel, and I agree. But, the longer you take, the more likely someone else might die. So please, don't take too long."

"I will not Eric."

As he was about to get back to work, I asked him," Do you have any tattoos Abel?"

"I do not."

He stood and made his way back inside, returning to his work. I was pretty sure he did have a tattoo, a meteor, but I had no way to force him to show me. I exited and since I hadn't eaten lunch, I headed over to a diner. As I walked over, saying hello and nodding at some of the citizens of Eagle, I had the feeling things were coming to a head. Maybe if Abel decided to talk and reveal his secret, we could catch the killer.

Of course we still had to talk with Harry Longbow and if we ever found Max Yellowfeather, we could talk with him. Between the three of them, we just might find out who the killer was, and why he was murdering Shoshone people. And of course, what he was after.

CHAPTER 46

Monday 4:30 pm

I was sitting in my office, trying to catch up on some paperwork when Chuck and Jimmy walked in. They both looked exhausted. After sitting down, and letting out big sighs, Chuck began.

"Well Eric, we have canvassed the city of Eagle from north to south and east to west," He stated. "There is no sign of Max Yellowfeather anywhere in town. We didn't go out to the res. I figured Bobby knew we were looking for him. If he came across his whereabouts or him, I figured he would let us know."

"Were you able to find and ask Liz?" I asked.

"We found her," Jimmy said. "She was just coming out of the men's restroom at Kelly's."

"Doing business as usual I suppose."

"Oh yeah. This guy came out right after her and he was zipping up his pants. When he saw our badges he high-tailed it out of there."

"So Liz had no idea where Max was?"

"Actually she said she had been speaking to Max right before he left."

"Okay. What had he said?"

"It took a bit of coaxing and the threat of bringing her in," Chuck said, "but she finally told us."

"Do I have to guess?"

"Sorry Eric. Liz said Max had been very upset about something. He wouldn't say what. Then he said he was going to visit a relative of his on the Fort Hall Reservation. It's in Idaho, in the Southeastern corner. I had to look it up."

"Well at least we now know where he is. Maybe we can get Bobby to send a message to the Tribal Police at Fort Hall. He can find out if Max is really there. Maybe even get him to come back home."

"You want me to head out to the res to ask Bobby?"

"I think it might be faster if I just call him Chuck."

"Duh. I must be really tired. Jimmy and I are going to go and write up a report on today's events, or I should say lack of events."

"Wait a minute Chuck, I need to discuss something with you. Thanks for all your good work Jimmy."

"Not sure it was good work, but thanks Sarge," Jimmy said and left, closing the door behind him.

"What's up Eric?" Chuck asked, and yawned.

"Looks like you need some rest Chuck," I said. "This won't take too long."

"No problem. I'm meeting Maggie for dinner, and I want to get a hot shower and a catnap maybe. So what do you want to talk about?"

"A few things. First I want you to be aware Chief Lewis knows you are seeing Maggie."

"How did he find out? Not that it's a secret."

"I told him during a briefing on the case. I thought it would be better if he knew, just in case down the road it becomes a problem."

"What kind of a problem?"

"Well that's the second thing I wanted to talk to you about. I spoke with Abel Bright Star today at his work. We discussed a few things, and he asked me a strange question."

"Okay, what was the question?"

"He asked me if I would ever break my oath."

"Your oath? Like to protect and serve?"

"Yeah, and I told him I would, if it meant saving someone I love from harm."

"Good answer. What did he say about that?"

"He told me he had taken an oath as well. He needed to think about it and decide if he could break it. I think he is going to tell us what he knows, only it will not be too soon. He sounded like he was going to take some time to think it over."

"Great. In the meantime, another person might be killed. But I suppose there is no way to force him to talk. What about Harry Longbow?"

"Harry went to Arizona to see his sister. I didn't even know he had one."

"Is it just a coincidence he left right in the middle of these murders?"

"No it isn't. He told Sam Gooding he was going to see her to show her a letter his father had written to him. It's connected to these murders. I'm sure of it now."

"So, we wait for Harry to return, Abel to decide if he will talk with us and for Max Yellowfeather to come back. Feels like we are spinning our wheels till then."

"I agree. One other thing Chuck."

"Yeah?"

"Will is retiring in September. The Chief wants me to take the Lieutenant's test and take over Investigations."

"Congratulations! But, doesn't he have to open the position to all the Sergeants?"

"Yes he does, but, as long as I am in the top six, he can choose who he wants. Which brings me to you."

"Me?"

"Well, if I become the Lieutenant in charge, my position becomes open. I want you to test for sergeant and get in the top six. Then I can choose you to be my Sergeant. What do you think?"

"I'm speechless Eric. I mean, you really think I could be a good second in command here?"

"I wouldn't have said so if I didn't believe you can. But, because of Civil Service rules, the test will be open to all police officers. Do you think you can get in the top six?"

"If I don't it won't be because of lack of trying. I'm going to get all the books for the test and start studying tonight!"

"I think it can wait a few days at least Chuck. Go home and get ready for your date. And keep this all under your hat. The Chief will decide when he is going to announce Will's retirement and the subsequent tests. Now get outta here!"

"Yes sir!" Chuck said and nearly ran into the closed door.

I supposed he was exhausted and excited at the same time. I knew he still had to pass the test and end up in the top six, and so did I. But Chuck was the best person for the job in my opinion. Perhaps in a few months I would be a Lieutenant and Chuck would be my Sergeant. But for now, we still had a killer on the loose. I picked up the phone and called Bobby, asking him to try and locate Max at the Fort Hall reservation. After hanging up I saw it was almost 5:30 and I too was exhausted. I decided to lock up and head home. I was wondering how Bell's meeting went, but soon I would know. It seemed between me becoming a Lieutenant and Bell becoming a city councilwoman, our lives were changing once again. But then again, I knew staying stagnant was no way to live life.

CHAPTER 47

Friday 1:10 pm

It had been close to a week, and we were no closer to finding the killer. Abel hadn't contacted me; Harry was still away on vacation and Max wasn't located at the Fort Hall res. I was getting frustrated and felt as if the Sword of Damocles was hanging over my head. Will was checking on our progress every day and reporting back to the Chief. Chief Lewis was not happy, which meant Will wasn't happy and therefore neither was I, Chuck Jimmy or even Bobby.

Bell had officially thrown her hat into the ring. She and her backers were meeting daily, going over her platform, events she should attend and a slogan for her campaign. She was extremely busy, but she was more excited than I had ever seen her. Well except for our wedding, the birth of our kids and once in a while, my sexual prowess!

The kids only had a week left of school and they were willing to pitch in to help. They were going to post flyers, and they even wanted me to put a big speaker on our car so they could ride around and proclaim their mother the best candidate. That idea was nixed. But I was happy and proud of them for wanting to help.

Chuck, Jimmy, and I met every day to discuss our options. I told them I was going to a judge to possibly force Harry to give us his letter. If he didn't want to let us have it, I was going to charge him with Obstruction in a homicide investigation. It would land him in jail temporarily if he refused, but I thought he would turn it over. We still had no idea what was written in the letter, but we all thought it might break the case open.

Earlier in the week, Bobby had asked us to help him with a small project. He had arranged for a family to move into Walks in Wind's teepee. He needed some help getting it set up and also to help move the family.

Chuck, Jimmy, and I had met Bobby on Wednesday morning with three pickups. We drove over to Running Bear's old home and loaded up all three trucks with an assortment of furniture, clothes, and personal belongings. Then we had gone to the teepee and began making it into a home, if only temporarily. By the time we were done, the place had looked pretty good. Much better than where Running Bear, Little White Dove and their children had been living.

Bobby surprised the family with some new toys for the kids, two large coolers to keep food fresh, some groceries and two portable heaters. Running Bear didn't know what to say, but his wife ran over to Bobby and gave him a big hug and kiss. Then she hugged us all with Running Bear following right behind her.

Finally, we had all gone to Bobby's house for a big meal his wife had prepared. There was a great deal of laughing and joking. Everyone had a great time, and I felt as if some new friendships had been made by all.

It had been the highlight of my week. There had been some more petty crimes including a robbery of a gas station on the outskirts of town. A pair of my detectives, Don Berry and Todd Cassidy had investigated it. The two people who held it up turned out to be a couple of kids who had a long rap sheet, even though they were only 19 and 20 years old. This time we were all hoping the judge would be a bit stricter when sentencing them.

I locked up and headed out, still thinking about the

murders. I stopped myself as I drove up the mountain for home. This weekend I intended to be focused on one thing only. My family.

CHAPTER 48

Saturday 8:20 am

Nihoono biitooeeihii couldn't believe his luck. He had waited outside Lewis Deep Water's apartment, hoping the big man would go fishing again. He hadn't had high hopes, but then at about 7:30 this morning, Deep Water had come out with all his fishing gear. He had loaded up his truck and driven off.

Nihoono biitooeeihii had followed behind just in case he went to a different lake or fishing spot. A half hour later, *Nihoono biitooeeihii* was thrilled to see him pull into the same little fishing spot on Tranquility Lake he had been at the week before. He was well prepared, but *Nihoono biitooeeihii* had to wait to make sure there was no one else around. He wasn't positive if when he confronted Deep Water how the man would react. Would he put up a fight or go along with his instructions? There was only one way to find out and *Nihoono biitooeeihii* was getting ready.

Nihoono biitooeeihii drove his car directly to the secluded spot. As he drove up, Deep Water turned and with an expression of concern, put down his rod and began to walk to the car.

"What are you doing here?" Deep Water asked as he got closer.

"There is no time to explain!" *Nihoono biitooeeihii* yelled out. "The lumber yard is in flames, and I knew you would be here fishing. Sam Gooding needs all employees to come to the yard!"

"Oh no!" Deep Water said, and immediately turned to gather his equipment. As he was bending down to get his things, he began to turn and said, "But how did you know I was here?"

Deep Water never got to hear any answer because *Nihoono biitooeeihii* grabbed him around the throat and pressed a cloth soaked in chloroform tightly against his mouth. Deep Water was amazingly strong and stood up with *Nihoono biitooeeihii* on his back, barely holding on. But the chloroform was doing its job, and soon the big man swayed, and slowly crumpled to the ground.

Nihoono biitooeeihii placed his hands on his knees, drawing in big gulps of air. After a few minutes, he went back to his car and retrieved what he needed. *Nihoono biitooeeihii* didn't think Deep Water had hidden the gift somewhere. A man of his strength and pride would carry the gift. He would believe it was the safest place for it. But if the gift was not on Deep Water, *Nihoono biitooeeihii* would search his home, tearing it apart to find what was rightfully his.

Nihoono biitooeeihii dragged the big man toward a stump of a tree. Before tying him up, he had done a quick search, looking for the gift. He didn't find it, but he was still sure Deep Water had it either hidden somewhere on him or close by. He sat him up and tied his body to the stump with thick rope. Then he tied his feet together, his legs together and his wrists and arms. Finally he placed a gag in his mouth so the big man couldn't cry out. He was making sure there would be no possibility of the man escaping.

Then *Nihoono biitooeeihii* waited patiently for Deep Water to awake. Once his head had cleared he would explain the situation. He would tell Deep Water how he knew about the gift. He would explain his great plans and try to get Deep Water to turn the gift over without having to torture him. But torture him he would if necessary. He was not going to leave Deep Water any choice. Sooner or later, *Nihoono biitooeeihii* would get the gift. It was Deep Water's choice whether or not he wanted to be tortured. Of course, he would have to die whether he revealed where the gift was by torture or not.

After a short while, Deep Water began to stir. As he awoke, he began to struggle against the ropes. Finally, breathing hard and with angry, wide eyes, he stared at his captor.

"I am sure you are wondering what is going on," *Nihoono biitooeeihii* began. "First let me alleviate your concerns about the lumberyard. It is not in flames, and all is well with it and Sam Gooding. Of course, the same could not be said of your situation. I will explain and then we will see if you need any further enticement.

A few weeks ago I overheard two people talking. One was Walks in Wind and the other his son. What I heard was fascinating and after a bit of encouragement, Walks in Wind told me almost everything about the gifts."

Deep Water renewed his struggling and looked even angrier than before.

"Oh I see you know about the gifts. But of course you do because you are in possession of one. Walks in Wind attempted to trick me, but I saw through his ruse. I found an ancient parchment telling the entire story of the gifts. It also told of the families down through over four hundred years who kept the gifts. Selfishly, I might add. So far I have obtained four of the gifts. Yours will make five. You have no choice but to give me the gift. Your only choice is whether or not you will be tortured or not, and if I shall let you live. So, what is it going to be Lewis Deep Water? Will you give me the gift without any fuss, or shall I get my tools ready?"

Lewis thought to himself how this man must be crazy. Yes he had the gift, and he kept it secret out of honor for his father and his father before him. He didn't believe the old legend. This crazy person really thought there was power in the gifts. Should he just give it to him, knowing it wouldn't help him at all? Or should he protect it and his oath to his ancestors? The choice was simple. He would not betray his honor, his oath, or his ancestors. Looking this crazy man in the eyes, he shook his head no.

"I suppose it is your choice," *Nihoono biitooeeihii* said. He walked to his car and brought out a large hard plastic box. Setting it down in front of Deep Water, he opened it and began to remove some tools. There was a tool for pruning branches, a small blowtorch and lighter, some pliers and a few other objects. Deep Water's eyes widened when he saw them.

Nihoono biitooeeihii said, "You have one more chance Deep Water. I will begin by slicing off your eyelids so you cannot close your eyes. Then I will snip off your fingers, one at a time. And if necessary, I will burn off your manhood. And believe me, that will be the most painful. So, for the last time, what will it be? Give me the gift now or suffer the torture?"

Lewis thought he was going to die for sure. Did he need to go through pain and die in the end anyway? But what of his oath? If he endured the torture, the pain, and did not give him the gift, what would he gain? He was sure this lunatic would search everywhere and everything he had. He would find the gift, of that Lewis was sure. He looked to the sky for some guidance from his ancestors. A sign or something to tell him what to do. There was nothing and Lewis had to make a choice.

Nihoono biitooeeihii said, "I think I have given you enough time to decide."

Lewis watched as he picked up a scalpel from the box. Then he moved closer to Lewis, bringing it close to his right eye. Lewis flung his head back and forth violently.

"Hmmm," *Nihoono biitooeeihii* said. "Maybe I will just have to use the chloroform again to keep you still. Then when you awake, you will feel the pain and realize I wasn't bluffing. You will never be able to close your eyes again. If I let you live, it will eventually make you mad. But so be it."

Nihoono biitooeeihii reached for the chloroform and Lewis realized he really had no choice. The gift would be taken but at least he would die whole. He tried to speak through the gag.

"You want to say something?" *Nihoono biitooeeihii* asked.

Lewis nodded.

Nihoono biitooeeihii removed the gag, but not before telling Lewis if he screamed out, the torture would begin. He also told him he wanted to hear one thing and one thing only. Where the gift was. He asked Lewis if he understood and agreed. Lewis nodded once again. *Nihoono biitooeeihii* removed the gag and allowed Lewis a second to breathe.

Lewis stated, "What you want is in the tackle box. There is a false bottom, and it is there. But you must..."

Nihoono biitooeeihii thrust the gag back into Lewis's

mouth before he could say another word. He checked his ropes and then walked to the water's edge. There, he found the tackle box. He opened it slowly and began to empty its contents. When it was empty, he searched for some kind of button or tab to pull open the false bottom. Finally, his finger felt something out of place. A small lip near the back of the box. He lifted it and there he saw a bag made of deerskin and decorated with some design. He carefully opened it. Inside was the gift!

"*Nihoono biitooeeihii* was elated and began laughing and howling like a wolf to the sky. Then he walked back to Lewis Deep Water with a smile and a glint in his eyes.

"You see!" *Nihoono biitooeeihii* yelled. "It is my destiny to gather all the gifts! Then I will lead our people to a new future. A future where we rule, and the white man is our slaves."

Lewis now knew this man was completely mad. Before he could even think another thought, *Nihoono biitooeeihii* grabbed the scalpel and drew it deep and fast across Lewis's throat. As his blood spilled down the front of his chest, Lewis prayed he would be forgiven. Then he thought nothing else.

CHAPTER 49

Saturday 10:00 am

We had gotten a late start because the battery on my truck had died. I needed to jump it with my G-ride, and it had taken a bit of time. Finally, the boys and I had gotten in the old truck and headed for our fishing spot. When we finally arrived, it was getting warm, and the mosquitos and other bugs were out in full force. I sprayed the boys down and then we got our rods ready, with the lines finally in the deep blue water.

The boys were extremely excited because Monday was the last day of school. It should have been yesterday, but because of a snow day which needed to be made up, the last day was in two days.

We got everything set up and began to fish. The boys were talking softly to each other, discussing all the things they wanted to do over the summer vacation. I heard them talk about getting together with a few of their friends every day, and riding their bicycles out to the mall, a bike race track at the edge of town, here to the lake and a bunch of other places.

To me, it sounded a lot like how I was thinking over twenty years ago when I had just turned sixteen. That summer was going to be my summer of independence. My parents had given me more freedom than I ever had before. Imp was leaving for Europe for the summer, but I had other friends to get into mischief with. Then it had all turned into the worst summer of my life. DeSade had come into my life. I shook my head and decided I didn't want to ruin today by thinking about the past.

Soon Ben had landed the first catch and a few minutes later, Bear caught one. I still hadn't caught any, so I got up to get different bait for my line from the truck. As I stood up, I looked around. There was something in another spot, a few hundred yards down from where we were set up. I strained my eyes, looking to see what it was in the spot. I saw a few fishing rods lying on the shore. But I didn't see anyone. Then I remembered Lewis Deep Water had been fishing in the spot last week. Suddenly I had a very bad feeling.

"Boys," I said, "I will be right back. I think I see a friend of mine fishing a bit over. You guys stay right here and keep fishing. If you get up to four or five, you can just sit here and wait for me to get back. Okay?"

"Sure Dad," Ben said, and Bear also agreed. Then they went back to fishing.

I decided it would be quicker to get over to the other spot with my truck. I backed out of our spot and headed down the road. When I got close to the other spot, I parked my truck on the side of the road. I wasn't sure why I wanted to approach carefully and silently, but something was telling me to do just that. It was a sixth sense which had served me well in the past, and I wasn't going to ignore it.

I approached and immediately saw my gut had been right. I saw Lewis Deep Water sitting against a stump. He had been tied up and I saw a gag hanging in his mouth. There was no rush because the front of Lewis' shirt was covered in blood. As I got closer, I saw a deep gash in his throat. Lewis had died quickly, and I hoped he hadn't suffered.

I walked back to my truck, took out my phone and got our people moving. I needed an evidence tech guy, and a few more cops to canvass the surrounding spots around the lake to see if anyone saw anything. Doc McAddams would have to come out. I got in touch with both Chuck and Jimmy and asked them to call Bobby right away. Then I called Bell and asked her to come to the lake to pick up the boys.

I didn't want to leave the body till someone else showed up. I walked to the water's edge and saw my boys were still fishing. I would keep an eye on them and wait for my men to show up. As I sat on a rock, I thought about the killer. Either he was extremely strong or very smart. Getting the drop on someone like Lewis Deep Water would have been tough. If he had used just his strength, there would have been a struggle. I couldn't see any marks on the ground, so I ruled it out. Lewis wouldn't have just let someone tie him up. So how did the killer do it?

I walked back to Lewis, looking to see if there was anything I could see. The gag in his mouth was hanging mostly out of his mouth. Before pulling it out, I took my phone and took a few pictures of it, so the scene was preserved. Then, I carefully removed it. I moved closer to Lewis' face to see if there was anything there. The wind shifted and suddenly I thought I detected a strange odor. Could it be some kind of knockout gas or liquid? Was that how the killer had gotten the best of Lewis? I would make sure the evidence tech and Doc knew about it. Maybe they would know what it was or could take samples to find out.

Looking around, I saw Lewis' tackle box. It was lying on its side, with everything dumped out on the ground. I moved it around with a stick since I had no gloves till I could look inside. There was a false bottom, with the lid slightly ajar. Whatever Lewis had been hiding inside it had been taken. It seemed this killer was on a winning streak.

Soon, Chuck showed up, followed by Jimmy, Mike Kowalski, our best evidence tech, and Doc McAddams. I told Chuck about the odor and asked him to pass it on to Mike and the Doc. Then I went back to the boys.

While I was gone, they had gotten five big fish.

"Looks like you guys are really getting the hang of this," I said.

"I got three of them," Ben said.

"Yeah, but mine are bigger!" Bear chimed in.

"Okay guys. Let's get them iced and put away," I said. "Bring in all the lines and get stuff together."

"Did you see your friend?" Bear asked.

"Yes son, I did."

Just then Bell showed up and the boys ran to her with their fish.

"Look Mom!" Bear yelled, "See all the fish we caught!"

"I know what we are having for dinner, great job boys!" she said. "You boys get in my car. Your Dad has something to do."

The boys got into Bell's car, and I walked over to her.

"It's bad, isn't it?" Bell asked.

"I'm afraid so Bell," I replied. "Another Shoshone murdered. Lewis Deep Water."

"Wasn't he the champion of the Shoshone games on the res? I remember how he tossed several men aside as he wrestled. He was big and strong. So who killed him?"

"I wish I knew but, I'm going to find out. I'll call you later and let you know what is happening and if we will still have a family weekend. Sorry about this love."

"Don't be silly Eric. You have a job to do. Now, give me a kiss and get to work."

I kissed her and then watched as she drove away. Luckily my boys hadn't seen anything. They could stay a bit innocent for a little while longer. But I knew, sooner or later, their innocence would be marred by some evil or vicious act. I just hoped it would be later, much later. Then I remembered how Ben had seen a boy jump to his death at the lake in Whispering Rock. Maybe it was impossible to keep evil away forever.

I sighed and got back in my truck. I drove back to the crime scene to see if anything had been found out yet.

I walked up to Doc McAddams first.

"Did Chuck tell you about the odor I smelled?" I asked.

"Chloroform Eric," he replied. "And from the lingering odor, I would say a great deal of it. As soon as Mike is done with his photos and collecting any evidence, I will transport him back. I suppose you don't want me to wait till Monday for an autopsy?"

"Well Doc, I don't think an autopsy needs to be a rush. But I do want you to go over every inch of him."

"You want to see if he has a tattoo?"

"You got it. I think he will, and I would like to know as soon as possible."

"Okay Eric."

I walked over to Chuck and Jimmy and began to discuss some ideas. As we were talking, Bobby showed up. He looked at Lewis' body and then walked over to us.

"Any tattoo?" he asked.

"Not sure yet, but as soon as Doc gets him on the table, he will look for one," I said. "There was a small false bottom in his tackle box. I suppose the killer got whatever Lewis had hidden. Damn it! I wish we knew what it was and why four people had been murdered. How about we all go back to my office and discuss this newest murder?"

"I'll meet you there Eric," Bobby said. "I will say a prayer for Lewis first, if that is okay with you."

"Of course Bobby. And maybe you can say another one for us, to catch this killer before anyone else gets killed."

Bobby nodded and walked over to the body of Lewis Deep Water.

CHAPTER 50

Saturday 12:30 pm

I had Chuck stop for some food, and then we all met in one of the conference rooms. Present was Chuck, Jimmy, Bobby, Mike, and me. We set up all the food and we each made a plate. Then after getting some bottles of water, we sat down. We ate silently, none of us in a hurry to tackle the murders. We didn't have much to go on, and we all knew it. So far this killer had murdered four people. He was smart and hadn't left any DNA, or fibers or fingerprints. He definitely knew how to keep a crime scene clean.

As I was finishing my food, my phone rang.

"Hello," I said.

"It's Doc, Eric," I heard Doc McAddams say. "I found a tattoo, again very small and done by an expert. It was the same size as the others. Lewis had it on his ankle."

"I figured he had one but it's good to confirm. Why don't you forget about the autopsy till Monday Doc and enjoy what's left of the weekend."

"Nah, I'm here so I might as well get it done. But I will wait till Monday for a report if that's okay with you."

"Fine Doc, and thanks. Bye."

"Bye Eric."

"I take it Lewis had a tattoo," Bobby said.

"Yes, on his ankle," I replied. "So now we know for sure he is a victim of the same killer. Everyone had the tattoo, and everyone was hiding something. If only we knew what it was."

"How about we get one of the white boards in here and list everything we do know," Jimmy said.

"Good idea Jimmy. Go get one."

Jimmy left and soon returned with a large white board on wheels. He set it up at the end of the conference table.

"You write Jimmy," Chuck said. "If I write, no one will be able to read it."

"Okay, what do we put first?"

"Start with the tattoos," Bobby said. "At least we know they all had one."

Jimmy put up a number one, and then TATTOOS.

"Put down they were all done by Painter Chief," I said.

"And the tattoo's look like a shooting star or meteorite."

Jimmy wrote Number four and looked to us.

"They were all hiding something small," Chuck said.

Jimmy wrote it down, then number five.

Bobby said quietly, "They were all Shoshone."

"Anything else?" Jimmy asked.

"Maybe we can come up with more Jimmy."

"We know some of the victims homes had been burglarized," I said. "except for Lewis Deep Water's. We also know Abel Bright Star's home was tossed. Therefore I think we can deduce Abel has a tattoo and is hiding something as well."

"I agree with you," Bobby said.

"Okay, so we know Max Yellowfeather came to me after Abel and Maggie's home had been tossed. Therefore, Max Yellowfeather either knows about what is being searched for, or he is another one with a tattoo."

"Hmmm," Chuck said. "I suppose you are right but, it is possible Abel doesn't have the tattoo, and Maggie does."

"Ummm, have you seen a tattoo on Maggie Chuck?"

Turning a bit red, Chuck replied, "No I haven't."

"Okay, so let's assume because Abel is the oldest and a male, he is the one with the tattoo," I said.

"What about Harry Longbow?" Jimmy asked.

"I think Jim Longbow was the target because he had the tattoo. But he did write a letter to Harry, a letter which Harry suddenly had to show to his sister in Arizona."

"Something is wrong with Harry going to see his sister," Bobby said. "Harry was an only child."

"Are you sure?"

"Yes I am."

"So where did Harry go?"

"For that matter, where did Max Yellowfeather go. I got in touch with the tribal police at Fort Hall reservation. No one on the res had seen Max."

"Is it possible Max and Harry met somewhere?" Chuck asked.

"It's possible but the only way we will find out, is when we find Max and Harry. Harry is supposed to be back to work on Monday. I'm going to ask Sam Gooding to send Harry over here when he reports for work on Monday."

"If he reports," Bobby said.

"I think what we need to do, is find Max, and get him and Abel and Harry together in the same room. Perhaps if we approach them all at the same time, we can get some answers. What do you guys think?"

"Seems like a plan," Chuck said, and Jimmy and Bobby agreed.

"Okay, looks like we will have to wait till Monday. I hate to ask you guys to work tomorrow, but we still need to find Max and Harry. I think we also need to keep a close eye on Abel."

"I'll keep an eye on Abel," Chuck said. "Maggie invited me over tomorrow for an early dinner. I will just show up early."

"Okay, good. Jimmy, I want you to search around town for Max again. If you find him, don't approach him. Give me a call. Bobby, I guess you will have to search the res again."

"Okay Eric," Bobby said. "And you? What will you be doing?"

"I'm going to be looking for Max as well. I know a few more people who might know where he really went."

"I guess it's all we can do till Monday," Bobby said.

The meeting broke up and I headed over to Doc McAddams. I knew what the tattoo looked like, but I wanted to see for myself. Plus, I felt like I should be doing something. As I drove over, the only thing I could think about was there were four people murdered. I didn't want there to be a fifth.

CHAPTER 51

Saturday 11:30 pm

Halfway up a small mountain on the Wind River res, there was a small cleft in the rock. It couldn't be seen from the ground, with small trees and brush hiding the opening. But if you climbed up and looked carefully, the opening could be seen. If you squeezed through the small opening, you would find a cave. The cave opened into a room the size of a small living room. On the walls were ancient paintings, depicting birds and animals. Paintings of Shoshone in hunting parties, hunting buffalos on the open plains. Near the back there were two more openings. One going right and the other left. Both of these additional rooms were small, just big enough for one or two people. There weren't too many who knew about the cave. But Abel Bright Star and Max Yellowfeather did. They had discovered the cave when they were very young. Two cousins exploring.

This night the cave was not empty, there was a small fire burning in the center of the room. There were packs on the floor which the two men had brought with them. They sat around the fire to discuss the murders and what they needed to do. They stared into the fire, looking for answers. Unfortunately, neither of them saw any answers to their problems.

"I remember coming here as children," Abel said.

"I do too cousin," Max Yellowfeather said.

"What shall we do?"

"It is obvious someone knows about the gifts."

"Yes and somehow has discovered the names of everyone who holds the gifts," Abel Bright Star said. "But how cousin?"

"I don't know, but we must face facts. Someone is killing us for the gifts."

"It is ridiculous for someone to think the gifts actually have some power. It is just an old legend, handed down through the ages."

"I agree but, stranger things have happened. But what are we to do? We do not know how many gifts there are, and we don't know who else might have them."

"True, so do you have a plan?"

"I have thought long and hard on just that cousin. I think we must go to Bobby Black Bear and to Sergeant Logan. Together."

"Are you sure? How will they be able to help? They know nothing of the gifts. They will be just as helpless as we are."

Max Yellowfeather took a deep breath. Then he said, "I trust Logan. He has been a decent man many times in the past with me. And I trust Bobby Black Bear. He is a good man, a good Shoshone. I do not believe we have another choice."

Abel stood and walked around. After a few minutes, he sat back down.

"I am not sure if going to them is the right path, but I must also think about my sister. If this killer were to come for me and she got in the way, I am sure he would kill her too. So, I agree cousin. When do we go see them?"

"We will go Monday morning at 9:00. I will get word to Bobby to be there. I am sure he could not refuse."

"Will you tell him we are both going to meet with them?"

"No, I will only say it will be me. This way they will not think you are involved. But once we both show up, it will be clear to them. But do not worry, it is the best plan. Once I get in touch with Bobby, he will then call Logan. They will both be at the Eagle Police Headquarters. One more thing Abel."

"Yes?"

"Bring the gift with you."

"It is with me always as is yours. Can we reveal it to these two? Maybe to Bobby because he is Shoshone. But Logan is a white man."

"Yes, he is a white man, but we must be honest with them if we are to stop these killings. Remember, we have no idea how many more hold the gift. We must do everything we can to stop the killings. Besides, the gifts hold no power."

"I hope you are right cousin. We will meet on Monday. Till then, where will you be?"

"I will stay here. I have food and water. But you must be very careful. Someone is hunting us and so far he has succeeded. I do not want to see you die."

"Nor do I want to see you die. Stay safe cousin."

"You too, cousin, stay safe."

CHAPTER 52

Sunday 1:20 am

Nihoono biitooeeihii paced around his apartment. He had been in a very good mood after getting the gift from Lewis Deep Water. He had gotten the better of the big man and everything had gone smoothly. It was more confirmation he was the one who should have all the gifts, he was the one who deserved the power. But now, his mood had changed.

Nihoono biitooeeihii still had more gifts to attain, but they would be difficult to get. He had searched for Max Yellowfeather for the past week. He couldn't find him, and he was very disturbed he was gone. Did he know someone was searching for the gifts? He couldn't have known who else had them. The parchment was clear. The only one to know everyone who held the gifts was the one with the parchment. A shaman. When the parchment was handed down, that person would again be the only one to know. He would add the names of the person to accept the gift, the next in a long line to safeguard it. So, could Yellowfeather know?

He didn't think so. But then why was Yellowfeather nowhere to be seen. *Nihoono biitooeeihii* thought Yellowfeather was either on the res, or at one of several bars in Eagle. *Nihoono biitooeeihii* had looked for him everywhere on the res and in town, but to no avail. Yellowfeather had disappeared. If he couldn't find him, his plans would have been for nothing!

He picked up a glass he had been drinking from and hurled it against the wall. It shattered, with pieces flying everywhere. He had to find him!

Taking a few deep breaths, he began to calm down. In the meantime, there still was another he could get the gift from. Again, it would be difficult. Even more so since the white detective started dating his sister, Maggie Bright Star. He didn't want to deal with both him and her, but he might have to. Killing a detective and Maggie Bright Star was not in his plans. Still, he would do whatever was necessary.

He began to clean up the shards of glass and while doing so began to formulate a plan in his head. It would have to be carried out carefully. He could do it; he knew. Afterall, hadn't he gotten five gifts? Didn't he pull off all of the murders without leaving a single clue? He was too smart for Bobby Black Bear and Eric Logan. Much smarter than the two of them combined. And they had no clue who he was.

Once he found Max Yellowfeather and gotten the gift from him, he would have the power. He knew it in his heart. It had to be. He was chosen and he would not fail.

CHAPTER 53

Chuck was sitting in Abel and Maggie's apartment, staring at Abel who was staring right back at him. Chuck was glad Abel was there because it made it easier to keep an eye on him. But ever since entering the apartment, Abel kept staring at him and then looking away. Chuck thought Abel wanted to say something. But what, Chuck had no idea.

"So Abel, how goes work at the lumberyard?" Chuck asked.

"It goes well," was the short reply.

"Ummm, Maggie and I are getting along well. I hope that makes you happy."

"It is good."

Geez, Chuck thought, it would be easier getting words from a mute.

Just then Maggie came out and told them the food was ready. Both men stood and went into the small dining room. Chuck waited for Abel to sit because he didn't want to take his regular chair. In fact, he didn't want to give Abel any reason to dislike him more.

On the table were plates with steaks, potatoes, corn on the cob and some biscuits.

"Looks great honey," Chuck said, which earned him a mean look from Abel. "I mean, looks delicious Maggie."

Looking her brother in the eye, Maggie replied, "I'm glad you like it...lover."

Chuck was too afraid to look at Abel after her remark. Instead he said, "Umm, why don't you serve yourself first."

"A guest is always served first," Maggie said. "Isn't that right brother?"

"Yes," was all Abel said.

Chuck helped himself to a bit of everything. Then Abel took some food, and finally Maggie.

After taking a bite of the steak, Chuck said, "Wow, this is delicious!"

"Thank you, Chuck," Maggie said.

Chuck was happy she had used his name this time. Abel was eating with his head down, obviously not interested in conducting any conversation.

"I heard Lewis Deep Water was killed out at Tranquility Lake," Maggie said.

Abel stopped with his fork halfway to his lips and looked very angry. Then he put a piece of meat in his mouth and silently continued to eat.

"Yes he was," Chuck said. "Sergeant Logan was fishing nearby with his boys and saw him. He wasn't sure who it was or if anything was wrong, so he drove over and found him."

"I hope Ben and Bear didn't see anything."

"They didn't."

"Bear?" Abel said. "Sergeant Logan named one of his sons Bear?"

"His name is really David, but at a young age he would walk around the house, growling like a bear. The name stuck."

"I see. Are you any closer to catching the man or woman murdering my people?"

"Well, it's an ongoing investigation so I can't really discuss the details. We are pretty certain it must be a man. We don't think a woman would have been able to overpower Lewis Deep Water. But I have worked several homi-cides with Sgt. Logan. No one is better at catching killers. I think it won't be too long till the murderer is caught."

"I understand."

"Well, I for one will be happy when this whole thing is closed and whoever is put away," Maggie said. "We Shoshone have enough troubles without someone killing us off, one by one."

"Let's talk about something else," Chuck said. "How are things going at your shop Maggie?"

They continued to eat and talk, but through the entire meal, Chuck couldn't help but wonder what Abel was thinking. He obviously had something on his mind. Chuck hoped it had nothing to do with him continuing to see Maggie. Abel never looked happy when he saw him, and Chuck was beginning to be annoyed by it. He under-stood he was only looking out for his little sister, but she was a grown woman, able to make her own decisions. If Abel continued to treat Chuck like an unwanted guest, he decided he would have a man to man talk with him.

During his time with Abel, he tried to see if he had a tattoo. But because it was so small and Abel could have it under his clothing, Chuck couldn't see one.

After dinner, Chuck wanted to take Maggie for some ice cream, but he had to keep an eye on Abel. He set-tled for some pie she had and then the three of them sat and put on a classic movie Maggie loved. Chuck liked it too and was interested to see if Abel would even break a smile during it. Anyone who could sit through Young Frankenstein and not laugh, just wasn't human.

CHAPTER 54

I had spent most of the day trying to locate Max Yellowfeather. No one seemed to know where he was, or if he was even in town. Bobby had called and told me he wasn't on the res. There was nothing to do but keep looking for him on Monday. At least Harry would be coming in early Monday morning. Well he would be if he reported to work. I believed whatever his father had written to him was important. It might just crack the case wide open. I had decided I wasn't going to use kid gloves on him anymore. He would either hand over the letter or tell me what was written in it. If not, I would lock him up for obstruction in a homicide case. The charge wouldn't stick, but maybe it would get him to give me the letter.

The evening was spent playing scrabble with the boys, and as usual, Bell won. She had put the game out of reach with a triple word score with *quizzes*. Even using a blank for the second Z didn't hurt her score any. Ben came in second with Bear and me coming in a very distant last.

Now the boys were in bed, excited for the last day of school. Summer was upon us and both boys had talked all night about their plans. They were both also excited about Paul, Caroline and their girls coming out soon. To be honest, I was wishing they could come earlier than planned. Maybe Paul would be able to help on the homicide investigation.

I got into bed, waiting for Bell to finish in the bathroom.

"What are your plans for tomorrow Eric," she called out.

"I have Harry Longbow coming in," I answered. "I hope I can get him to hand over a letter his father had written him before he was killed."

"Do you think it says something about why these killings are taking place?"

"I do. Besides, even if the letter has nothing to do with Jim Longbow's death, I have to find out. Other than that, I have to still find Max Yellowfeather, and I want to bring Abel Bright Star in for questioning as well."

Slipping into the bed, Bell said, "You don't think he has anything to do with the murders, do you?"

"I don't think he is the killer, actually the opposite. Abel and Maggie's home had been burglarized and he acted very suspicious about it. Also, Max Yellowfeather is a cousin of theirs and he came to me about their burglary. He was very mysterious about the whole thing. I think the only way to solve these killings is to get either Harry, Max, or Abel to speak."

"Well I hope they will, and you can catch this maniac."

"So far, whoever is doing these killings has been especially careful. He has not left any DNA, or fibers or anything we can use to identify him. Plus, whatever he is after is still a mystery. I wish I knew what the victims had been hiding. I also think Abel and Max may be hiding something as well. I also had an idea about who our killer might be, but for now it is just a hunch. I will discuss it with Chuck and Jimmy tomorrow. Maybe talk to Bobby about it as well. But enough about the case. What's new in the world of politics?"

"The backers hired someone from Denver to come up and run my campaign."

"Oh, and who might that be?"

"Did you ever hear of James Breckenridge?"

"Wasn't he the guy who ran the governor's campaign in Colorado several years ago?"

"Actually, it was closer to fifteen years ago. And for some reason, he agreed to run mine."

"Pretty amazing, but not to be a wet blanket, why would Breckenridge agree to run a City Council campaign? I'm surprised he isn't retired or dead. If I remember him clearly, he was pretty old when he ran that campaign."

"He was a bit old back then, and he did retire from running any campaigns. But he is also a very close friend of Teresa Benton's. She asked him for help, and he agreed. Isn't it great?"

"Sure is. Looks like you are going to be the next City Councilwoman. And I couldn't be prouder!"

"He came up with a slogan for me."

"So fast? Okay, lay it on me."

"It is, 'You CAN handle the truth, and Belinda Logan will always tell you it.' What do you think?"

"I like it."

"Not too corny?"

"Nah."

"He also came up with, ' Belinda Logan is a BELL which always rings true'."

"I think I like that one even more. I can't wait to see them on posters all over town."

"It's getting exciting. I just hope Graham Stone doesn't run a dirty campaign. It's what he has done in the past."

"Don't worry about it honey. There is nothing he can sling at you. Have you heard anything from Stone since you announced you were running against him?"

"He actually sent over to my temporary headquarters at the paper, a bouquet of flowers with a note saying good luck."

"Seems like a nice gesture."

"Yeah, but when I turned the note over it said, you're gonna need it!"

"Ummm, yeah I guess not so nice. But I wouldn't concern myself with Stone. You will have many people wanting you to win, and an honest campaign will carry the day. I'm sure of it. Now, how about coming over here and let me hold you."

"Hold me? I can think of something much better than that."

Then, the phone rang, and I thought our night would be ruined. I silently prayed no one else had been killed. In fact it was just the opposite.

"Hello," I said into the phone.

"Sorry to call so late Eric," Bobby Black Bear said. "But I just got word through a third party. Max Yellowfeather is back in town, and he wants to meet with you and me at your office, first thing tomorrow morning."

"Terrific! Maybe we can finally find out what is going on. I have Harry Longbow coming in as well if he shows up for work."

"Okay, Max said he will be there at nine, so I suggest we meet a bit earlier. I will be there about 8:00. See you then."

"See you then Bobby and thank you."

"What's going on?" Bell asked.

"We finally may have gotten a break. Max Yellowfeather is back in town and wants to meet. With him and Harry coming in, we might be able to get a break on the case. I wonder if I should get Abel Bright Star to come in as well. Maybe I should call Chuck and have him suggest for him to join us as well?"

"I think you should forget about the case for now."

"Okay lover, as usual you are right. Now, what did you say about something better than a hug?"

Bell gave me a mischievous smile and began to show me what was better than a hug. She was absolutely right, again.

CHAPTER 55

I was looking forward to finally questioning both Harry and Max this morning. One or both must know something. Whatever they knew I was determined to find out. Bobby, Chuck, Jimmy, and I were sitting in the conference room, talking over our strategy.

"Maybe it would be better for Jimmy and me to not be in the meeting Eric," Chuck said. "They might not be so willing to talk in front of us. Max knows you better and I'm sure Harry wouldn't want us there."

"You might be right Chuck," I said, "but I'm tired of skirting around them with kid gloves. They are going to talk, one way or another. If I have to lock them both up on a charge of conspiracy, I will."

"Let us hope it will not come to locking them up Eric," Bobby said. "After all, it was Max who called me and asked for this meeting. He obviously wants to talk about something. I suggest we let him have his say. If he withholds anything or we think he is playing us for whatever reason, then it will be time to as you say, take off the kid gloves."

"Okay Bobby. But it has gone far enough. He and Harry will talk to us."

Jimmy asked, "What about Abel Bright Star? Is he still being covered by someone?"

"I had Mike Kowalski stay in plain clothes this morning. He should be outside Abel's apartment right now. He will shadow him all the way to work. Then he will pick him up again at lunch if he leaves the lumberyard."

"What about Maggie Eric?" Chuck asked. "She might be in danger as well."

"I have one of our female officers, Gloria Vance following her when she heads to work. She will shop around the mall, keeping an eye on her. No worries Chuck."

"Thanks Eric. So what time is Max supposed to come in?"

"He told me at nine, but Max is not very reliable when it comes to being on time," Bobby said.

We sat around eating some donuts and coffee, trying to come up with anything new. We discussed the entire case from beginning to end, and knew we were stuck. We needed some new information and hopefully, Max or Harry's letter would bring the necessary spark to get moving again. I hadn't discussed my hunch with Chuck or Bobby yet. After our meeting, I figured it might make more sense. I would tell them it, even though I thought I might be way off base.

Just then Mike Kowalski opened the conference room door.

"Aren't you supposed to be following Abel?" I asked.

"I did," he answered. "He is waiting in the lobby. He said he will speak with you, but not until his cousin arrives."

"I guess we will have all three here at the same time," Bobby said. "Do we want to separate them or talk with all three, if Harry shows, together?"

"I think we keep them together," I said. "Them seeing Harry here as well, might have an effect on Max or Abel. Maybe not but we can try. If no one speaks we will separate them all. Bobby will talk with Harry, Chuck and

Jimmy to Abel, and I will take on Max. How does that sound to you guys?"

"Sounds like a plan Eric," Chuck said, "but I have a feeling it won't be necessary. Yesterday, Abel looked as if he wanted to say something to me. He kept on starting to speak and then he would be quiet again. Plus, I don't think Max would have set up this meeting if he didn't want to talk."

"Let's hope you are right," I said. "Mike, could you check if Max or Harry have shown up yet?"

"Sure thing Sarge," Mike said and went to check.

A few minutes later, Mike came back in with a small grin on his face.

"What's up Mike?"

"They are all here, sitting and staring at each other," Mike said. "I'm not sure if they are going to be friendly or there will be war, but they must have something on their minds. Good luck to you Sarge."

"Thanks Mike, "I said. "How about bringing them all in for me? Well guys, this is going to be interesting."

CHAPTER 56

Monday 9:15 am

Max, Abel, and Harry entered the room and took seats opposite Chuck, Jimmy, Bobby, and me. At first it looked as if their faces had been carved from stone. None of them said anything at all. They just took their seats and sat there staring across the table. They were offered drinks and food, but they all shook their heads no. Well, we weren't going to get anywhere like this.

"*Behne*," I said to them, and Bobby did the same. Chuck and Jimmy just nodded.

Grudgingly, Max and Abel said, *Behne* back to us and Harry said good morning. Well, at least they said something.

"Max, I'm glad to see you," I began. "I'm also glad Abel and Harry are here too. As you well know, there have been four murders, here in town, and on the res. All the victims have been Shoshone. They all appeared to be hiding something valuable to someone. What that was, we don't know. We also know each victim had a tattoo. The same tattoo on all of them."

"You have discovered much," Max said.

"A tattoo?" Harry said. "What kind of tattoo? I don't think my father had one."

"It is extremely small Harry," Bobby said. "All of the victims had one. It appears to be a shooting star possibly."

"It is a meteor," Max said.

"Okay," I said. "A meteor. My first question is, do any of you have a tattoo of a meteor on you? And was it done by Painter Chief?"

Max stood and turned around. Then he lifted his shirt and pointed to the small of his back. There, we all saw the same tattoo which was on all the victims. Then he motioned to Abel, and he too stood. Lifting his foot onto a chair, he removed his shoe and sock. On the back of his heel was the tattoo.

"Don't look at me," Harry said. "I don't have any tattoos."

"Maybe Max or Abel can tell us what those tattoos stand for," I said. "Unless something in your father's letter Harry, has explained it. Which of you wishes to go first?"

Harry said, "The letter my father left me was about an ancient legend. About a meteor falling on the res. He mentioned there was something of great power I was to dig up. There was a small map and directions where to find this object. But I suppose, whatever it was had been discovered by the killer. He didn't write anything else, except I wasn't to talk about it with anyone. I was supposed to safeguard it and then before my death, I was to pass it down to my son or daughter if necessary. I guess I never got the chance. But none of it makes any sense to me."

"Where did you go Harry?" I asked. "We know you have no sister."

"The death of my father and the letter he left for me had me questioning my choices. I left the way of my people, and I now wasn't sure I had made the right decision. I needed to be away, to think. I went away where no one knew me."

"And have you made a decision?" Bobby asked.

"I still have much to think about."

Max looked to Abel, nodded, and then stood. He opened his shirt and removed what appeared to be a grayish stone, on a leather strap, from around his neck. Abel stood and reached to his waist. Then he removed another stone, looking very much like the first one. They placed them on the table before me, and then sat back down.

"Are you telling me, someone has been killing people for these...stones?" I said. "Do they have something inside of them? Maybe gems or diamonds? What makes them so valuable that four people have been killed?"

"I will tell you all, but you must promise never to say anything to anyone else about the legend," Max stated. "It has been kept a secret for over four hundred years. Do you all agree?"

"We agree Max," I said, and everyone nodded in agreement. Finally, we were going to find out the reason behind the killings.

Max looked to Abel, who nodded. Then he began his story.

"Four hundred years ago two young Shoshone witnessed a meteor falling from the night sky. Their names would mean nothing to you, but Sarah Tall Tree was a direct relative of one of them. The meteor hit our sacred mountain about halfway up. The boys knew they were forbidden to climb the mountain, but being young, curious and a little stupid, that is what they did.

They climbed up and finally found where the meteor had crashed. It wasn't very big, possibly the size of a softball. But it was very hot. So the boys formed a cradle made of leaves and branches and carried it down to their village. They presented it to their Chief.

Before a decision could be made, one of the boys touched the meteorite. He immediately fell backwards, his eyes rolling into his head, unconscious."

"And you believe it was the touching of the mete-orite which made the boy unconscious?" Chuck asked.

"I am not sure what I believe Chuck," Max said. "I only know what the legend tells me."

"Please continue Max," I said.

"The boy recovered, but before the Chief and his shaman could decide as to what to do with it, it was taken. The boy who touched it had to have it for himself. He managed to put it into a leather pouch and placed it on his shoulder. He stole it but before he could get away, he was followed by the boy who had first found it with him. The boy carrying the meteorite ran and ended up by the cliffs. When he tried to climb down, he slipped and fell to his death. But the strap of the small pouch he had the mete-orite in, got caught on a stone. It was recovered and brought back to the Chief."

"Okay, so what did they decide to do with it?" Jimmy asked.

"I'm guessing they broke it into pieces," I said.

"Yes they did," Max said, "but not before the shaman had held it. The shaman had fallen to the floor, in convulsions. When he finally was calm again, he told the Chief it must never be allowed to be possessed by any one person. There was great power in it."

"But you have worn it around your neck Max," Bobby said. "And you too Abel. So why are you both not affected by its power?"

"The shaman told the Chief the power will be gone if it were broken up. The separate stones would hold no power. But if all the pieces were brought together again, it would have the power again."

"So, whoever has been killing people and collecting the stones, thinks if he gets all the pieces and brings them together, he will have some kind of power. Right?"

"Yes, at least he believes it, "Max said.

"This is crazy!" Harry said. "Ancient legends from people who were afraid of their own shadows. Afraid of the gods and omens they think they saw. They had no idea what a meteorite even was. They probably thought one of their gods had sent it to them as a..a..kind of gift!"

"Yes Longbow," Max said. "You are not wrong but if you honored your father and his beliefs, you would be in possession of one of these gifts right now."

"That may or not be true," I said as Harry began to stand, anger in his eyes. "You cannot know if Harry ever would have been given the stone, and if he had, he might have been one of the victims. It is not important Max."

"You are right Eric," Max said, and apologized to Harry in his native tongue. I thought Harry wouldn't accept it, but then he said something back to Max in the Shoshone language as well. Whatever he said made Bobby smile. I would have to ask him later.

"Okay," Chuck said, "we now know what the killer is after, and two of the people who still have it. But how many others have this so called gift?"

"We do not know," Abel said. "In order to protect the stones and the people holding it, none of us know how many pieces there were and who has them. There might be many more or it's possible we are the last."

"But someone must have known?" I said. "There must have been someone who kept a kind of record. Who would that be?"

"I think it would have been a shaman, Eric," Bobby said, "and an elder. There are three shamans in the Shoshone nation right now. One is Dark River; one is Red

Cloud and the last is no longer with us. He has passed."

"Who would that be?"

"It was Walks in Wind."

"I wonder if Walks in Wind didn't die a natural death. And if he didn't, it might be possible our killer found not only a stone, but something which has led him to all the other victims."

"I will get in touch with Walks in Wind's son. He might know something. But I think we should go with your theory. Someone got a list or the story of the gift from Walks in Wind."

"But, how could the killer have even known about Walks in Wind having a stone and a list of the others?" Jimmy asked.

"A good question Jimmy," I said. "Okay, for now we at least know of two who have the stones. Both of you must leave the stones with..."

"No," Max said.

"No, we will not," Abel stated. "The stones must stay with us."

"We will be very careful Eric, but we will not give up the stones."

"I think you are both being a bit foolish, but we will honor your wishes," I said. "But from now on, until we catch the killer, you both will be under police protection. And don't worry, they will be very discreet. In fact, maybe Bobby can have two Shoshone police officers watching you both."

"I can spare one man but not two Eric," Bobby said.

"Then one of the officers will be one of my men. I think Abel can be watched by Chuck. With him dating your sister Abel, it wouldn't look too strange for him to be seen around you."

"I suppose it will be okay," Abel said, staring at Chuck.

"And I can get Daniel Red Shirt to watch over you Max," Bobby said.

"An Arapahoe Bobby?" Max asked.

"Yes Max, but a good officer."

"As you wish. Is there anything else?"

"No but I want you both to be alert to anyone who looks suspicious," I said. "Remember, so far our killer has killed four and possibly five Shoshone. Which means he is smart, careful, and probably very strong as well. Lewis Deep Water would not have been an easy target."

"We will stay alert."

"Also, no more disappearing. You too Harry. You might not have a stone, but the killer might be after you if he knew about the letter your father left. In fact, I will put Jimmy on you for your protection. Now, all of you can go. Don't suddenly change your routines but stay alert. And Max?"

"Yes?"

"No getting drunk."

"Hmmm, I suppose I can stay sober for a while. A short while in any case."

"Jimmy and Chuck will be with you two soon at the lumberyard. There are still some things we need to discuss. Max, where will you be?"

"I will be at my home on the res Eric. Thank you for all you are doing. I will pray to my gods for your success. *Abisha'i.*"

Abel said *Abisha'i* as well and Harry said goodbye. Then they left.

"Okay guys, we have a lot to discuss and then Chuck and Jimmy will begin to shadow Abel and Harry," I said.

I thought about all we had heard, and I was surer than ever about my hunch. Maybe after I discussed it with everyone, we would have a better chance of stopping the murders and catching our killer. I truly hoped so.

After Max, Abel and Harry had left, I asked Bobby what Max and Harry had said to each other.

Bobby smiled and then said, "Max had told Harry whether he followed the way of the Shoshone, he was still a brother to him."

"And what did Harry reply?"

"Well, Harry said Max was right, and in front of white devils they should be united."

"White devils!" Chuck said.

"It is just an expression Chuck, and one you might hear again seeing how you are with a Shoshone woman."

"Well then you better tell me how to say it in Shoshone so I will know whether or not who I might need to beat up!"

Laughing, Bobby said he would write it down.

"Okay guys let's put our heads together and figure out our next move," I said.

CHAPTER 57

Our meeting lasted a few more hours and then finally broke up. Chuck and Jimmy headed to the lumberyard to watch over Abel and Harry. Bobby went back to the res to assign Danny Red Shirt to watch over Max. He would also track down Walks in Wind's son, Matt Jones. If he couldn't find him on the res, I would locate him here in town.

We had kicked around my hunch for a while, and even though they all agreed it was a good possibility, there was no way to be sure. Bobby had not agreed with it for now. Still, I had decided I was right. But they were right about one thing, it didn't really help us, at least not right now.

We had coverage on Max, Harry, and Abel, as well as on Maggie Bright Star for now. But we couldn't keep a watch on them for very long. There were still cases which needed to be looked at, and both Bobby and I didn't have the resources for 24 hour coverage. We could only keep an eye on all of them during the day. The nights would leave them unprotected, but at least they would be more vigilant.

There were only three ways we were going to catch the killer. The first was if he tried anything while we had protection around them. That to me was doubtful. I didn't think whoever the killer was, he would want to kill a police officer, especially if my hunch was right. So far the killer had been very careful and smart, and I didn't think he would make a mistake now.

The second way would be to set up some kind of a trap. But setting one up would be difficult. We would need one of our gift holders to go along with it. Plus we would need a secure location. But hardest of all, would be getting the information to our killer. It would have to be done where he wouldn't suspect a trap. Plus, how do we get it to him in particular? We didn't know who he was.

Finally, the third way was just plain dumb luck. There were plenty of cases solved in that way, but I couldn't rely on it happening.

I racked my brain for a few more hours and then headed home. I knew Bell had planned a very busy day with her new campaign manager. I sent her a text and told her I would pick up some Chinese food for dinner. This way she wouldn't need to cook. Her reply was for me and the boys not to wait for her. She might be a bit late.

Oh well, I thought, I better get used to some dinners without her. If she got elected, there would be plenty of missed dinners. But I couldn't blame her and besides, I had missed more than my share of dinners, parties, and school events. I shut down my computer and lights and headed for the parking lot.

As I was about to get into my car, Liz Butler sashayed up to me. She was wearing a skirt which barely covered her backside and a blouse with a deep neckline, showing off her natural assets. With everything she had been through, she still was a very good-looking woman. How she was walking in what looked like six inch heels was beyond me. I sure hoped she wasn't about to make an indecent proposal to me.

"Evening Liz," I said.

"Hi handsome," was her reply.

"What can I do for you Liz?"

"Well, I know last week you and some of your men were looking for Max."

"He showed up today Liz but thank you."

"I haven't said anything yet to thank me Eric," she said and huffed.

"Sorry Liz. What did you want to talk with me about?"

"Well, besides you there were several other people who had been looking for Max."

"Like who?" I asked, knowing Chuck, Jimmy, and Bobby had been looking for him. But I didn't want to offend Liz again.

"Well, let me think...."

I reached into my pocket and pulled out a twenty. Even though I didn't believe anything Liz was going to tell me would be informative, I knew there were times when she did have good information. Plus, I didn't mind helping Liz out every once in a while. Twenty bucks was worth it.

"Thank you sweetie," Liz said and actually batted her eyes. "Now let me think. There was your partner, Chuck whatshisname. And that young detective, ummm..."

"Jimmy?"

"Yeah. Jimmy. Now he's someone I might do for free."

"Ummm, go on Liz."

"There was also the tribal police guy."

"Bobby Black Bear Liz. Thanks. I have to go now."

"Well, he was one of them, but there was someone else from the reservation too."

"A Shoshone or an Arapahoe?"

"C'mon handsome. How the hell would I know?"

I thought about that and decided I would have to ask Bobby if he had asked anyone else to look for Max, or if he knew of any other Shoshone searching..

"Okay Liz, what was his name?" I asked.

"Would it be worth another twenty?" she coyly asked.

Sighing, I reached for another twenty.

"The name first Liz," I said, holding the bill in my hand.

"Better I whisper it to you sweetie."

Liz moved closer and I was almost overwhelmed by her perfume. I leaned over and she pressed her lips to my ear.

"Now let me think. It was something like ran, or can? No maybe something like that, I think. Or it might have been Carl. No, maybe Sam. I'm not sure but I still think I helped. How about the other twenty?"

I handed her the other twenty and she leaned in to give me a kiss. I politely backed off and she sashayed away, the same way she had approached me. She glanced over her shoulder and gave me a wink.

Now I had a lot to think about. Liz had been somewhat of help but not enough to break open the case. Still, I had more than I had a few moments ago. I would give it the night, and then I would get in touch with Bobby in the morning. I didn't think anything would happen tonight and wanted to mull over what Liz had just revealed.

I got into my car, went to the local Chinese takeout, getting eggrolls, spareribs, lo mein, General Tso's chicken and some spicy garlic beef. And a few fortune cookies for the boys. I then drove home. I was so consumed with thinking about what Liz had said, I couldn't remember doing anything once I drove away from the station, but I arrived at the house without driving off the mountain.

I set up dinner, called down the boys and we ate together. Then they headed out to some friends till about nine. Since I was alone in the house, I got myself a beer and sat outside on the patio. I had a terrific view from here of the town, the mountains, and the sky. I stared at the twinkling stars for a few minutes, imagining a meteor falling through the sky. Then I set my mind to thinking about how I could use the new information from Liz. It was going to be a long night.

CHAPTER 58

Monday 10:30 pm

I was still sitting outside, with three empty beers on the floor when Bell finally came home. She grabbed a beer from the fridge and sat down heavily next to me.

"Long day baby?" I asked.

"Sure was," she replied, "but exciting too. Are the boys in bed?"

"They should be. They were over by the Andrews boy's house most of the evening. Then they got home about an hour ago and headed upstairs. They might still be up if you want to say goodnight."

"I think I'm too pooped to get up right now."

"I think they will understand. They're not babies anymore."

"No, they aren't. I'm sorry I got home so late."

"Don't give it another thought. How many dinners and other events have I missed because of work. It's your time to take a shot at something you want, and something important. So what did you discuss?"

"Everyone was there, including James Breckenridge. We went over some of my opening speech for this weekend at the local fair. We also tried to nail down some of the things I want to accomplish."

"Sounds like a great start. Are any of your backers giving you a hard time?"

"Actually, once we started to discuss our plans, they realized they wanted the same things which I did. They were really behind me on most things."

"Most?"

"Well, Cummings and Trask were against one thing I was adamant about."

"And what would that be?"

"A new police building. And before you say anything, I don't want one just because I am married to the best detective in town."

"Hmmm, are you sure?"

"I know how cramped your department is. Plus, I think all of us agreed we need to hire at least twenty more officers in the next two years. So, you need the room, and I am going to fight for it."

"Well, I do agree with you on everything you just said. Especially the part of being the best detective."

"Oh really? That was the one thing I might have exaggerated about!"

We sat outside for about another hour and then we both went inside to bed. We were both too exhausted to do anything but sleep. Bell was fast asleep within minutes, but my mind wouldn't stop thinking about who Liz had told me about. Sometime in the night I finally drifted off and had some wild dreams about meteors, and tattoos and a killer who I thought we were getting closer to.

CHAPTER 59

Tuesday 1:30 am

There was someone else who wasn't sleeping. *Nihoono biitooeeihii* paced around his apartment, trying to come up with a solution to his problem. Now that the last two Shoshone who possessed the gifts were being guarded, there was no way he could figure out how to get the gifts from them. He knew if he killed any of the police officers guarding them, he would be hunted down. Cops didn't like other cops being killed.

He thought up several scenarios and just as quickly dismissed them.

Maybe I could incapacitate an officer, he thought. This way I could get the gift and not kill a cop. But no, how could I get an officer incapacitated while either Max or Abel were around? It would be likely I would be caught or forced to kill them both. No way will that work.

Nihoono biitooeeihii slammed his fist into the wall, cracking the cheap plaster board. He didn't even notice the cut on his hand and the blood dripping from his fingers. He continued to pace long into the night. By the time the sun began to rise, he had no idea what he was going to do. He decided he would just have to wait for the right opportunity to show itself. Until then, he would have to bide his time.

He jumped into the shower to wake himself up. He had stayed up all night without realizing it. He was so close. He had five of the gifts and they were tucked away under his floor. The parchment was there as well. Before he began his day, he took them all from the hidden spot. Holding the stones, he thought he could almost feel their power and he knew when they were all together, they would once again form one stone, filled with unimaginable power. Holding the stones renewed his desire to get the last two gifts, no matter what it took. If nothing happened to allow him to work out how to get the gifts, he would take drastic measures. Even if it meant killing one, two or every police officer on the res and in town!

CHAPTER 60

Nothing had happened all week with the case. No new murders and we were still no closer to figuring out what to do next. There had been other crimes, and I had to pull Chuck and Jimmy off guard duty. Two people had robbed a convenience store, and for some reason, had killed the cashier. He was a boy I knew, only eighteen years old with his first summer job. It became a priority with the Chief, and I didn't disagree.

I had gotten two uniform officers to watch over Abel and Harry at the lumberyard. Bobby had also had a bit of a crime wave on the res. Two men had gotten into a fight and had drawn knives. One was Arapahoe and the other Shoshone. They had both been drunk, which was a good thing. Neither of them was able to cut the other and after a short while, they had given up the fight. Unfortunately, they had both gone into hiding and Bobby needed to find them before they sobered up and tried again.

Then he had two young native girls go missing as well. It was a sad thing, but native women going missing was not very unusual. Bobby had been angry about it and had pulled all of his men to search. Max was told he wouldn't have any protection, and he said he wasn't worried. He told Bobby he was going to go to a secret place, somewhere only Abel knew about. Bobby wasn't thrilled with his decision, but figured there was nothing he could do about it.

Earlier in the week I had met with Bobby out at the res. I told him about what Liz had told me. At first he wasn't sure if he knew of anyone else searching for Max. He told me he would have to give it some thought.

I had left it like that, not wanting to put more pressure on him. He had enough to go around at the moment. I had decided to try and figure out who the person was that Liz had told me about, sort of. The names she said had made no sense. I did a lot of footwork all week long and now I was sitting in my office going over it.

I pulled the large whiteboard we had used earlier in the week into my office and began listing each of the killings, in order. The first one I listed was Walks in Wind. His body had been exhumed with permission from his son. Doc McAddams had done a full autopsy on him. It was not conclusive, but because of a few signs, like petechia in his eyes, Doc thought he had been strangled or smothered. He had also found some dirt in his throat. It was good enough for me. Walks in Wind was the first victim. I also thought besides one of the stones, the killer had gotten a list of who else had the stones from him. I knew being a shaman meant he would have been trusted with a list of the people who possessed the stones. It made sense.

I listed all of the other victims, the times we believed they had been killed, and the locations. I still had a thought as to who our killer might be. So then I listed where our killer, at least who I thought was our killer, had likely been at the times. It was missing several times where he had been, but he hadn't been ruled out by what I had found out. I was beginning to think of him as the murderer of at least five Shoshone.

I sat back looking at the board and stopped myself for a minute. Was I making him fit the crimes or was I making the facts conclude he was the killer. It was never a good thing to get tunnel vision. To forget about anything else but what fit one person. I didn't have what added up to proof positive at all. And I reminded myself I really had no proof at all.

I was looking at the board again, trying to find one thing which truly led to the man I now thought of as our killer. As I sat there, the phone rang.

"Hello," I said, "Sergeant Logan here."

"Hello Eric, it's Bobby."

"Anything new with the missing girls?"

"Not yet, and as is often the case, I don't know if I will ever find them. They may be two more girls lost to their families."

"I'm sorry Bobby. Look, if you need anything from me or my department, just ask."

"Well, maybe you could spread around some flyers in town and pass them out to your men. I can supply as many as you want."

"Absolutely, send me over two hundred and I will personally see they get put up around town and to my men. Anything else I can do?"

"Not about the girls for now."

"What ever happened with your two natives fighting?"

"One of them found the other and killed him. He is now sitting in my jail."

"That's too bad but at least you caught him. Have you had a chance to figure out the other thing?"

"Why I'm calling. I am not sure it is who you think, but I never asked him to look for Max, especially not in town. Now it doesn't mean he didn't go looking for Max just to help out. On his own initiative. But, I'm doubting it."

"Plus if we are right, it might explain how he is getting away with every kill without leaving anything behind. No fingerprints, no fibers or DNA."

"I agree with you Eric. So what do we do next?"

"I think we should get together with my men and Max, Abel, and Harry. It's time to set up a trap."

"I will have to get Abel to get in touch with Max. He is the only one who knows where he is. Might take a day or so."

"Okay, let's plan on getting together at my house Saturday morning. Better than at your place or my police building."

"I agree. I will let you know if we have everybody on board. Thanks again for the flyers Eric."

"No problem Bobby. Speak soon."

"One more thing Eric,"

"Yes?"

"As you are aware, the res is Federal land. Therefore crimes committed on the res sometimes means the FBI get involved. With three murders happening on the res, I have been contacted by them."

"Are they sending out a Special Agent?"

"The agent who usually is in contact with me is not available. I went over all the information with a senior agent. He has decided to not interfere with our investigation. But he wants to hear about anything new we discover."

"Sounds fine to me Bobby."

"Good. Again thank you for putting up the flyers."

I hung up and decided now that we were on the same page, what type of a trap could we lay? It was something I would have to give a lot of thought to. Afterall, a trap was only good if we could catch our killer without getting anyone else killed.

CHAPTER 61

Friday 4:30 pm

I was sitting in Chief Lewis' office, along with Chuck, Jimmy, and Will, and we were waiting on our District Attorney, Imp. As soon as he arrived, I would begin to lay out everything we knew and what we were planning to do. Bobby wanted to be here as well, but he was still looking for the two missing girls.

Imp finally arrived and we sat around a small conference table. The Chief gave me a nod, and I began.

"First I want to let you know the FBI have contacted Bobby Black Bear about the murders," I said. "He gave them all the information we have so far. They have decided to let us continue the investigation but want to be kept in the loop. We now know more about the reasons behind the killings. It might sound crazy, but apparently over four hundred years ago, a meteor struck the side of a mountain inside what is now the Wind River reservation."

"A meteor...over four hundred years ago?" the Chief asked. "What could a meteor have to do with four Shoshone being killed?"

"Their legend states the meteor had great power. It was broken up and passed down through the generations. Oh, and it's five victims now Chief."

"I didn't hear of another murder."

"Actually, the first victim, a Shoshone named Walks in Wind, was recently discovered. He was a tribal shaman, and we believe he had a piece of the meteor as well as a list of anyone else who had one. That is how our killer is picking his victims."

"Do we have the list?" Imp asked.

"I'm afraid we do not. But we do know the names of two Shoshone who have the pieces passed down to them. One is Max Yellowfeather and the other Abel Bright Star."

"Bright Star?" the Chief asked. "Isn't that the name of the young lady you are dating Detective Blackwell?"

"Ummm, yes it is Chief," Chuck said, slightly blushing, "But it isn't interfering with the investigation sir. In fact, it is helping because it gives me the opportunity to keep an eye on Abel, I mean, Mr. Bright Star."

"Hmmm, okay."

"A few days ago we received a lead on a possible suspect," I said.

"A lead from who?"

"Ummm, well Chief, from Liz Butler."

"Liz Butler! I'm not sure she is a very reliable source Sergeant."

"I understand Chief, but in the past Liz, ummm, Miss Butler has provided me, I mean the department, with good info. In any case, it is something to look into."

"I suppose you are right Sergeant. Okay, I have a meeting to get to so keep doing what you are doing. I want you to give Lieutenant Tolliver any new information as soon as you have it. That will be all."

We all stood and walked out of the Chief's office. Then Chuck and Jimmy went out to work on the convenience store robbery and murder. Will went back to his office, so Imp and I went to mine.

After sitting down, Imp said, "Sounds to me as if you aren't too sure about Liz's tip."

"Why do you say that Imp?" I asked.

"For one thing, you never mentioned what Liz had told you. To me, it means you aren't willing to give out the info...yet."

"You know something my old friend, you would've made a great detective. But you are right. She gave me a sort of a name, but nothing conclusive. We think we have a person in mind, but there isn't any proof yet. Bobby Black Bear is working on running down some things, just as I have been doing all week. Once I have something, anything to confirm, I will let you know."

"Okay Eric but remember this maniac has killed five people and has left nothing behind. No evidence at all tying him to the murders. For me to prosecute him you will either have to catch him in the act or get him to confess. One other thing."

"Yes?"

"You better stay safe. But if you happen to get yourself killed, I will take care of Bell and the kids."

I picked up a pen and through it at my oldest and longest friend.

"I bet you would!" I said. "Speaking of my wife, what do you think about her chances?"

Tossing the pen back to me, Imp said, "I think she has a better than even chance to win. She has a great campaign manager now, and all the backers are falling into line. I know this Saturday at the fair when she officially throws her hat into the ring will only be the beginning. There are a lot of people who know she will be running, but at the fair it will be official."

"Have you heard her opening speech?"

"Nope, she and Breckenridge are the only people working on it. And it is being kept secret from everyone else. Unless she shared it with you?"

"Not with me either."

"You are going to be there to support her on Saturday, aren't you?"

"I certainly plan on being there, but you know how it is. If something happens in our fair city I might miss it. What about you?"

"I wouldn't miss it for the world."

"Good, then at least either her husband, or future husband will be there!"

"Uh huh. Well, I have to go to work, which is something you better do as well. See you on Saturday, I hope."

"So long Imp."

I called Bobby and told him he would have to get Max and Abel to my home early Saturday morning. Bell was going to make her speech at the fair at about noon. I really didn't want to miss it. Bobby told me he would get on it and hopefully Abel would be able to get in touch with Max.

There wasn't much more I could do, so I picked up the pile of undone paperwork sitting on my desk. Besides my own, I had to read all the reports my detectives had written, as well as anything from patrol which had been sent to Investigations. Sighing, I began and knew I was going to be working on it till I finally went home.

CHAPTER 62

Saturday 8:00 am

Bobby had shown up at the house early, and we were waiting on Chuck, Jimmy, Abel, and Max. Bobby had told me Abel had spoken with Max, and he would be here. We decided we didn't need Harry for our plan to work.

Meanwhile, Bell was up in our bedroom, rehearsing her speech for about the hundredth time. She wouldn't let me hear it, saying she wanted it to be new when she said it later on today. As for the boys, they were full into enjoying their summer. They had taken out their bikes and gone to meet up with a bunch of their friends. All they needed to do was to be home by ten so we could all go to the fair.

I heard the doorbell and went into the house from the patio where Bobby was sitting. Opening the door, I saw Chuck and Jimmy. I was hoping Max and Abel would show up soon. I told Chuck and Jimmy to help themselves to some breakfast and coffee in the kitchen, and then to go out to the patio. I waited at the door, looking anxiously for our two other guests.

Ten minutes later, I saw Max and Abel coming up the drive in what had to be Abel's car. Max didn't own one.

They got out, and we shook hands.

"Come on in," I said, and escorted them to the kitchen. "Please take whatever you want and if you don't see something, just ask."

"Thank you Eric," Max said. "You have a very nice home. This is the first time I am here."

"I guess so Max and thank you. Let's go out to the patio."

We went outside and took seats around a fire pit I had made a few years before.

"First off," I began, "have either of you seen anything suspicious this past week?"

"Nothing," Max said, and Abel shook his head.

"Bobby and the others and I have been working out a plan to catch our killer. It hasn't been completely worked out yet, but we have the beginning of an idea. The thing is it will put both of you in some danger."

"It doesn't matter Eric," Max said. "Living in hiding is nothing I want to do for much longer. If we do not catch this person, I will come out of hiding and take my chances."

"I agree," Abel said. "Being in danger and catching this killer is fine with me. But I do not want my sister involved in any way."

"She definitely will not be involved," Bobby said.

"That is good. So, what is the plan?"

We sat and talked and tried to work out something which would place Max and Abel in as little danger as possible. There were several things that needed to be done. Once again, they both refused to give up their stones, even though I said they would be safe and protected. Max said it was a matter of honor and his oath. Abel agreed with him.

Chuck and Jimmy came up with a few good ideas and by the time we were finished, a plan had been made. At least, the beginning of a plan. We still had not decided how to spring it on our suspect without him becoming suspicious. It would still have to be resolved.

By 10:00, everyone had left. Bobby was still working on the missing girls. Jimmy was working the convenience store murder alone for today. Chuck was going to take Maggie Bright Star to the fair and then later in the day, he would meet up with Jimmy. As for Max and Abel, they wouldn't say where they were going, but Abel would keep in touch through Chuck. I was surprised because when they left, Abel had put his arm around Chuck and wished him goodbye and to stay well. I guess Abel was becoming used to the idea of Chuck dating his sister. I wondered if he would still be okay with Chuck if there was an engagement.

The boys had come home, and they were bouncing off the walls, excited about the fair. I went upstairs to Bell who I found sitting on the bed, papers in her hand.

"Are you okay?" I asked.

"Just a few jitters I suppose Eric," she replied.

"Honey, you are going to do just fine. I think you were meant to be our next councilwoman and there are plenty of other people who think the same way. Do you want to say your speech to me first?"

"Nice try buster! Let's get ready to go. I want to walk around the fair a bit before I give my speech."

"By the way, where will you be giving the speech from?"

"You wouldn't believe me if I told you. Come on, let's get going."

I wondered what Bell had meant by that, but decided I wouldn't push her. This was her big day and all I needed to do was to be with her and support her. It was going to be an amazing day.

CHAPTER 63

The fair was in full swing by the time we got there. We had looked at some exhibits, some old pictures of Eagle when it was just a small town filled with cattle ranchers and farmers. We passed an exhibit with animals which could be petted and also one with a few large bulls. After passing all of the food vendors and exhibits, we bought the boys all day passes to get on the rides. As soon as the passes were on their wrists, they had taken off as if they had been shot from a cannon.

As we walked around, we met up with Imp, Chuck, and Maggie. I was wondering where Bell was giving her speech, but at ten to noon, she went into the main arena where the rodeo would soon be starting. She had told me to go in and get a good seat. The boys showed up just in time and we all went in and found some center seats.

Before Bell began her speech, I asked Chuck if he had heard from Abel or where he and Max had gone. He replied he had no idea and neither did Maggie. I was hoping Bobby knew where they had gone but I didn't have high hopes.

I still didn't know where or when Bell would give her speech, and I kept looking around. Then a cowgirl on a huge white horse came into the ring, holding the American flag. After she made a full circle of the ring, the National Anthem was played. I was happy to see my boys and most everyone else stand and sing along. There was definitely something about growing up in Wyoming.

Once the song ended. I looked down and saw my wife walking to the center of the ring. I don't know how this had been arranged, but Bell had a huge crowd to hear her speech. I sat up and waited for her to begin.

Speaking into a mike, Bell started with a great big, " Howdy All!"

The crowd cheered back, "Howdy!"

"What a great day this is going to be! Some of you may not know me but my name is Belinda Logan, and I am running for City Councilwoman. Now I know no one wants to hear a big speech. So all I am going to say is all of you, CAN handle the truth, and I will never tell you anything but the truth! It is time for some new blood, some new ideas from our city council and I am going to be that new blood. My name is Belinda, but to all of you I am Bell. And believe me when I say, this Bell will always ring true! Thank you and let's get this rodeo started!"

The crowd erupted in applause and Bell walked off. The rodeo then got into full swing and soon Bell had found us in the stand.

"That was a great speech honey!" I said.

"It sure was," both Ben and Bear chimed in.

Maggie took her hand and said, "You are a natural Bell."

"You have my vote Bell," Imp said and kissed her on the cheek.

"I was scared to death," Bell said. "Did I look nervous out there?"

"Nah, you looked as if you were meant to give a speech before a few thousand people," I said.

"A...a few thousand?" Bell said and looked as if she were about to faint.

"Don't sweat it Bell, you were made for public office and public speaking. Now, how about we enjoy the rodeo, future councilwoman."

We watched the rodeo for about an hour, and then the boys were begging us if they could go back on the rides. We all left the main arena, and as we did Bell was stopped over and over again.

"Great speech young lady, You have my vote, Terrific," were just some of the remarks from the people we passed. By the time we stopped to get some burgers, Bell had gathered a crowd around her. I think she was amazed and embarrassed at the same time, but she gathered her nerve and spoke to the crowd.

"Hey everyone, you have made me extremely happy from all of your confidence in me," she began. "I wasn't sure if I was making the right move by running, but after today, after all of your good wishes and support, I say...full steam ahead and Graham Stone...I'm coming for you!"

The crowd let loose with a roar and then finally dispersed.

"Do you believe those people?" Bell asked.

"Looks to me like those people are sick of Graham Stone and want some change Bell, and you are it!" Imp said.

"I think if today is any indication, you are going to win Bell!" I said and meant every word.

The rest of the day was spent by Bell shaking hands and smiling the biggest smile I had ever seen on her face. The fair was great and around five, we got the kids, said goodbye to Chuck and Maggie, and Imp, and headed home.

Chuck was going to take Maggie home and then he, Jimmy and I were going to head out to the res to meet with Bobby. We had to come up with a plan to set a trap to catch our killer. I had a few ideas, but I wanted to get everyone involved in the planning. It had to be foolproof, or Max and Abel would be in danger. One thing I didn't want was another murder.

CHAPTER 64

Saturday 7:30 pm

Nihoono biitooeeihii was worried. He had been waiting all week for some kind of an opening to get the two gifts still held by others. But Max Yellowfeather and Abel Bright Star had disappeared again! There had been no opportunity to get to either of them. At least no one was guarding either of them any longer.

For the past few days, he had been devising one plan after another. But after thinking about each one, he dismissed them as being too risky. At this point the one thing he didn't want was to be caught before he had the power.

He slammed his hands down on the table in frustration, thinking, damn! How will I get the two remaining stones! He tossed things around, throwing anything and everything his hands grabbed onto.

Calming down, breathing heavily, he slowly began to pick up everything he had thrown. As he did, a thought came to him. Maggie Bright Star was the sister of Abel's, and she was also the cousin to Max Yellowfeather. She might be the perfect leverage to get the stones, from both of them. But how was he going to get to her.

Nihoono biitooeeihii sat down and began to think of how he could kidnap Maggie Bright Star. He knew she was under protection from some female cop. But that was only at the mall. Once she left work and arrived home, she was alone. Except when her boyfriend, Detective Chuck Blackwell showed up. But there was a small window when *Nihoono biitooeeihii* could get to her.

He would have to be very careful and time it all to the minute. But he could do it, he thought. I will get her and then those two with the stones will come to me! Of course, I will most likely have to kill them all. So what, he thought with a smile spreading on his face. What are three or four or however more I need to kill matter? Once I have the stones and the meteor reforms, I will have the power! I will be the One True Chief, I will be *Nihoono biitooeeihii* in more than just name!!

CHAPTER 65

We decided it would be best to meet at Bobby's home instead of the tribal police building. There were too many eyes and ears there. Chuck and I drove out together. Jimmy had caught the convenience store suspect and couldn't be with us. Before we had headed out, he had given me a quick briefing.

The suspect was a high school kid who had a bad drug habit. Even in our small town there were plenty of people on drugs, and plenty of places to get them. The kid had been strung out and had no money. So he had taken his father's gun and without much thought, had robbed the store. Unfortunately for him and the cashier, he had been forced to kill him when he had gone for a gun under the counter. Now one kid was dead and another's life ruined. It was a sad situation and one we had all seen before and would see again.

Chuck had given him a big pat on the back and told Jimmy what a great job he had done. I had agreed and after congratulating him, had headed out to Bobby's home.

Bobby had met us outside as we drove up. He indicated we should take a short walk. Not knowing where we were going, I shrugged, and Chuck and I followed.

After a few minutes' walk, we were standing at the top of a large ravine. Below us we could see movement, and after a short time and our eyes adjusting to the dark, we saw a small pack of wolves. There were about ten wolves, with a huge gray male leading the pack. He was obviously the alpha male of the pack. We looked in the direction they were heading and saw a huge bull moose with a large full rack of antlers standing by a small stream. As we watched, the pack spread out to surround the moose. I wasn't sure how they signaled to each other, but all at once they attacked. But this time, it looked as if they might have bitten off more than they could chew. The moose hadn't run but he did do some damage with his big rack of antlers. He was snorting, turning in circles, and using his big hooves to fight off the wolves. When he nearly gored the alpha male, the attack was called off. The moose bellowed and stomtped his hooves as the wolves retreated.

"Wow Bobby," Chuck said, "I've never seen anything like that!"

"I have seen it many times Chuck," Bobby replied. "Those wolves have tried before to take down this moose and each time they have failed. I come up here a lot to see if they will succeed."

"But if the moose keeps getting attacked, why doesn't he move on?" I asked.

"The moose is much as we Shoshone are. This is his home; his land and he will not be run off. He would rather die than give up his land. So he stays, and fights. Many of my people should see this and learn the lesson. But enough of my silly talk. Let's sit and discuss what we came here for."

I understood a little more how Bobby and the other Shoshone or any Native American thought. It saddened me but the reality of the situation was I could do nothing to change it.

"How goes the search for the missing girls?" I asked.

"Thankfully," Bobby replied, "the girls were found. They had wandered off the res into some mountains to smoke cigarettes and drink some wine they had found at their father's home. Then of course, they had gotten sick from both and hid out. When they finally felt better, they realized they were lost. They wandered around and were found by one of my deputies. I think they were going to be even sicker when they got home."

"At least they were found, and they were not injured," Chuck said.

"Yes, I was grateful they did not end up as so many of our girls do."

"Okay, so let's get down to coming up with a plan to trap our suspect," I said.

"I still find it hard to believe who you think our killer is."

"I know it is hard to imagine, but after checking him out, the times he could have been at the killings and his behavior as of late, I think he is the one. "

"I suppose we could still be wrong, but I agree. It would explain a great many things."

Chuck said, "Yeah like leaving the scene clean, no prints or DNA, and getting away without being seen."

"So far it has been his game, and he has been one step ahead," I said. "It's time to change all of that. We need to be ahead of him this time and we will be. Let's figure out how to trap him."

We sat there, each of us putting forward some ideas and nixing others. We spent a few hours working it out, and finally, we had our plan. We would have to arrange a few things before we could spring our trap, but I think we were all satisfied it would work. If it didn't, there might be one or two more Shoshone dead.

As we got up to leave I looked down and saw the bull moose again. He was a magnificent animal, and what

Bobby had said about him standing his ground resonated with me. I felt as if I had just learned something about the Native Americans on the reservation. It was a lesson everyone should learn.

CHAPTER 66

Sunday 6:45 am

I had gotten home late Saturday night and went immediately to sleep. The weather was supposed to be good Sunday, and Bell and I promised the boys we could take a ride. I had slept well considering we had finally nailed down a plan. On Tuesday or Wednesday, we would set some things in motion. First we had to get in touch with Max and Abel and tell them of our plan. We needed to meet with them, lay out our trap and make some preparations. If they didn't agree with it, we would be back at square one.

We had gotten up early and drove out to the Double T ranch. As always, waiting for us with our horses saddled and ready was Tom Brown Shirt. After saying good morning, Tom had went over to Bell. He handed her something which I didn't see, and Bell had given him a kiss on the cheek. Then she had placed whatever it was in her waist pouch she was wearing.

We had saddled up and then taken off at a good pace, letting the boys lead the way. After about an hour of riding, we found a great spot near a small lake. We tied off the horses so they could graze. The boys wanted to explore, but before they did, Bell reminded them we weren't on a city street. So they had to keep both their eyes and ears open. No looking under tree stumps or rocks. Bell advised a rattlesnake bite was both deadly and painful. The boys promised they would be careful and took off.

Bell lay down, resting her head in my lap. I bent over and gave her a kiss.

"You know, I am so very proud of you," I said.

"Thank you Eric, I'm kinda proud of myself too," she said. "Running for office is going to be a long haul and a lot of work. I'll probably miss some things, and I might get a bit grouchy, but I am glad I decided to run. I hope down the road you will not regret pushing me on."

"I promise I won't regret a single moment on one condition."

"Don't tell me I have to give you a campaign promise?"

"Well, not a campaign promise and in fact, not a promise at all."

"Okay, so then what?"

"All I ask is for you to remember, even when you get busy or have a hectic schedule or day, you have a family who loves you, is proud of you, and only want you to succeed."

"I can definitely do that."

"One more thing."

"Oh?"

"Don't forget you have certain spousal requirements, and you need to make sure you don't forget about them."

"Hmmm, so I still have to make time for you to make love to me?"

"Definitely."

Bell sat up and we had a quick make out session until the boys showed up and started groaning.

"Gee guys, can't you stop kissing?" Bear said.

"Yeah, I'm just glad nobody can see you," Ben chimed in.

"Okay, let's saddle up and head in, unless you want us to start in again."

"NO!" was the resounding answer from both of them.

We headed back to the stable and even though Tom was willing to take care of our horses, I insisted we would unsaddle them, cool them down, brush and feed them. The boys had to learn if they wanted to ride it wasn't all fun and games. They had responsibilities and they needed to honor them.

A few hours later we had gotten home, and the boys immediately grabbed their bikes and headed off to meet their friends. Where they got their energy I hadn't a clue. I was bushed and so was Bell. We decided to go upstairs to bed and take a short nap.

As we got into bed, I asked Bell, "By the way. What did Tom give you."

"Tom said he had heard I was running for office," Bell replied. "He said if I kept it close to me at all times, it would bring me good luck and keep me safe."

"It? What exactly is this mysterious object?"

"I'm not really sure. It was small and had some writing on it as well as a small figurine carved of an eagle. It is very pretty."

"Do you really believe it can bring you luck and keep you safe?"

"I'm not sure but there are a great many things out there we cannot prove or disprove. I think it pays to have an open mind."

I thought about the stones which had led to five deaths. Could there be something to them having a power? I supposed Bell was right. It would be better to have an open mind.

"So lover, are we going to nap or not?' Bell asked with a grin.

"No nap for you young lady," I said.

All in all it was turning out to be a great day.

CHAPTER 67

Monday 9:45 am

I had just finished outlining our plan to Chief Lewis and Will. They had a few reservations and also a few ideas on how to make the trap better. Anything to make it come off without any hitches was fine with me.

Then I headed to my office to do some paperwork and look at reports from the weekend. Other than a few fistfights at the fair, the weekend had been a quiet one. I was happy about it.

There was a knock on my door and in walked Chuck and Jimmy.

"Good morning Sergeant," Jimmy said.

"How about Eric when we aren't in public or in front of any bosses?" I said.

"Okay, Eric."

"What's up for today?" Chuck asked.

"I need to check in with Bobby out on the res. He hasn't been able to get in touch with Max or Abel and we need them both to come in to hear our plan. But we want them to come in after dark. When he gets word to them, we will meet at Bobby's house again."

"How will he get in touch with them?" Jimmy asked. "Aren't they in hiding somewhere?"

"I have no idea Jimmy, but I know if anyone can get in touch with them, it will be Bobby. Now, how is Maggie, Chuck?"

"She was a little annoyed with me," Chuck replied. "She spotted the policewoman who had been shadowing her. She didn't understand why she was there. Maggie told me, if anyone was going to protect her, it should be me."

"Actually Chuck, I think I agree with her."

"But I can't be with her all day and night."

"Why not? Call off her shadow and you stay with her. Our plan should be ready to go in a day or two, and Jimmy can handle any new calls. I will have Mike Kowalski partner with him for the next few days. Maybe you can get Maggie to take a day or two off. This way it will be easy to protect her. But don't go anywhere too far away and keep in touch. Understood?"

"Absolutely Eric!" Chuck said and was on his way before I could say another word.

"I think Chuck is in love," Jimmy said.

"I do too," I replied. "It looks as if we might have a wedding to attend one of these days. Okay, you get in touch with Mike and tell him I said he was to get into plain clothes and work with you for a few days."

"Does that make me the senior detective over him?"

"Don't get carried away Jimmy. Mike has more than twenty five years on the job. If I were you, I would try to pick up a few pointers from him."

"Yes sir," he said, and left my office.

I worked on some reports and then after about two hours, I headed out to the res. The ride out to the res never failed to impress me. The mountains, the open plains and the deep blue sky reminded me of why I lived in Wyoming.

I pulled up in front of the tribal police building, and headed in. At the front desk was Sgt. Betty Slow River, and at her feet was Geronimo. Standing around drinking coffee were a few more officers who I knew. Daniel Red Shirt, Tommy White Hair and a woman named Cindy Black Crow. A few other officers had just headed out for a patrol.

"*Behne* Betty," I said. "I see you still have the dog by you. I thought Bobby said he wasn't going to allow a dog to stay in his building?"

"Do you really believe the Lieutenant has any say over what I do?" she replied. "Geronimo stays." Turning to the three officers, she said, "And the three of you do not need to stay, you better get out on patrol."

They put down their mugs and headed out quickly. Betty obviously ran the show around here.

"No, I suppose I don't. Is he in?"

"He is Eric, and he is expecting you."

I stopped for a second to give Geronimo a rub on his head which made Betty smile, and then walked to Bobby's office.

I knocked on the door and saw Bobby on the phone. He waved me in, and I went and sat down.

"Yes my friend, it must be done quickly," Bobby said. "They must meet me at my home tonight at 9:00. Thank you my friend."

"Talking about Max and Abel?" I asked.

"Yes. I was speaking to an old friend of mine, Lucas Storm Cloud. He knows every inch of the res and he is also a great tracker. He will find where Max and Abel are hiding."

"I thought Abel was supposed to stay in touch... somehow."

"He was Eric, but either he has decided not to get in touch, or something has happened. Of course, knowing Max, perhaps the two of them are just plain drunk."

"I hope they aren't. Drinking on the res is against the law," I said with a very serious face.

Bobby looked at me and then the two of us broke out laughing.

"You know Bobby," I said, "It felt good to laugh."

"I agree, there hasn't been too much laughter around here lately. I will hear from my friend soon enough. Hopefully before tonight. When I do, I will get in touch with you. Then we can all meet and tell Max and Abel about our trap."

"Sounds like a plan. Oh by the way," I said as I stood.

"Yes?"

"I see your orders were followed to the letter."

"What orders?"

"You know, the one where you said Geronimo couldn't stay in the office with Betty!"

Bobby threw a book at me as I ducked and headed out. I knew even though he tried to play the stoic boss, he had a heart of gold. I was sure he even gave Geronimo a snack or two when no one was looking.

I stopped by to pet Geronimo one more time and headed back to my car. On the ride back into Eagle, I thought about our plan. I also thought about who we believed was our killer. I just hoped we were right, and all of this would soon be over.

CHAPTER 68

Monday 6:15 pm

We were all sitting down to eat dinner. Bell had made fried chicken, with mashed potatoes, green beans, and biscuits. Everything looked delicious and as soon as I took a bite, I decided I had been right. It was delicious. As we ate I wondered how many of these meals would be missed in the future. Between me and my work, and Bell getting elected, which I now thought of as a sure bet, there would be many times meals and other events might be missed by one or both of us. At least the boys were no longer babies and could fend for themselves. But I made a mental note to talk with them about the future. I wanted them to be prepared and also wanted to hear their opinions.

We were halfway through the meal, with the boys telling us about all the things they had done today. Besides bike riding, they had played basketball and street hockey, skipped rocks out at the lake, teased a few girls and had malteds down at the soda shop in town. That had only been the morning! Where they got their energy was beyond me. I wondered if I had been the same at their age and thought I probably had been.

As they were launching into their afternoon escapades, my cell phone rang. I got up from the table and answered it.

"Sgt Logan," I said.

"Hey Eric, Bobby here," I heard Bobby say. "My friend contacted them, and they are meeting me at home at about ten tonight. They said they couldn't make it any earlier."

"Ten will be fine Bobby. How did your friend find them?"

"He wouldn't tell me. He said it was an old Indian talent; one many Shoshone have forgotten. I think he was trying to bring a bit of shame on me for not going with him hunting for a long, long time. As soon as this is over, I will have to make amends to the situation."

"I suppose we all tend to forget our friends doing this work. I will be there at ten."

I hung up and finished our meal and then helped Bell clear the table. The kids headed out but were told to be back by nine.

"Do you believe all the things those boys did today?" I asked.

"I know," Bell said. "What in the world are they going to do tomorrow?"

"I have no idea but I'm sure they will come up with something. I have to go out tonight. I'm meeting Bobby and our two stone holders later tonight."

"Is this whole thing going to end soon?"

"I sure hope so. We are pretty sure we know who our suspect is, but we have no proof. He has been very smart, leaving no prints or DNA at any of the murder scenes. He hasn't been spotted by anyone as well."

"So how are you going to get him?"

"We came up with a plan, but a lot depends on if Max and Abel are willing to go along with it. A lot depends on if we are right on who our suspect is."

"What about Maggie? Isn't she in danger as well?"

"We think she might be, which is why I assigned Chuck to stay with her 24-7."

"Oh, I'm sure he is hating that assignment!"

"Yeah, he and Maggie seem to be getting along well. Do you think there is a wedding in their future?"

"Well, Maggie is in love, she told me at the fair. And from how Chuck looks at her, I would say it was a good bet."

"I hope so. What are your plans for the week?"

"Tomorrow I am having some photos taken to make some flyers and posters. And everyone wants to put up a few large billboards around town as well. But I'm not sure I would be happy with my face being so large for everyone to see."

"Honey, anyone who gets to see how beautiful you are will be lucky. I think it is a great idea."

"Well, we will see. Now you better get going if you are driving out to the res."

"I didn't say anything about going out to the res. How did you know?"

"Don't you think I have picked up a few talents from you along the way? Now get going."

I gave her a kiss, grabbed my cuffs, gun and badge, and headed out. As I drove out to the res, I hoped Max and Abel would agree with the plan. If not, I had no idea what else to do.

I arrived at Bobby's home and as we waited outside, we did not speak. We both had a great deal on our minds. The sky was clear with a full moon shining above. A few minutes later, Max and Abel appeared silently. We greeted each other and walked over to the same ravine Chuck, and I had gone to with Bobby. As we looked over the edge, I once again was able to make out the big bull moose. I didn't see any wolves.

"That big moose fought off a bunch of wolves a few nights ago," I said.

"Yes, the *Baadihiya*, is a mighty creature," Max said. "We have seen this particular one on the res for many years."

"How do you know it is the same one?" I asked.

"Can you see the antlers on the right side of his head?"

"Yes, but what am I looking for?"

"Near the center, just below the tips , if you look closely you will see what looks to be a five sided star. I have seen this *Baadihiya* many times. He is mighty and wise. I don't believe any wolves will ever take him down."

"Does he have a name?"

"Yes, we call him his rightful name, Shoshoni."

We watched Shoshoni move below us and then we finally sat down on the ground to talk about our plan. Bobby and I outlined what we wanted to do. There were a few things Max and Abel would have to do for it to work, There was also a bunch of things I and Bobby had to do as well. After some discussion and refinements, we agreed to spring the first part of the plan on Wednesday morning. Then we would have to be ready after that.

Max and Abel stood and shook both of our hands. Then as Abel and Max began to leave, Abel took a step toward me.

"You are a good man Eric Logan, and I am putting my trust in you," Abel said. "I have never trusted a white man before. I am also trusting Chuck Blackwell to protect my sister. He seems to be a good man. You may tell him... tell him I said he would be welcome in my family."

"Thank you Abel, and I will tell him."

Abel and Max took off and Bobby and I sat looking into the ravine for a bit.

"For Abel to say he trusted you must have been difficult," Bobby said.

"I'm sure it was," I answered. "But it meant a great deal to me, and I know it will mean a lot to Chuck as well."

"Maybe something good will come from all of these murders Eric."

"Maybe," I said, "maybe."

CHAPTER 69

Tuesday 5:30 pm

Nihoono biitooeeihii sat at a table in the mall, watching Maggie Bright Star and Chuck Blackwell. They were sitting close together, holding hands and every once in a while, kissing. It angered him a great deal. A Shoshone should not be with a white man. Nor should an Arapahoe or any other of the People. It was wrong and once he had the power; he would put a stop to all of the intermingling between his people and the whites.

He was sitting far away from them, a hat pulled low on his head, hiding his hair and face. He decided he better not push his luck; he didn't want to take a chance of being recognized. He got up and moved quickly away and out of the door. He got into his car and drove away.

He had planned on kidnapping Maggie Bright Star. He knew the policewoman who was protecting her would not have been a problem. But then it all changed. Chuck Blackwell hadn't been away from her for more than a few minutes. Even when she was at work, he would sit on a bench directly outside of the store where she worked. Then they would leave together and go to her home. He would stay all night and *Nihoono biitooeeihii's* anger grew with the thought of what was probably happening inside!

Now as he arrived back at his home, he thought how he needed a new plan. He had to find Max and Abel and then no matter what, get the stones from them. But how, he thought for the thousandth time. He didn't even know if they were together, wherever they were. What if they had left the reservation? One or both of them could have gone to another res. Perhaps down south or even to Florida. Then how would he get the stones?

He paced and paced, but he couldn't come up with any plan which would work. But he must! If he didn't get the last two stones, the meteor would never reform, and he wouldn't get the power.

Finally he decided he would have to be patient and began to breathe deeply and calm down. There was no point in getting angry and maybe sloppy as well. So far he had done everything perfectly. Now was not the time to screw up.

He would keep his ears and his eyes open. He would eventually hear something and then he could move. It was not going to be easy, but *Nihoono biitooeeihii* decided he would have to be as patient as he needed to be. Yes, he thought, he could wait. It was his destiny to have the power, of that he was certain. Soon, all the pieces of the gift would be his.

CHAPTER 70

Wednesday 8:15 am

We were going to meet at my office to lay down the trap. Right now, Chuck, Jimmy, Mike, and I were going over everything once again. It would have to sound convincing if we were going to pull it off. Bobby would be coming out with Tommy White Hair, Daniel Red Shirt, Sgt. Betty Slow River and Cindy Black Crow. He would also be bringing a few other officers who were available. The room was going to be crowded. We would be using the large conference room.

I quickly went over everything for my guys one more time. Bobby and his officers would be arriving soon, and I didn't want any mistakes. While Chuck was here, Maggie Bright Star was at my house with Bell. We figured it would be a safe place in case we were wrong about who we suspected. If we were wrong, all of this would be a waste of time.

One of the uniforms came in with some food for our guests. There was coffee, tea, donuts, bagels, and assorted fruits. I wasn't sure what everyone wanted so I had splurged a bit. I set up all the food on a side table and then we sat and waited for our guests.

"You really think this is going to work Eric?" Chuck asked.

"I certainly hope so Chuck," I replied. "If it doesn't I'm afraid we will be at a loss to keep protecting Max, Abel, and Maggie. They can't hide out forever and I can't have you protecting Maggie all the time. And then sooner or later, our killer will strike."

"What if they gave up the stones and we kept them locked up here?" Mike asked.

"Bobby and I have tried to get them to give us the stones but both of them refuse. They say it is a matter of honor, a vow they took and respect for their ancestors."

"I suppose I can understand their reasons, at least partly," Jimmy said.

Just then a uniform came in and told us Bobby and his people were waiting in the lobby. I had asked Bobby to wait when he first arrived to give us time to be ready. I told the officer to bring them in.

When Bobby walked in he said hello, and each of us returned the greeting.

"I'm not sure if everyone knows each other, so before we get to introductions, grab some food and then we can get started.

Everyone took something, and with plates in hand, found seats around the table.

"I think it would be easier if we go around the table," I said. "I am Sergeant Eric Logan."

Next to me, Bobby said, "I am Lieutenant Bobby Black Bear of the Wind River Reservation Tribal Police."

We continued around until everyone had introduced themselves. Then we began to lay out our trap.

"As you all know, there have been four murders of Shoshone Indians in the last few weeks."

Bobby and I had decided not to include Walks in Wind as a victim. We figured it might make the killer forget all about going after his son. Plus we wanted to make the killer believe he was smarter than we were. Maybe he would make a mistake if he thought we knew less than we did.

"So far, this killer has been very smart. He has left no fingerprints, no DNA, not one fiber and hasn't been seen at any of the murders."

"Sounds to me the killer is a ghost," Chuck said, right on cue.

"Do not joke about the spirit world Chuck," Bobby said. "You may not believe, but I have seen many things I cannot explain."

"Umm, sorry Bobby, I mean Lieutenant," Chuck said, remembering we had guests who might not like for us to be too informal.

"As I was saying, we do know some things which might help in capturing the killer, whoever or whatever he might be. Lieutenant, why don't you continue."

"Thank you Sergeant," Bobby said. "We know what the killer is after. We have worked it out from some of the evidence, such as the tattoos, and…"

"Excuse me Lieutenant, what tattoos?" Cindy asked.

"I am sorry, I forgot some of you may have no clue about some of our findings. Each of the victims had a tiny tattoo of a shooting star."

Once again, Bobby and I had decided not to call the tattoos a meteorite. We didn't want our killer to know exactly how much we actually knew.

"The reason for the tattoos is still a mystery but we do know what the killer is after. It seems each of the victims had been hiding and keeping some sort of stone. We believe within the stones there must be some rare gems. Maybe diamonds, or emeralds. But whatever is hidden in the stones, they must be very valuable."

"How many stones are there?" Jimmy asked.

"We really have no idea. But, we do know of two Shoshone who are hiding the stones."

"If you don't mind Lieutenant, I will explain how we came to find them," I said.

"As you wish Sergeant."

"Max Yellowfeather and I have been friends for many years. Several nights ago, I found Max pretty drunk outside Kelly's Bar. This unfortunately, is not a rare occurrence. In any case, I was going to drive Max to the res and on the way he began to talk about the stone he was carrying. Being drunk, it sounded like a crazy story, and he wasn't making any sense. He even showed me the stone he kept on his person, wearing it around his neck. He even told me his cousin, Abel Bright Star had one too. He wore his around his waist."

"What did the stones look like?" Daniel Red Shirt asked.

"Oh they weren't very big, a dark gray color mostly. In the dark in the car I didn't get a great look at it. But as I was dropping off Max, he told me about the tattoo he and his cousin Abel had. I knew about the tattoos from our other victims. I figured Max and Abel might be on the killer's list."

"So that's why Max, Abel and Maggie Bright Star had been under police protection," Betty said.

"Correct Sergeant Slow River. Unfortunately, we cannot continue to keep them under police protection. First of all, we don't have the manpower or the money for round the clock protection. We also do not know if there are other Shoshone with stones. We can't protect everyone, especially out on the reservation."

"So what is our next step," Chuck asked.

"Lieutenant?"

Bobby stood, looking each of us in the eyes and then said, "What I am going to tell you must remain confidential. I know I can trust all of you, because lives are at stake. I have spoken with Max and Abel, and they have decided to hide out in a cave on the res. The mountain is in the west, and it is known as *Numu-Tsa*, or little sister. It is called so because it is much smaller than the other mountains surrounding it. The other mountains protect her, like big brothers. Halfway up, there is a small slit in the mountain. There is a very small cave within. It is not very large, but it will accommodate Max and Abel easily. Max and Abel have decided to stay there for the next month, or longer if necessary. They are bringing in supplies and will be fine there. No one besides us will have any idea where they are."

"We aren't too happy about their decision," I said. "But there really was nothing we could do about it. Lieutenant Black Bear will be checking up on them from time to time, maybe once a week. But we wanted all of you to know where they were in case the Lieutenant couldn't get out to them."

"What about Abel's sister, Maggie Bright Star?" Tommy White Hair asked.

"She will be guarded 24 hrs. a day for now by Detective Blackwell."

"Sergeant Logan and I have come up with a plan to possibly bring out the killer," Bobby said. "We will spread the word to all of the res that I have one of the stones. We must spread the rumor carefully, but each of you for the next few days will tell everyone you see. You will say it is part of an ongoing investigation, and you are asking if anyone else might have such a stone. You will all have to sell it."

"As for my guys, you will tell the same story to any Shoshone living here in town," I said. "We are hoping the killer will take the bait and try to get to Lieutenant Black Bear."

"Might that be a bit dangerous?" Betty asked.

"The Lieutenant will be staying with me for the next few days, at my house. I will be staying home as well. This way there will be no danger involved. But maybe, our killer will slip up and go looking for him."

"Are there any questions?" Bobby asked. "Remember, for this to work, you all must keep everything we have said confidential. Do not talk about it to anyone else, not even other officers."

"Okay everyone, if there is nothing else, we better get back to work," I said.

"Sgt. Slow River," Bobby said, "you will be in charge for the next three days. I will be available on my cell only."

"Okay Bobby," Betty said, "but I sure hope you know what you are doing. Will you be coming back with me now or are you staying here?"

"I will be staying here. Make sure my vehicle stays at the station. I probably will not try to contact you, so do the best you can."

"No problem Bobby. Good luck to you and you too Sergeant Logan."

"Thank you Betty," I said and soon only Bobby, Chuck, Mike, and Jimmy were left in the conference room.

"Do you think we hooked him?" Chuck asked.

"I'm not too sure but if our killer is who we think he is, he will know the story about Bobby having a stone is false," I said.

Bobby said, "And he will know the trap we are setting for him will be at Eric's home."

"What if he isn't who we think he is?" Jimmy asked.

"Then we are screwed, so let's keep our fingers crossed."

"Chuck," I said, "you better get Maggie to work. Stay with her just in case, although I don't think she is any danger now. At least not if we are right. Jimmy, you, and Mike work anything that comes up. As for now, you will report directly to Lieutenant Tolliver. The other detectives in our unit will be advised I will be away for a few days, and they will report directly to Lieutenant Tolliver, as well. If there isn't anything else, I guess it is time to get the show on the road."

"Good luck Eric, Bobby," Chuck said.

Chuck, Mike, and Jimmy left, and Bobby and I sat down once more.

"What do you really think Eric?" Bobby said.

"I think this is our best and last shot to catch our killer Bobby," I said, "and if it doesn't work, we are back to square one."

"I still am having a very hard time believing who our killer might be. But it all fits. Still, I will only believe it when I see it for myself."

"Well then, I suggest we head to my home just as we said we would do."

We left the building and drove directly to my home. We weren't sure if we had been watched as we went, but it was necessary to show we were doing as we had said. Maybe the killer would take the bait, or maybe he wouldn't. Only time would tell.

As we arrived home, we passed Chuck and Maggie leaving to take Maggie to work. Bell was waiting outside and after parking we walked up to her.

Hello Bobby," Bell said. "I guess we are hoping the killer is watching. Kind of gives me the creeps."

"Don't worry honey," I said. "Even if he is watching he is only doing so to confirm where Bobby and I are. He will soon be heading out to where Max and Abel are staying."

"Still sends a chill down my spine."

"I suggest we bring in my pack just in case he is watching," Bobby said. "I can't stay here for a few days without a change of clothes."

We all went in to the house, Bobby bringing a large pack which looked as if it was full. I wanted to look around, to see if I could spot anyone spying on us, but I resisted the temptation. As I closed the door, I could only hope our little ruse was going to work.

CHAPTER 71

Wednesday 11:30 am

Nihoono biitooeeihii had a great deal to think about. He was sure Bobby and Logan were trying to lay a trap for him, but which one was the trap? He was surprised at how much they had discovered but at the same time, was happy about some of their conclusions.

They obviously knew nothing of the true story behind the stones. They thought they contained gems! Ha! How stupid of them. And they knew nothing about Walks in Wind. They had not found out he had been the first victim.

But was it possible they were laying the trap out on the mountain where Max and Abel were hiding out? Or was the trap at Logan's home? If they believed telling everyone on the res that Bobby had a stone, to get to the killer, then the trap would be there at Logan's. But if that was just a ruse, it would mean they knew who I am. Or at least they might suspect. But if they suspected, why wouldn't they just arrest and question me?

All of these thoughts were running around *Nihoono biitooeeihii's* brain, driving him into a frenzy. Slamming his hands on the car's steering wheel, he pulled over to the side of the road. He had been spreading the rumor about Bobby having a stone all morning to anyone he saw on the reservation. Of course he knew it was a lie, just a story. But did Bobby and Logan know he knew? He didn't think so. He had to look as if he was following the directions given to them all in the meeting.

After their meeting had broken up, *Nihoono biitooeeihii* had taken a backway up to where Logan lived. He had arrived in time to see Chuck Blackwell arrive and take

Maggie away. Then he had seen Logan and Bobby arrive. They had met with Logan's wife. He had seen Bobby take in a large bag which looked to be filled. It made sense he would need some clothing and other things if he were staying for several days. Then *Nihoono biitooeeihii* had slipped away and driven to the res.

Now, as he sat by the side of the road on an old tree stump, he began to think everything over once again. Bobby and Logan did go to his home, and it appeared Bobby had brought things for a few days stay. Chuck had gotten Maggie and taken her to work. He decided they were hoping the killer would hear about Bobby having a stone and would come out to Logan's house to get Bobby's stone. They had no clue as to his identity. Of this he was sure now.

He smiled thinking how they had given him the information he needed to get the two last stones. He knew exactly where Max and Abel were. He knew where Little Sister was, and how to get there. He would have to wait for a day until he was not working. He would go to the mountain in the dead of night. Both of them would not be on guard thinking they were safe there. He would climb up and shoot them both dead as they slept. Both men were too big and strong to take any chances. Then he would get the stones. One from around Max's neck and the other from Abel's waist. Then he would have them all!

Nihoono biitooeeihii got back in his truck and continued to drive around the res. He would keep spreading the rumor about Bobby and keep asking anyone he saw whether or not they had a stone. It was a complete waste of time, but he wanted to look as if he was doing his job.

Then, tomorrow night he would make his way to Little Sister and finally have the power he was destined to have. Once the stones had reformed and he had the power, he knew there would be nothing to stop him. Nothing at all.

CHAPTER 72

Thursday 1:30 am

Chuck and Maggie were sitting up in her apartment, neither one able to sleep. He was holding her on the couch in his arms. They had tried to watch a movie, but both of them had no patience for it. There was too much to think about.

"Do you really think this will all be over soon?" Maggie asked.

"Well, I have worked with Eric for a long time now," Chuck stated as he slowly stroked her hair. "He is definitely one of the smartest cops I have ever known."

"But the killer seems to be even smarter."

"Nah, he is smart but smarter than Eric, or Bobby? Not a chance."

"My brother's life is hanging out there for the killer to take. If the plan you told me is to work, the killer must go to Little Sister. He will go there to kill Max and Abel. What if he is successful?"

"He won't be, I promise you. Eric and Bobby have worked everything out and there will be no danger to your brother or Max. Now, how about we try to get some sleep?"

"Okay Chuck, I believe you. I know you have faith in Eric. I will have faith in you."

Maggie and Chuck made their way to her bedroom and got into bed. Maggie rested her head on Chuck's chest, and as he held her, he felt her relax and fall asleep. Chuck on the other hand was wide awake.

He thought, now that I have promised Maggie her brother will be safe, I hope I am right. If Max or Abel were to be hurt or killed, he wasn't sure Maggie would ever forgive him. He knew he was in love with her. He had even planned on asking her to marry him after all this was over. But if it didn't go well, he was sure all his plans for the two of them would just disappear.

But he did have faith in Eric and Bobby. He had never let him down and telling Maggie he thought Eric was the smartest cop he knew had not been a lie. Still, he was worried. He sat up until the light of morning came through her window. She stirred and he made believe he was still sleeping. Then she lightly woke him and gave him a light kiss.

"Maybe today will be the end of all this Chuck," she said as she got up.

"I'm sure it will," Chuck said.

She went in to take a shower and Chuck began getting breakfast ready. He could imagine doing this for the rest of his life. Somehow, he needed to make it happen. He wanted Maggie to be his wife and for them to live together every single day of their lives.

But he thought, all I can do is wait and see how the plan worked out.

CHAPTER 73

Thursday 8:30 am

Bell was putting a breakfast together for me and Bobby. We had stayed up in the den, talking about our plan, most of the night, wondering if we had made the right decisions. We had gone over everything we knew, starting at the beginning. We had laid out all of the murders, the tattoos, the stones, and anything which we thought we had missed.

"Come and get it," Bell called out.

"Your cooking smells delicious," Bobby said as he sat down.

"I know your wife is a great cook Bobby, but Bell might just edge her out," I said and gave her a kiss. "Where are the boys?"

"They left while you two were busy in the den," Bell said. "They are going fishing with a few other boys at Tranquility Lake. Their friend's dad is driving them out there. They are going to camp overnight."

"I suppose it will be okay," I said.

"Are you being a nervous father Eric?" Bobby said with a big smile.

"Maybe a little bit, but I'm sure they will be fine. Now, what are your plans for the day?"

"I am going into town to look at two billboards going up with my face plastered on them," Bell said nervously.

"I don't think you have any reason to be worried Bell," Bobby said. "You are an honest and true hearted woman. Plus, don't tell my wife, but you are also very pretty."

Bell blushed slightly and said, "Why thank you Bobby. I won't tell her."

We finished breakfast and Bobby, and I cleared and washed the dishes. Bell went upstairs to dress and get ready for the big unveiling of her billboards. Her picture and slogan had been plastered all around town and people were sure to know she was running against Graham Stone.

Stone's manager had contacted Bell's and asked her to agree to a debate. He said they wanted to unmuddy the waters as to who might be the best person for the job. Bell had discussed it with her backers and me, and decided she would debate him in three weeks. He had agreed. Hopefully I thought, the investigation would be far behind us by then.

Once the dishes were done, Bobby and I went out front and had some coffee, sitting at a table we had out front. We both had to keep up the appearance of both of us being at my house. We couldn't be sure if the killer was checking up on us or not. The other thought was, if we were wrong about who we suspected, the killer might hear about Bobby having a stone and come looking. Either way, we had to play the game.

Bell came out looking like a million dollars.

"Okay boys, I guess I better get going," Bell said.

"Good luck Bell," Bobby said, "but I doubt you will need it."

"Why thank you Bobby."

"Knock em dead honey," I said, and gave her a big kiss.

Bell got into her car and waved and then drove away.

"I'm a lucky man Bobby," I said.

"We both are Eric," Bobby said. "Let's keep it that way."

I couldn't help but look around as we drank our coffee. I wondered if the person we thought was the killer was out there right now, watching us. Maybe Bobby was thinking the same thing. We had to play it out and hope we were right. We also had to hope Max and Abel would be ready.

CHAPTER 74

All of Bell's backers and her campaign manager were standing patiently at the intersection of Main Street and Eagle Avenue. Above, a large tarp covered the billboard. They were waiting for noon, when there would be a great deal of traffic from people going to lunch. Her manager, James Breckenridge, had told her the best way to get people to look at the billboard was to make a big show of unveiling it.

The clock on the banks tower, a block away, indicated it was now noon. Right on time, people began leaving their offices for lunch. As they walked about, Brett Trask raised a megaphone to his lips and began to speak.

"Ladies and gentlemen of Eagle!" he began. "For those of you who have not heard about who is going to be our newest councilwoman, let me show you!"

Trask then gave a wave to two workers high above the ground, standing on either side of the billboard, and they pulled the covering aside.

Looking up, Bell saw her giant face and the slogan in huge letters, "You CAN handle the truth, and Belinda Logan will always tell you it!" Then it said in smaller letters, "Belinda Logan, you're new City Councilwoman! Vote for Belinda Logan!"

The crowd cheered and Bell felt both excitement and embarrassment at the same time. Then some of the people started shaking her hand and patting her on the back. There were a few who said, "You got my vote Bell, and It's about time old Stone was tossed out!"

Soon the crowd thinned out and Bell was talking with James when she felt a tap on her shoulder. Thinking it was another person wishing to congratulate her, she turned with a big smile. It quickly disappeared as she saw Graham Stone standing there, a big smirk on his face.

Stone looked as if he had come dressed for a party. He had on an immaculate blue pinstripe suit, with a light blue shirt on. A deep blue tie and matching pocket square, beautifully folded. His shoes were a deep black and you could see your face in them if you wanted to. He was close to seventy years old but judging by his dyed hair and trim body, he easily passed for sixty. He sported a thin moustache which looked ridiculous to Bell. He was alone and stood there, looking up at the billboard.

"Hello Mrs. Logan," he said in a deep bass voice.

"Hello to you Mr. Stone," Bell said.

"Quite a big billboard and if you don't mind me saying, you look very beautiful up there with your face twenty feet high."

"Thank you Mr. Stone."

"I would think you or your husband might mind your face being so open to the public like this."

"Oh I don't mind at all, and I have the full support of my husband."

"Still, it will take a lot more than a pretty face and billboards to win an election. The people of Eagle know me and know how I have been their servant for over ten years now."

"Maybe they want some new blood Mr. Stone."

"Maybe, but I doubt it. I wonder how they will feel when I reveal at our debate some interesting things I have found out, about you and your husband?"

"There is nothing you can say which will hurt my or my husband's reputations. But, if the only way you think you can win is to play dirty, by all means, do so. I on the other hand will not get down in the gutter with you Mr. Stone. I will tell the people the truth and what I plan to do to make this city better. I will win by being the right person for the job. You on the other hand, have nothing to offer the people of Eagle but some dirt you think you have. Good luck with that Mr. Stone."

Bell hadn't realized she had a crowd standing behind her as she spoke to Stone. Suddenly a cheer went up behind her and some clapping. She looked at all the people and was overwhelmed with pride. Then she looked back at Graham Stone and saw only anger on his face.

"We will see Mrs. Logan, we will see," he said and stormed away.

"Looks like you won round one Bell," James Breckenridge said, "but we have a long way to go. Still, it couldn't have worked out better."

Her backers and Breckenridge moved off to some vehicles and proceeded to the second billboard they had put up. It was right near the mall and this time Bell didn't feel as worried about it. She was excited by the reaction of the people, and for the first time, really thought she could win. She couldn't wait to tell Eric about it when he came back. Still, she was a little worried about the dirt Stone had. Maybe he was lying in order to scare her out of the race. But Bell and Eric had decided together there was nothing Stone could say to keep her from running.

CHAPTER 75

Thursday 5:45 pm

Nihoono biitooeeihii sat a few hundred yards down from Eric Logan's home. He had some powerful binoculars and saw Logan and Bobby sitting out front. It appeared as if they were both relaxed, with some kind of drinks in their hands, and cigars in their mouths. He was happy to see them both there. It confirmed they were sticking to their plan. They were still setting the trap for the killer at Logan's home. He was sure of it now, seeing them both there.

He watched until they had put out their cigars and once again entered the house. Then he slipped away and made his way back to his truck. As he drove back to the res and his apartment, he silently congratulated himself on his being smarter than them. He knew he would soon have the last two stones.

Once he arrived back home, he carefully removed the stones he had gotten from the space under his cabinet. He spread them out on a table. It was amazing, he thought, how such simple looking stones could hold such power! He even felt some of it when he held them in his hands. He did not know where the power had come from, but he knew the legend was true.

When the stones were placed together, they would reform. They would come together to their original form and the power would be his and his alone.

He placed the stones into a leather pouch and then began to prepare for tonight. He had purchased a very powerful set of night goggles, many months ago. He had gotten them to hunt elk and deer, but now he would use them to hunt bigger game. He knew where Little Sister, the small mountain surrounded by bigger ones was, but had never climbed it. The goggles would help him a great deal. He didn't want to step in a crevasse or onto a sleeping rattlesnake. He had to climb the mountain silently. Maybe there was a trail leading up to the cave where Max and Abel were hiding, but it didn't matter. He would climb the mountain away from where the cave was. Then when he felt he had climbed high enough; he would circle to the cave.

He then laid out all the gear he would be bringing with him. He had a semi-automatic H & K weapon, equipped with a silencer. He laughed for a moment, thinking how silencers were illegal. It was equipped with .40 caliber bullets, strong enough to knock big men like Max and Abel to the ground. But he didn't think it would be necessary to knock them down. He was sure they would be sleeping in their beds of blankets, unaware of the death they were about to meet.

He also laid out three wicked looking knives which he would hide on his body. If for some reason, the guns didn't kill them both or one of them, he might have to fight. He knew he would be able to kill anyone with his knives. He was very proficient with them.

His clothing was lightweight and all black. A hood would cover his head, and on his feet he would wear strong black boots. No one would be able to see him as he climbed up the mountain.

He checked everything again and when he was satisfied he sat down to eat a light meal. He was anxious to get started but knew he would have to wait several more hours. He needed the two men to be fast asleep when he entered the cave. But if for some reason they weren't, he had no doubt he could kill them and get his prize.

After eating, he returned to where everything he needed was laid out. He checked it all again, looked at the clock, and rechecked everything.

Soon he thought, very soon now his name would be true. He would be the One True Chief, and he would lead his people to a new world.

CHAPTER 76

Max and Abel were sitting on the edge of the cave, looking out at the night sky. The sky was clear of any clouds and the moon was very bright in the night sky. With their eyes adjusted to the darkness, they were able to see all the way down the mountain and a great distance away from it.

"I do not believe anyone will be able to climb the mountain without us seeing them," Abel stated.

"I agree, but we cannot stay awake forever," Max replied. "We have stayed awake for a long time, and I for one am very tired. I am sure we will be safe."

"I am tired too, so I think maybe we should get some sleep. We can wake after a short time and then once again keep watch."

Let's wait a bit longer. The sky is putting on a show with all the stars shining, and the air is warm."

"I wonder if we will be able to return to our lives soon."

"I trust Logan and Black Bear, and they will soon have the killer in jail. All we can do now is hope for the best."

The cousins sat quietly, looking out from the cave. They saw some animals at the base of the mountain, while an eagle soared overhead. Unlike the whites, the two cousins felt connected to the animals, the trees, the mountains and the earth and sky. Even though they no longer were truly free and able to live as their ancestors did, they both tried to keep the traditions and heritage in their hearts and minds.

As they looked at the night sky, a shooting star flew over their heads.

"I wonder if the stones truly have any power," Abel said.

"There are many things we will never understand," Max replied. "Did our ancestors understand things we no longer believe? Or were they just superstitious people, afraid of omens and things falling from the sky? Perhaps we will never know. Maybe it is time for the passing down of the stones to end. When this is all over, I will decide what to do about mine."

"But what of our vows? What of honoring our ancestors? For over four hundred years the stones have been handed down, kept safe and secret. Can we abandon them now?"

"The stones have caused much sadness and death," Max said. "Five Shoshone have been murdered and many families no longer have them in their lives. Is keeping a stone secret worth those lives? And we do not know if there will be more. No, there can be no more deaths. I will rid myself of the stone once this is over. I believe you should do the same."

Abel sat there thinking and finally said, "You are right cousin. We will both rid ourselves of the stones and the legend. Now, I am going to sleep."

The two cousins went into the cave and added some wood to the fire burning inside. Then they laid out their blankets and lay down to sleep. It was only a short while later, both men were fast asleep.

If they had stayed up a few hours more, perhaps they would have seen a man dressed all in black, stealthily climbing up the mountain. Perhaps not, but as it is with all things, it was fate for them to have gone into the cave to sleep. There they lay on the heavy blankets with the fire slowly getting smaller. They slept deeply, assure in their minds they were safe.

CHAPTER 77

Thursday 1:10 am

Nihoono biitooeeihii had taken three times as long to make the drive out to where Little Sister was. He drove through the darkness with his lights out on his truck. He didn't want to be seen by anyone who might be out in the night. There was always a chance a tribal police officer would be out on patrol, or a Shoshone or Arapahoe out and about, perhaps returning to their home. He knew the road leading to Little Sister and was sure he could do the drive with his lights out.

It had taken close to three hours to arrive near the mountain, when during the day the ride would've taken only an hour. But *Nihoono biitooeeihii* didn't mind the extra time it had taken. He used the time to think of the killing he would do tonight. He thought of the stones, finally together and reformed. He thought of the power he would attain and all the things he would do.

He drove to the far side of the mountain, parking his truck under some trees. He was sure no one would see it even if they passed by close. Then he took everything he needed out of the truck. He secured the pouch with the five stones under his shirt, keeping them close to his heart. He believed the five stones would want to be reunited with the last two and would guide him along. Next he made sure his knives were secure, and his gun filled with the ammunition he would need. He checked the fitting of the silencer. Although he was sure no one would be around to hear the gun, he knew it was very loud. Plus with the silencer, when he fired into one of the sleeping men, the other would not be alerted. The last thing he took out of the truck was a pair of high powered night goggles. They would make the climb easy, taking the darkness away. He didn't believe he could make the climb or find the cave without them. Then he began his climb up the mountain.

The going was slow and more than once, *Nihoono biitooeeihii* nearly slipped. But he was not worried about falling. His destiny lay above and in a cave, and nothing would stop him.

He would have to climb up but also around the mountain. He decided it would be best to climb halfway up and then begin to circle around to the cave.

He was breathing heavily and had to rest. He found a boulder and sat down. He couldn't resist removing the stones and feeling them in his hands once again. Perhaps he would need to take the reformed meteorite and place it into a crown or necklace. The stones he had were so light they almost didn't weigh anything. It would not be hard to wear the reformed stones around his neck. Then everyone would see his power and they would obey his words. They would follow him back to glory. He carefully replaced the stones in the pouch and placed it under his shirt again. He could almost feel them pulsating against his chest.

He looked up into the sky and decided he couldn't waste any more time. He needed to be at the cave before the sun began to rise. He hurried up and soon decided he had climbed high enough. Now he needed to circle the mountain and end up at the cave. He wanted to be above the cave entrance when he finally found it. He was sure he was high enough and he had to go slower and silently along. He could not make any noise which would warn the two men inside. He knew the cave was not very deep and had only one room. Therefore, the two men would be sleeping close to the entrance.

He moved quietly and soon saw a bright area below him. The night goggles had picked up a fire the two men had made inside the cave. He was about twenty feet above the cave entrance. Using the goggles, he decided on the route he would take down. There was a slight overhang above the entrance to the cave. He would climb down to it, and then hang by his hands from it. Then he would drop quietly, remove his gun, and kill the two men before they even had a chance to wake.

He moved even slower than before. Each foot was placed carefully as he climbed down. Although it was only twenty feet below him, it took *Nihoono biitooeeihii* almost an hour to make the descent. Finally he was on the small overhang above the cave entrance. He removed the goggles and sat quietly, waiting for his eyes to adjust to the darkness. He was ready.

He made sure the gun was near his hand, and he hung down from the small ledge. It was only a drop of three feet to the floor of the cave. He let go and dropped silently, making no noise at all.

Quickly, he grabbed his gun and began firing rounds into the two men huddled under their blankets. There had been no sounds emitted from the men and *Nihoono biitooeeihii* moved in closer, shooting them both several more times, emptying his weapon.

He had done it! He had made the climb, found the cave, and killed the two last men who had the stones! He decided there was no longer any reason to be quiet and let out a loud yell. The stones would be his now. The power would be his.

Nihoono biitooeeihii moved into the cave, and with both hands, grabbed onto the blankets covering the now dead men. With one mighty tug, he pulled the blankets off!

CHAPTER 78

It couldn't be. He was stunned for the moment, unable to move, unable to breathe. The gun fell from his hand and as it hit the floor. Then two men came running out from the back of the cave, yelling at him.

"It's over Daniel," Bobby Black Bear yelled. "Put your hands up now!"

He didn't understand what had happened. How could Bobby Black Bear be here? And with him, Eric Logan? He had seen them at Logan's home, and they were staying there, to spring the trap on the killer.

Logan pulled Daniel's hands behind his back and placed handcuffs around his wrists. Then he pushed him down, sitting on the ground. Only then did Max Yellowfeather and Abel Bright Star come out from the back of the cave.

"So you were right Eric," Yellowfeather said. "It was Daniel Red Shirt."

"Well, I had a fifty-fifty chance of being right Max," I said. "It was either him or Tommy White Hair. But I didn't think Tommy would be able to kill his own people. Daniel being Arapahoe sealed the deal for me."

Bobby moved in front of Daniel and began removing any weapons the ex-officer had on him. Then he pulled the leather pouch from around his neck.

"You cannot stop me now!" Daniel cried out. "I am the one who must have the power! I am the one who will lead our people back to their former glory!"

"The only thing you will be leading is the line in prison to get your meals," Abel said. "If it were up to me,

I would throw you from the mountain myself."

Bobby shook out the five stones into his hand. He held them for a second and then laid them down on the floor.

"Will you place your stones here, next to them?" Bobby asked.

I watched with unexpected nervousness as Max and Abel removed their stones. Would the stones reform and have power again, as described in the legend? And if they did, what would be done with it? It would have to be dealt with by the Shoshone council and the tribal police. I wondered quickly, what would happen?

Max knelt down first and placed his stone on the floor of the cave, close to the others. Then Abel knelt, and carefully, with some shaking of his hands, placed the last stone down. Then he stood and backed up, perhaps afraid of what would happen.

We all looked on, eyes wide and holding our breath. And then, nothing happened. There was no reforming of the meteorite, no movement or glow. There was no power. The stones held no mysterious power at all.

Nihoono biitooeeihii was struggling with his cuffs. He fell forward, using his head to push the stones closer to each other.

"It cannot be!" he cried out. "I felt the power! It is real! They must reform!"

Bobby and I lifted him away and placed him in one of the back rooms of the cave. We left him there, babbling, screaming about the power, and how he was *Nihoono biitooeei-hii,* the One True Chief. He was the one who would lead his people! He yelled louder and kept on without stopping.

"Well I guess it's over," Max said.

"So much death for nothing," I said. "I wonder how Daniel found out about the stones and the legend?"

"Perhaps he will tell us, or maybe not," Bobby said. "It doesn't really matter now. Listen to him babbling back there. He might never stop."

"Perhaps he has lost his mind after seeing the stones held no power at all. Only time will tell, but if he has lost his sanity, he cannot stand trial. He will be put in a mental hospital for the criminally insane. Either way there will be no more killings."

"What of the stones?" Bobby asked.

"Abel and I were discussing it earlier," Max said. "Did you hear us?"

"Bobby and I were way back in the cave and couldn't hear a thing," I replied. "Good thing Daniel believed there was only one small room in this cave."

"Good thing he also never saw us leave your house and get out here," Bobby said. "Hiding my truck under some brush and making the climb took longer than we thought. I think we made it just in time."

"So Max, Abel," I asked, "what about the stones."

"Abel and I decided we would rid ourselves of the stones, and let the legend die," Max said. "We made the decision, even before we found out the stones held no power. There has been too much tragedy and death associated with them. Will you take them for us Bobby?"

"Of course I will," Bobby said.

I watched as Bobby placed all seven stones into the pouch taken from Daniel. He then placed them inside a pocket and sat down.

"I think we might as well wait for daylight before we bring Daniel down," I said.

Max looked at me and said, "You, Chuck and Jimmy have been faithful friends to us. You are good and honest. Abel and I will soon call you all out to the reservation where we will make you our blood brothers. There will be a special ceremony in front of the tribal council. It will be a great honor. Will you accept?"

I smiled and shook both Max and Abel's hands, and then said," It would be a great honor to consider you both my brothers."

"One more thing Bobby," Max said.

"Yes?" Bobby asked.

"Wherever you put the stones, wherever you take them, do not reveal their location to anyone. Let their secret die and hopefully, it will never cause any pain again."

Bobby said something in Shoshone, and I figured it must have been some kind of promise. I sat back thinking of all the deaths and pain an old legend had caused. I couldn't believe in this day and age; someone truly believed the stones held any power. And yet, for over four hundred years, the holders of the stones had kept them hidden, passed them down along with the legend. Maybe sometime in the past the stones had held some kind of power. Perhaps being separated for so long, let the power within them die. I didn't know the answer and figured I never would.

We waited for daylight, each thinking our own thoughts. Finally as the sun came up, Bobby and I led Daniel out of the cave. Max and Abel stayed behind, saying they wanted to cleanse the cave of the evil Daniel had brought into it.

We made our way slowly down the mountain, with Daniel mumbling about the power. I was not sure if he would ever stop his rambling, if his mind had really snapped. For some reason, I felt some pity for him. He had been a member of the Tribal Police force, an honored position and one which was not for everyone. It demanded long hours, was sometimes dangerous but had the trust of his people. Daniel had betrayed his oath and all the people who knew him. And for what? A legend about a meteor, a tale told for over four hundred years and ended up being a false tale. There had been no power.

Bobby parked outside his building and another two officers escorted Daniel into a jail cell.

"Guess we got him," I said.

"Yes, but there is a great deal left to do. I will get a search warrant for his home. You will also be asking for him to be held responsible for the murder inside of your jurisdiction. There will be a ton of paperwork."

"No kidding, but what else is new," I said and laughed. "One more thing Bobby."

"What is it Eric?"

"What will you do with the stones?

Bobby smiled but didn't say a word.

I shook Bobby's hand and then got into my vehicle. As I drove away I thought of everything which had happened. I decided it wasn't worth thinking about right now. Bell was running for office, I had to study for the Lieutenant's test, my boys were home for the summer, and I wanted to spend as much time as I could with them. Then there was the arrival of Detective Paul Saunders, his wife and two girls. Things were definitely not slowing down for me, and I wouldn't have wanted it any other way.

CHAPTER 79

Several weeks later, early morning

It was quiet as the lone man placed his small canoe into the waters of Tranquility Lake. He began to paddle his way out slowly. There was no rush, and the man took in the quiet and the beauty of the lake. It had been properly named, and the canoe moved steadily through the still waters.

As he paddled, the man heard the sounds of many animals. There was the hoot of an owl, getting ready to sleep away the day. And the call of a moose perhaps to his mate somewhere on the shore. In the water there were signs of life as well. The man saw the signs of fish below the surface and perhaps a turtle diving for food.

He slowly made his way further on, till he was approximately in the middle of the lake. Then he stopped, resting, and catching his breath. He looked all around; sure he was alone but making doubly sure just in case.

He thought back to sitting outside of Eric's home. When Eric had gone inside, he had looked around and found two stones which were similar to the ones Max and Abel had shown him. It was a good thing Max and Abel had shown them their stones. Bobby now knew what they looked like and how big they were.

He removed a leather pouch from his shirt and slowly poured out the contents. There were seven ordinary stones in his hand. They were plain and held no power. They were just stones after all. He began throwing them into the lake, each in a different direction. Then, when all seven had sunk into the lake, he carefully removed two more stones from another pouch.

As he had taken the five stones from Danial and held them in his hand, he pocketed two of them subtly.

Then he had taken the stones he had gathered from the front of Eric's home, mixing them with the others. When Max and Abel had placed their stones next to the ones Bobby had put on the floor, he was sure there would be no reaction.

In the weeks that followed, Bobby had been tempted to put the true seven stones together, but he had resisted. It wasn't up to him to see if the legend was true. Nothing could be gained from it. So, he had kept them separate and finally come out to the lake to dispose of them.

Now looking at the two remaining stones, he said a quick silent prayer, and then heaved them both as far in opposite directions as he could. He finally felt relieved of the pressure of holding onto the stones. Now they would rest on the bottom of the lake for the rest of time.

Bobby slowly began to paddle back to shore, smil-ing and singing an old Shoshone song. It told of an old chief who had saved his people long ago. Perhaps Bobby thought he had just done the same thing.

Epilogue

A few weeks later

Daniel Red Shirt had been deemed insane and unable to stand trial. He had been transported to a hospital for the criminally insane where he would spend the rest of his life. In the event he ever became sane, he would then stand trial for the crimes he had committed.

Will Toliver had retired earlier than expected which left both the position of Lieutenant and Sergeant of Investigations open. Chuck and Eric had both passed their tests and Eric Logan was now the Lieutenant of Investigations for the Eagle Police Department. Chuck Blackwell was his second in command, being made Sergeant in a dual ceremony with Eric.

Paul Saunders had arrived and decided along with his wife and girls to relocate in Eagle. He was going to be the newest detective in the department and Jimmy was his new partner.

Paul's wife Caroline jumped right in to help Bell with her campaign and seemed to love the new work she was doing. As for the girls, Ben and Tara had spent a great deal of time together. As for Abigail, she and Bear had a more contentious relationship than Tara and Ben but were getting along somewhat. Both families had been horseback riding, and Eric had found a great home for them only a few houses away from their own.

All in all, things couldn't have been better for both the Logan and Saunders families.

But right outside of town, in Tranquility Lake, something was happening under the surface. There on the bottom of the lake, seven small pieces of stone which had once arrived from far away, had begun to move. Ever so slowly, dragging through the silt and mud on the bottom, the stones were drawn to each other. It had taken a long time, but finally, all seven stones came together.

There was a bright light emitted from them as they somehow fused together. There on the bottom of the lake, the stones were once again together, pulsing with a glow and a power unseen by anyone.

THE END